A Seductive Interlude

Michael bent to retrieve her bag. "You shouldn't be here, darlin'. Come on, I'll take you home."

"If you loved me, you wouldn't send me away."

He tried not to sound as angry as he felt. "When I own a real home, Beth Waverly, and you're dressed in a white wedding gown all tricked out with lace and orange blossoms, with my ring on your finger, then and only then will I have you."

In a manner unlike her at all, she taunted him. "I never knew you were a coward, Michael." She turned away and headed for the door.

He grabbed her by the shoulder and spun her around. "I'm not a coward, nor am I a saint. Just what do you want from me, Beth?"

She shook free and slid her arms up around his neck, then raised herself on tiptoe until their lips met. "I want this," she whispered against his mouth before she kissed him in a way he'd never dared to kiss her. When it was over, he bent down, swept her into his arms, and carried her to the narrow iron bed . . .

—*from* "Faithful and True"
by JILL MARIE LANDIS

Books by Jill Marie Landis

ROSE
SUNFLOWER
WILDFLOWER
JADE

Books by Jodi Thomas

NORTHERN STAR
THE TENDER TEXAN
PRAIRIE SONG

Books by Colleen Quinn

WILD IS THE NIGHT
DEFIANT ROSE
(Coming in March)

And by Maureen Child

RUN WILD MY HEART
(Coming in March)

LOVING HEARTS

BY
JILL MARIE LANDIS
JODI THOMAS
COLLEEN QUINN
MAUREEN CHILD

DIAMOND BOOKS, NEW YORK

LOVING HEARTS

A Diamond Book / published by arrangement with
the authors

PRINTING HISTORY
Diamond edition / February 1992

ISBN: 1-55773-666-9

Diamond Books are published by The Berkley Publishing Group,
200 Madison Avenue, New York, New York 10016.
The name "DIAMOND" and its logo are trademarks
belonging to Charter Communications, Inc.

PRINTED IN THE UNITED STATES OF AMERICA

10 9 8 7 6 5 4 3 2 1

FAITHFUL AND TRUE

by

Jill Marie Landis

Dear Reader,

Is there any woman alive who doesn't remember receiving her first *real* valentine—that special card or heart-shaped box of candy from her first love? I'll bet there are even a few of you out there who might still have those mementos tucked away somewhere. I know I do. I'll never forget the way my heart pounded and my face flushed with embarrassment when I was a sixth grader and the boy I had a crush on knocked on my front door, shoved a valentine and a box of candy at me, and then walked away without a word. His name was Mike, and in honor of that first real valentine I have named the hero of this story "Michael."

Many actual experiences inspire my stories. A dear friend collects turn-of-the-century Valentines, most of them postcards, all of them beautifully created with lace and cut-outs, hearts and cherubs, or lithographs of paintings. Some have handwritten greetings on them. I've had a lot of fun reading the inscriptions, imagining lovers of days gone by exchanging sentiments.

The rhyme in this tale comes directly from one of those old cards.

I decided early on that Beth Brown, the heroine of "Faithful and True," named after my niece, Beth, would somehow be involved in the manufacturing of valentines. Then, when a book about the history of valentines virtually fell into my lap as I sat in the university library near my home, I was certain what Beth Brown should do. Rather than have her labor on an assembly line in a crowded workroom as was common according to my research, she would be an artist, able to create lovely paintings for her greeting cards anywhere.

Telluride, with its Victorian homes and quaint buildings secluded high in the mountains of Colorado, seemed the perfect place for Beth to hide the secret she keeps from Michael for so long.

So, that's how this story came to be. I sincerely hope you enjoy "Faithful and True." And that not just on Valentine's Day, but every day, your heart is filled with love.

Wishing you joy and peace,

—Jill Marie Landis

I enjoy hearing from you. Write to me at

    P. O. Box 3533
    Long Beach, California 90803

Colorado, 1895

Everyone Michael Shaughnessey knew had told him that January was no time to travel to Telluride. He ignored them and dressed for harsh weather.

Perfectly fitted gloves fashioned of the finest leather protected his hands from the bite of the cold, but even through the rich material, he could still feel the folded scrap of paper he held between his thumb and forefinger. He had stared at it so often he was sure he could make out the penned words with his fingertips. As he shoved the bit of paper down into the deep pocket of his wool coat and closed his fist around it, Michael ducked his head, hoping his hat brim would shield his face from the bite of the wind-driven snow.

There was no one else on the platform, no other passengers who were willing to brave the cold to wait outside for the train. Instead, they huddled around the wood stove inside the sparsely furnished building. Now that he was this close to his goal, impatience stretched his nerves as taut as a bowstring. The close air in the waiting room, the smell of tobacco smoke and wet wool, mingled with the complaints of the anxious travelers and the whining of restless children, had driven him outside.

His associates in Denver had advised him to wait until spring to travel to the out-of-the-way mining town in the San Juan Mountain Range. But Michael Shaughnessey had never been one to take advice; if he had, he'd still be trapped in the Irish slums of Boston doing manual labor in the mills like his older brothers.

"They'll keep ye down, Mick. Jest wait 'n' see. Ye'll end up back here like all the rest." His brothers had often spouted such dire predictions over tankards of ale in the local tavern until Michael heard them in his sleep. But if anything, their words had done more to spur him on than to discourage him in his attempt to better himself. While they let life keep them down and bemoaned their fate, Michael had fought to change his. He'd taken jobs sweeping out stores and working nights as a bartender to earn enough money to put himself through the university and still provide for Ma and the girls. Gifted with a good ear for accents, he soon dropped the Irish brogue that marked him as an immigrant and took note of the manners and dress of his classmates.

"Puttin' on airs, Mick, will do nothin' but alienate ye from your own," his mother had warned. "There'll come a day ye'll have to choose which world ye want to live in."

What he had wanted was both—and until Beth disappeared, he had been certain he could have them.

He let go of the paper scrap and pulled his hand out of his pocket. Cupping one hand over the other, he blew down the core between them to warm his fingers and then turned his collar up against the wind. The whistle of the steam engine whined through the low-lying gloom, and he stepped forward in anticipation.

Maybe I should thank Beth, he thought as he raised his face into the wind. If she'd never left him, perhaps he wouldn't have been driven to accomplish all that he had. It seemed fitting, now that he owned the largest department store in Denver, that he had finally discovered where to find Beth. He could go to her and prove he had gained all the wealth he had promised her long ago. He peered along the tracks, straining to see the engine. There was no sign of the train, but again a mournful whistle sounded, much closer now.

He'd waited six years for this. He could wait a few minutes longer.

He wondered what she'd look like now. Had Beth changed as much as he? Were her eyes still as large, as brown? Did her smile still light up a room when she entered? No doubt Beth Waverly-Brown still had reason to smile and to enjoy life. Michael, on the other hand, couldn't remember the last time he had truly enjoyed himself.

Until he saw Beth's cousin two weeks ago, he had made time for nothing but work. Driven by the need to succeed, he spent almost every waking hour pushing himself and his employees. He owned not only Allgoods but also a grand home and a stable full of thoroughbred horses. He had a butler, an upstairs maid, a downstairs maid, and the satisfaction of knowing his mother and

sisters would never want for anything again. He
had succeeded in leaving the poverty and the
burden of his Irish heritage behind.

The one thing he didn't have was Beth—but at
least now he knew where to find her.

When he did, Michael Shaughnessey planned
on asking her only one thing. *"Why?"*

Someone was knocking.

Beth Waverly-Brown frowned at the interruption and put her brush down on a turpentine-
soaked rag beside her paint palette. There was no
hope for the mess surrounding her on the dining
table, so she didn't even attempt to clean it up.
Preliminary sketches were scattered about the tabletop. One had drifted to the floor. Among the
drawings were paintings in various stages of completion. Curly-headed winged cherubs smiled up
at her from each and every painting; some held
bouquets while others climbed into or out of
baskets of flowers. Cherubs played on swings,
splashed in waterfalls, drifted gaily on clouds. She
smiled down at the collection, started toward the
door, then paused, unable to resist picking up her
brush again and adding a blush of pink to one
round-faced cherub's cheek and wings.

The knocking commenced again. "Beth, are you
there? I'm freezing out here."

She recognized Charles Massey's voice and put
her brush down immediately. "Coming," she called
out, wiping her hands on the apron she wore over
her faded peach gown. A quick glance in the hall
tree mirror as she flew past assured her she had
looked better, but her appearance couldn't be

helped, not with her publisher waiting for the valentine collection. He'd wired again yesterday. The deadline for completion had already been extended twice, but although he had been sympathetic, there would not be a third delay. She had to get down to business, complete the paintings, and have them on the train by the end of the week or face losing the fee they had agreed upon.

Beth reached the door and recognized Charles's tall silhouette through the oval window and the lace curtain draped over it. She opened the door halfway to block the winter's cold from whirling in and stepped back to allow him entry.

"I'm glad you're home," he said cheerfully as he doffed his tall, stately hat.

Beth couldn't help but smile. "And where else would I be? I'm working and can't spare a moment."

"Exactly why I came by. I thought perhaps you'd be in a romantic mood, seeing as how you're concentrating on valentines." He took off his hat and then began to shrug off his overcoat and shake it out over the worn rug that lay in front of the door.

Beth put her hands on her waist. "I'm really busy, Charlie. Could you come back later?"

He ignored her, ducked beneath his scarf, and then peeled off his gloves. His light blond hair was powdered with melting snowflakes; his green eyes shone brightly as he smiled down at her. Charles Massey shook his head. "How much later?"

"Next week?" Beth laughed.

"I was afraid you'd say that." He rubbed his hands together. "It's freezing in here." Charles moved toward the low fire in the grate and held his hands over the rising heat.

Beth rested a hand on the woolen coat he had draped over one of the chairs near the door. "Wood is costly."

His smile never dimmed as he reminded her, "If you'd marry me, you wouldn't have to worry about money ever again."

"If I get these paintings finished and shipped on time, I won't have to worry about money for a good while. Then I'll have ample time to think over your proposal."

"Until just before Easter. Then there will be Christmas and New Year's and you'll have more paintings due for each." His cheeks still reddened from the cold, Charles walked toward her. "Your life is just one big holiday after another, Beth Brown."

She smiled at his humor. They both knew her life was anything but a holiday, but at least she enjoyed her work. Three years ago Beth had thought her worries were over when George C. Whitney of the Whitney Company in Worcester, Massachusetts, agreed to buy her first cherub paintings and publish them as exquisite lithographed greeting cards. The money she made was enough to get by on, but there was little to spare at the end of every month.

Marrying Charles would indeed solve her problems, but as he stood in the middle of her front parlor looking larger than life, more handsome than any man had the right to look, Beth knew that for now, her answer was still no.

With a thumb beneath his jaw, he smoothed his

thick blond mustache with his forefinger. "How about a cup of coffee?"

She sighed. Charles Massey hadn't become one of the richest landowners in Telluride by learning to take no for an answer. There would be no moving him until he was good and ready to leave. She gave up prodding him in that direction. "All right, there's coffee on the stove. If you pour some for us both, we can talk while I work."

He started across the parlor, passed through the dining room beyond on his way to the kitchen in back. If the mess on the table bothered him, he said nothing, accepting it as he did the rest of her humble surroundings. "Where's the imp?" he called out over his shoulder as he disappeared through the swinging kitchen door.

"With Mrs. Fielding, who very kindly volunteered to keep her out of the way so that I could work." When there was no response, she called out again, "Did you hear that?" Beth raised her voice. *"So that I can work."* Beside the table once more, she picked up her brush and dipped it into the blue paint on her palette.

Within moments he pushed his way out of the kitchen carrying two steaming cups of coffee.

"Don't get those near the table," Beth warned, glancing from the full cups to her completed work.

"Follow me." He led the way back to the parlor, and Beth rolled her eyes. Once more she laid down her brush and followed Charles. They took familiar places, he in the wing chair near the fire, she on the settee across from it.

"Have you eaten today?" he asked.

"Why?"

"Have you?" He handed her a cup and saucer. The coffee was blended with just the right amount of milk and sugar.

"Yes."

"Good. Just checking."

Beth blew on the steaming coffee and then set the cup back on the saucer. He'd been her husband's friend. Now he was her guardian angel. "You're a dear friend, Charlie."

"But not quite marriage material." He stretched out his long legs and crossed them. His eyes were serious as he stared at her over the rim of his cup. "It's been three years since Stuart died, Beth. You've mourned him long enough."

She quickly dipped her head and concentrated on the cup in her lap. The discussions were always the same of late; Charles had proposed and now on every occasion politely argued her decision to decline. Because she valued his friendship, because he was good to her daughter, she listened, but she never told him the truth. She had already been married to a man she didn't love; she wouldn't do it again.

"Beth?"

"What?" She looked up.

He was waiting.

"I'm sorry. I was just thinking. Please, Charlie, let's not complicate things."

"I'm not getting any younger." He was not smiling now. In fact, he looked downright serious for a change.

Beth knew a moment of unease. "How about if we wait until spring? Ask me again then."

"What exactly are we waiting for?" He drained the cup and set it on the table beside him.

Beth wasn't sure. She saw him glance up at the ceiling and hoped he wasn't thinking about the peeling paint on the crown molding that bordered the walls. It was an eyesore, but then again, so was the faded wallpaper. She met his gaze and shrugged. "I can't yet. That's all, Charlie."

He leaned toward her, reached across the space that separated them, and took her hand. His touch was warm and comforting, but it sent no shivers down her spine. She knew a marriage between them would be the same—warm, comforting, but lacking the special spark she knew could exist between a man and a woman.

He let go of her hand and stood up. "I can wait, Beth Brown. At least until spring. But I can't promise I won't try to persuade you to marry me long before then."

Relieved to find that he was ready to leave, she stood up and followed him to the door. Beth waited quietly while Charles put on his heavy coat, wrapped his tartan scarf around his throat, jammed on his hat, and worked his leather gloves over his fingers.

"Can I at least take the two of you to dinner tomorrow? It's Sunday, after all, and you have to take time to eat."

Beth started to decline, then thought of Emma and how much the child would enjoy the outing. "All right. But I can't be gone long."

He put his hand over his heart. "I promise."

"Good." She took him by the shoulders and turned him toward the door. "Good-bye, Charlie."

"I'll come by tomorrow at noon. We'll go to the Sheridan Hotel."

Beth opened the door and stood back. "Wonderful."

Charles stepped out onto the porch. "How about a kiss?"

Laughing, she shook her head. "See you tomorrow."

"You're a cruel woman, Beth Brown."

"One of the worst."

"Where's your Valentine's Day spirit? At least recite one of the rhymes you're writing."

"'When your heart grows lonely, think of me, and then how happy you will be.'" Beth shut the door in his face and smiled when she heard his shout of laughter and his retreating footsteps. She might not be desperately in love with him, but Charles Massey would make an admirable mate.

"Next stop, Telluride! Telluride, next stop!"

The conductor's shout roused Michael from a restless sleep. His neck was stiff; an aching crick on the left side couldn't be eased by mere rubbing. The woman across from him continued to stare out the window, avoiding contact with his eyes as she clutched her handbag. He wondered if he looked the suspicious sort. He tried to glimpse his reflection in the frosted glass as he ran a hand over his dark, waving hair. Black Irish, they called him, with hair as dark as coal and just as shiny. Even in winter his skin held the kiss of summer that made his deep blue eyes that much more distinct.

He stared at the woman again, caught her eye when she glanced his way, saw her redden. If there had been somewhere else to sit in the crowded car, he'd have changed seats and put her at ease, but there wasn't a spare place to be had, and besides, he had nearly reached his destination. He settled back and let his mind wander.

Why, Beth?

The question continued to plague him. *Why?*

He couldn't wait to ask her to her face. He would demand an answer, even if her rich husband objected. They'd have to throw him out of the house, for he was that determined not to leave until he had heard it from her own lips.

Holy Mary, he'd been a fool seven years ago— only twenty-two-years-old and ready to whip the world. The woman across from him forgotten, he remembered the night he'd first met Beth. It seemed a hundred years ago.

He'd been invited to attend what his friend Randal Nelson had described as "just a small gathering. One of those Valentine affairs women are so fond of." Michael had no notion of what the evening would entail, but decided to accompany Randal and see for himself. With his shoes polished to a high, gleaming shine, his hair slicked down, and his one dress suit newly pressed, he knew he could hold up his head in any crowd. He'd been accepted at the university, made new friends easily, but had little time to attend social activities. This night would be his first outing, a great leap into that other new world in his life.

As he moved with Randal through the grand rooms of the elegantly appointed home, Michael had forced himself not to gawk at the wealth surrounding him. The cost of one of the silver candlesticks on the table would have fed Ma and the girls for months. He remembered he was adjusting the sleeve of his coat around his shirt cuff when Randal elbowed him and whispered, "See anything you like?"

At that, Michael looked up from where they paused in the ballroom doorway and took stock of the ladies and gentlemen moving around the dance floor. Silk and satin, lace, and French faille creations adorned the female dancers. The men were all in black. The resultant contrast was stunning. The room was alive, pulsing with music and color. In bustled gowns of wine red, deep green, yellow, and cream, the ladies moved through the steps of the dance in the arms of the somberly garbed gentlemen. He had never seen anything like it—nor anyone like the vision in white that was swiftly moving toward them.

She was petite; the crown of her head just reached his shoulder. Her hair was rich, shining brown, done up in a creation of curls and ringlets and topped by a feather aigrette that bobbed merrily as she moved. A white and rose lace fan dangled from her wrist. She was smiling, hurrying toward them, her dark eyes flashing. Michael knew a moment of acute despair when he realized she was rushing up to greet Randal and didn't stop until she planted a kiss on the man's cheek.

For the life of him, Michael didn't know why that innocent exchange had angered him so much.

Then, although her gaze kept straying to him, she said, "Randy! I'm so glad you're here. I was about to die of boredom."

Nelson introduced them by saying, "This is the

friend I was telling you about. Michael Shaughnessey, this is my cousin, Beth Waverly."

For the first time in his life Michael had been tongue-tied, but within two minutes he recovered enough to ask her to dance.

As they whirled about the dance floor she said, "Randy talks about you so much, Mr. Shaughnessey, that I just had to meet you."

"Please, call me Michael." The pronouncement delighted him. "I'm afraid he kept you a surprise, Miss Waverly."

She laughed up into his eyes. "Then I have you at a disadvantage. Please call me Beth and tell me what you would like to know."

He wanted to know how she had come to be so beautiful. Instead, he asked, "May I have the next dance?"

The sound of her merry laughter threaded itself about his heart. "This dance isn't even over yet."

"I like to plan ahead," he told her.

"People will talk if I dance with you all night."

He dared to pull her closer. "And would you care?"

Without a moment's hesitation she shook her head. "No, but I'm afraid my parents would."

"And where might they be?" Michael looked around.

"Father's in the card room. Mother is that worried-looking woman standing beside Randy at the champagne table."

As they waltzed past, Michael smiled at her mother. The woman returned a cool nod.

"Don't mind her," Beth assured him. "She's

always like that when I'm dancing with someone she doesn't know."

"Does she know everyone here?"

"And their lineage."

A feeling of impending doom swept over him before he stemmed it and tightened his grip on her hand. This was America. He was as good as any man in the room. Better, he told himself. For what they'd been born to, he was willing to fight every step of the way.

They danced another dance. When she prettily declined a third, he tried to understand. Although Randy attempted to persuade him to go ahead, Michael elected not to dance with anyone else all evening. Instead, he silently sipped champagne as he watched one gentleman after another lead Beth onto the dance floor. There was not a moment during the rest of the evening when he didn't know exactly where Beth Waverly was and with whom she was dancing. Even though he had little more than a chance to say a hurried good-bye, he went home content, his heart singing. He knew he had just met the girl he would marry.

There was no money to spend on flowers, but he did manage to have a card sent to her on Valentine's Day. It cost him more than he should have spent, but it was grand. Edged in paper lace with a print of a dark-haried woman plucking flowers from a tree burgeoning with blossoms, it contained a verse that he had committed to memory: "If ever a heart were faithful and true, it's the very heart I'm offering you."

When he finally saw her again, Beth told him she would keep the valentine forever.

Their courtship had been hampered by his need to work every evening and at week's end, but when he could spare an occasional hour or two, Beth met him on the Common. She told him she knew how precious his time was and she had decided to make the most of their stolen moments without interruption. Her cousin Randal was always willing to carry the notes they exchanged.

Winter ebbed, and on warm afternoons they spent private hours on the Common, walking amid the blossoms and new spring leaves. No more than a touch of hands or stolen kiss had ever passed between them until one Sunday afternoon when Beth arrived, her dark eyes shadowed, her brow marred by lines of worry.

"What is it, darlin'?" he asked, intentionally using his brogue—one of the things that she told him she loved most about him. He would have done anything to put the roses back on her cheeks and the sparkle in her eyes.

Beth shook her head. "It's nothing," she whispered as she gently laid her hand alongside his cheek. "I had a hard time getting away today."

"Come," he said, grabbing her hand without thinking, his heart racing as he started to lead her out of the park. "It's time I talked to your father. This has gone on long enough. I'll meet him face to face and tell him of our plans to be married."

"No!" Her objection was so vehement he let go of her hand.

"What is it?"

"You can't talk to Father. Not just yet."

Anger welled up inside him. Anger coupled with humiliation and pride. "I've put up with the sneakin' and the secret meetin's long enough, Beth. If you're ashamed to have me face your parents, say so and I'll be gone."

In the middle of the well-worn path beside the pond, she pulled him to a halt. "Never even think it, Michael. Never. It's just that you don't know my father. He's . . . he's set in his thinking."

"You mean he's like the rest of these highbrow Bostonians? Does he have a 'No Irish' sign hangin' in the window of his bank?"

Her face had paled. "Please, Michael, don't do this."

He tried to calm down, forced himself to let his temper cool. The woman clinging so very trustingly to his hand meant the world to him. There was no obstacle he would not overcome to have her. If that meant doing as she asked a while longer, so be it.

Finally, in control of himself again, he agreed "I'll do what you think best, Beth. But I won't put this off forever."

She had come to him the very next day.

When he heard the tentative knock on the door of his one-room flat, Michael had looked up from his books, arched his back, and stretched as he went to answer the summons. When he opened the door he found Beth standing in the dim hallway. He stood speechless for a moment, and after making certain there was no one in the hallway, he ushered her in. She moved inside. Her gaze took in every aspect of the bare room. Michael shrugged into the suspenders hanging from his waistband.

Dressed in a fitted canary-yellow gown and a

forest-green capelet, she was a touch of spring brought indoors. She stood immobile, her hands pressed open against her rib cage.

Afraid she was about to tell him she could see him no more, he took a step toward her and halted. "What is it? Has something happened?"

She flew into his arms. "Hold me, Michael. Just hold me."

He tried to make light of the way she was trembling as he willingly wrapped his arms about her. "You're shaking like a leaf in the wind."

She burrowed her face against his shoulder. "I love you, Michael."

Relief coursed through him. "As I love you," he assured her.

Then she pulled back and held his face between her hands. "Then love me now, Michael."

"Beth, I . . ." His mind raced with the overwhelming ramifications of her request.

Her fingers were working their way through the thick curls at the nape of his neck. Her soft breath at his throat was sending chills down his spine. He was already hard with the intense need that filled him.

"Don't you want me?" There was a catch in her voice, a sorrowful sound that tore at his insides.

There was no way he could look down into her deep brown eyes and deny his wanting. He pulled her close. With a hand at the small of her back, Michael pressed her so very near that there was no doubt in her mind about his desire.

She let the strings of her reticule fall, and the bag hit the floor with a soft thud. Still trembling, she began to unbutton his shirt. Michael closed his eyes and sighed as her breath followed her fingers down his chest all the way to his waistband. He grabbed her hands in his and held her away.

Her eyes were wide, her expression one of fright mingled with determination.

"This isn't the way it should be, Beth. Not here." He looked around at the yellowed walls of the room, at the scarred table and two chairs that were the only pieces of furniture in the small flat except for the narrow bed that stood in one corner. His books and papers were spread over the table where, in the gloaming, an oil lamp waited to be lit. His dress suit, along with two spare shirts, hung limply on the wall near the door.

He had never imagined her in such humble surroundings. It was merely a stopping-off place for him, a room not far removed from the Irish ghetto and still very far from where he intended to be when they finally married. She was a lady, as out of place here in her fine gown and her expensive cape as a whore in a cathedral.

He didn't know what had driven her to come to him, but Michael knew it was up to him to stop this foolishness. At least that was what his head told him. His heart and his traitorous body were telling him something else altogether.

He escaped her hands and bent to retrieve her bag. "You shouldn't be here, darlin'. Come on, I'll take you home." When he started to close his shirt, he heard her swift intake of breath.

Almost frantic now, she asked, "You don't love me, do you?"

"What are you talking about?" Wasn't he making

the greatest sacrifice a red-blooded man could make?

"If you loved me, you wouldn't send me away."

He tried not to sound as angry as he felt. "When I own a real home, Beth Waverly, and you're dressed in a white wedding gown all tricked out with lace and orange blossoms, with my ring on your finger, then and only then will I have you."

In a manner unlike her at all, she taunted him. "I never knew you were a coward, Michael." She turned away and headed toward the door.

He grabbed her by the shoulder and spun her around. While his fingers tightened on her upper arms, he leaned close. "I'm not a coward, nor am I a saint. Just what do you want from me, Beth?"

She shook free and slid her arms up around his neck, then raised herself on tiptoe until their lips met. "I want this," she whispered against his mouth before she kissed him in a way he'd never dared to kiss her. When it was over, he bent down, swept her into his arms, and carried her to the narrow iron bed.

After he deposited her in the center of it, he leaned down, planted his hands on either side of her, and trapped her between his open arms. "Is this what you want?" Daring her to say yes, he prayed she would say no.

"Yes." The word was a mere whisper, but as loud as a cymbal crash in the silent room.

"Then we'll do it my way."

He undressed her then, slowly, gently. When her newfound bravado all but failed, he asked her if she wanted him to stop. "No," she assured him. "No."

As the twilight deepened, he taught her with his lips and his hands. They came together amid sighs and whispers during an interlude he never wanted to see end. Like every other moment in time, it was all too brief, but he knew he would hold the memory in his heart forever.

Afterward, when it was over and he had helped her dress, she refused to let him take her home. He led her downstairs and hailed a hack. When the carriage door closed, Beth leaned out of the open window and rested her hand on the frame. He put his hand on hers. "I'll come to your house tomorrow night, and we'll face your father together."

Her eyes had brimmed with unshed tears. "I'll see you then, my love," she had promised.

That was the last time he had laid eyes on her.

The hum of the wheels against the iron rails brought Michael out of his reverie. He picked his hat up from the seat beside him and brushed it off with his sleeve. The whistle shrilled, announcing their arrival in Telluride as the conductor, in his navy blue uniform, made his way down the aisle.

Michael looked out the window and tried to make out the station in the dense, low clouds that had settled over the mountains. It looked like any other stop along the line, but for him this one was different.

Beth was somewhere in Telluride, and he didn't intend to board a train back to Denver until he found her.

"Mama? I'm home."

Beth finished cleaning the last of her brushes and set them aside. The dining table had been cleared, the completed paintings lined up across the back of the sideboard. "I'm in the dining room," she called, immediately recognizing the sound of her six-year-old's impatient footsteps running across the kitchen floor. The door between the rooms swung wide, and her daughter entered, ebony curls bouncing, blue eyes flashing.

"Timmy pulled my hair," Emma Brown complained, but instead of looking truly dismayed, the smiling child climbed up on a chair and then dramatically planted one hand on her hip as she shook her head. "Do you believe it?"

"And what did you do to Timmy?" Beth couldn't resist reaching out to straighten the oversize bow in Emma's hair. Eyes as blue as the sky on a clear day smiled back at her.

"Nothing, Mama."

"Nothing at all?"

"Almost nothing," the little girl said softly. "I called him a mule."

"Aha!" Beth dropped a kiss on Emma's nose as she headed for the kitchen to fix them a late supper. "Then I guess there's no need for me to march over there and tell his mama he needs a spanking, is there?"

Emma followed her into the other room and stood beside Beth as she added wood to the stove. "I guess not. Mrs. Fielding said that if you're still real busy tomorrow I can go back again and play. May I, Mama?"

"Maybe in the afternoon." Then Beth recalled Charlie's visit and his invitation. "Mr. Massey is taking us to dinner tomorrow at the Sheridan Hotel. Won't that be nice?"

Emma shrugged and scuffed one toe of her shoe over and over. "Yes."

Beth recognized the hesitation in Emma's voice. She set aside the bowl of eggs she'd taken off a shelf and knelt down, eye to eye with the youngster. "You like Mr. Massey, don't you? If you don't want to go tomorrow, I'll tell him we can't."

"I miss Papa."

"I know, muffin." Beth drew Emma close and held her tight. Her heart climbed into her throat as the little arms clasped her about her neck. She wondered if the child actually missed Stuart Brown, who had died when Emma was not yet three, or if it was merely the idea of not having someone to call Papa, like all of her friends, that she missed.

"If we go to dinner with Mr. Massey, you'll be able to order whatever you like."

"Even the tapioca?"

"Even that."

"Then I think we should go." Her worries momentarily forgotten, Emma gave Beth one more bear hug and then skipped away. While Beth turned back to the eggs, Emma dragged a kitchen chair across the room so that she could stand beside her mother and chat. "When will we make the paper valentines?"

"It's still too early," Beth told her. "I have two more paintings to complete for Mr. Whitney, and then we can decorate the special ones for our friends." It had become their tradition to make old-fashioned valentines adorned with paper cutouts, lace and foil, stamped cupids and flowers and bits of ribbon, much like the ones sold fifty years before. Beth collected trimmings all year, and then she and Emma worked for a week before Valentine's Day making just the right card for each of their friends and acquaintances.

Beth cracked an egg into a small bowl, intent on making an omelet for dinner. Emma chatted on. "Is Massachusetts very far? How come you sent your paintings there, but we never get to go see this Mr. Whitney?"

Her hands paused in midair as she held an egg over the crackled pottery bowl. Boston. It was another lifetime away. She would never go back.

To Emma she said, "Mr. Whitney doesn't need to see us, that's why. All he cares about is my work, and all I care about is the money he's promised to send me in exchange for the paintings."

"Why don't you put your whole name on them? No one knows you're the B. Brown who makes all the cards they send for the holidays."

Whisking the eggs together, Beth leaned over and bussed Emma's dark crown. "Thank you for the compliment, muffin, but B. Brown is nearly as popular as Kate Greenaway these days. Whether they know who I am or not, people still enjoy the pictures, and that's what counts, isn't it?"

Unconvinced, Emma shrugged. "I guess so." She leaned an elbow on the counter and watched Beth closely. "Mama? If you married Mr. Massey, would he be my papa?"

Beth sighed. She didn't need both of them nagging her to make a decision. "I suppose he would."

"And I could call him Papa?"

"*If* I married him, you could ask his permission."
She glanced over and hated the worry that marred
her daughter's perfect features. "I'm sure he'd be
delighted. *If*," she reemphasized, "I do decide to
marry him."

"Mama?"

"Yes, Emma."

"Do you think you could hurry and decide? I'm
the only one I know without a papa."

Beth gritted her teeth and beat the eggs a little
harder.

The storm had lifted. Telluride was carpeted
with a fresh layer of snow, the sky as deep a blue
as lapis, the air cold and crisp enough to break.
The pines were frosted with ice and snow; their
branches sagged with the weight.

The Sheridan Hotel was crowded with Sunday
diners who had been willing to brave a trip through
the cold to enjoy a sumptuous repast. The elegant
hotel and adjoining opera house had been built in
an attempt to lend respectability to a town that had
begun as a rough-and-tumble gold and silver mine
camp.

With Charles seated on her right and Emma on
her left, Beth had a clear view of the entire dining
room and the lobby beyond the heavy velvet
draperies swagged open with gilt cords to frame
the doorway. She brushed a crumb off the bodice
of her green serge gown, which was a good three
years old. She hadn't purchased anything new
since Stuart's death, but the dress was one she
rarely wore and so it was still like new. She
suspected that the serge—with its tightly fitted

sleeves and waistline slightly pointed in front and rounded in the back—might be out of style in Boston, but the West was always forgiving where fashion and availability went hand in hand.

Barely able to reach the table, Emma wriggled on the gilded chair. "Can I sit on my feet, Mama?"

Beth quickly responded. "Well-bred young ladies do not sit on their feet."

"Not in public," Charles added with a wink to Emma.

"Then can I have another tapioca?"

Charles laughed.

Beth smiled and shook her head at them. "You are both incorrigible." She singled out Emma. "What does sitting on your feet have to do with tapioca?"

"I've been very, very good." Emma looked to Charles for support. "Haven't I, Mr. Massey?"

"Good as gold, muffin." He waved the waiter over and ordered another tapioca.

Beth watched him as he and Emma chatted. In his gray striped wool suit and crisp-collared white shirt that emphasized skin tanned golden by the winter sun's reflection off of snow, he was a man whose looks commanded the attention of every woman in the room, young or old. Not only was he handsome, but his open charm was guileless. Any woman would be lucky to have a man like Charles Massey propose to her. If she had any sense at all, Beth told herself, she would—

Her mind froze in mid-thought. The sound of Charles's and Emma's voices faded as all sense of time and place dropped away. Her breath caught in her throat, trapped there by the erratic beat of her heart. Beyond the draped doorway that led to the lobby stood Michael Shaughnessey—or a man who looked so much like him that her physical response had been instantaneous. Her heart began to ache with a pain she thought had long since died.

The man was older than Michael. He carried himself with a self-assurance and quiet dignity that Michael, in his youth, had not yet achieved. The man's hair was coal black; his eyes, even from a distance, shown brilliant blue. But there was a cold, sarcastic glint in them that Michael's had never possessed.

That chilling glance quickly swept over the crowded dining room as the man turned away from the reception desk, crossed the lobby, and started up the stairs.

"Beth?"

Charlie's voice floated to her from somewhere far away.

"Beth? You're as white as the tablecloth. Are you all right?"

Blinking, returning slowly from somewhere deep within herself, Beth turned to him as she lowered her shaking hands to her lap. "Yes." She cleared her throat and glanced once more in the direction of the lobby. "I'm sorry. I just need to get home . . . to get back to work." Her voice faded to nearly nothing.

Charles immediately stood and motioned to the waiter. Obviously concerned by the sudden change in her, he put his hand on the back of her chair and helped her stand. Emma hopped down unassisted, and wove her way through the maze of tables and chairs, and waited for them by the door.

Outside the hotel, with her hand tucked into the curve of Charles's elbow, Beth felt relatively safe as they made their way down the well-worn path through town. Snow, banked along the edges of the narrow lane, dusted the hem of her skirt as she passed. Emma ran ahead, inspecting every twig, every rock, anything that had fought its way to the surface of the snow.

The short, brisk walk home helped clear her head, but Beth couldn't shake the mingled feelings of overwhelming sorrow and dread she'd experienced when she saw the man who so reminded her of Michael Shaughnessey. Wagons and carts, carriages, and mounted riders moved up and down the street past the shops which were closed on Sunday, but even the presence of so many sights and sounds couldn't dispel her sense of impending doom. She needed desperately to be alone, to come to terms with her fear and put it aside. Michael was not here. He would never find her. Why should he, after all, even want to look for her after what she had done?

Of course it couldn't have been him, she told herself. He was hundreds of miles away in Boston.

But what if . . . what if he had found her?

"Charles, could you please walk Emma down to the Fieldings'? Marjorie has invited her over again and I'm nearly finished."

He frowned, watching her carefully. "Will you be all right while I'm gone?"

She nodded. "Of course. I'm fine now. I just

need to get these paintings on the train, and the sooner I finish them, the better."

When they reached the walk that led to her front porch, Charles stopped and took both of her gloved hands in his. Their frosted breath mingled on the icy air. Still worried about her, he said, "I'll be right back."

"Please," she begged, "don't bother. I'm fine, really. I just need to—"

"You're pushing yourself too hard, Beth, and I won't have it. Stuart wouldn't have wanted you to live this way."

"Stuart isn't here to do anything about it, is he?" she snapped. Piqued, she was about to say that Stuart, who had been more of a guardian than a husband, should have provided better for her and Emma.

Charlie frowned.

"I'm sorry," she said, glancing back toward the hotel. "I'm not myself today. Emma!" She called out to the child bundled in a long wool tweed coat, thick stockings, and high-button boots. "Mr. Massey will walk you to the Fieldings'." Then she cupped her hands around her mouth and added, "Be nice to Timmy!"

"Terrible Timmy at it again?" Charles asked.

"As usual." She took his hand. "Thank you, dear friend."

He sighed dramatically. "You're breaking my heart, Beth."

"Get on with you." She let go and started up the walk he had shoveled clear of snow. As Charles followed Emma down the street, Beth shoved her hands deep into her coat pockets and watched them go.

Once she was alone in the house, she shed her coat, added a log to the almost dead fire, and went upstairs to change into her work dress. The house was silent; the closed-up winter smells of cold and mustiness were heavier upstairs. As she moved back and forth across the floor of the front bedroom she had moved into after Stuart's death, the floorboards groaned in protest.

The memory of the sight of the man who reminded her of Michael would not leave her. Nor would her reaction to him. As she slowly squirmed and stretched to work open the hooks and eyes down the back of her green serge gown, the image of Michael undressing her in his flat in Boston came to her unbidden.

She closed her eyes, willing the thought to leave, but the darkness only intensified the scene. His hands had been warm and gentle, his caresses tender. She could still remember her canary-yellow dress, the gay slippers of the same shade, the way he had slipped the gown slowly off her shoulders until it pooled about her ankles and then had drawn it off and carefully draped it over the foot of the old iron bed.

Beth covered her face with her hands, her task forgotten, as her mind raced back over every detail of that fateful visit so many years ago. She had been eighteen then, a shy virgin willing to risk everything to ensure a future with the man she loved.

But unused to high-stakes gambling, she had

taken a great risk without thinking of the conse-
quences.

And she had lost.

Taking a deep breath, she wiped away a single
tear and sat down on the edge of the big four-
poster. Outside the frosted windows, a jay foraged
for something to eat in the snow-shrouded boughs
of a tall pine. She would have to remember to put
crumbs out for the birds.

Birds had been singing the day she had gone to
Michael and begged him to make love to her. Why
had she been so certain her foolish plan would
work? Why wouldn't the truth have done just as
well in place of deception?

Now, seven years later, things looked much
clearer. Back then, when her father found out
about her clandestine meetings with Michael, she
could think of no alternative. Alexander Waverly
was used to having everyone—his employees, his
wife, and most certainly his only child—meet his
demands.

When she balked, he had become irrational. "Do
you know how I felt when Clemmens told me his
wife had seen you and that Black-Irish devil on the
Common?" He didn't give her time to reply. "Betrayed, that's how. Thoroughly betrayed. If my
sister's idiot son Randal wants to make an issue of
befriending the downtrodden, that's one thing,
but I will not have my daughter anywhere near a
degenerate drunken Irishman."

"Papa, Michael's not—"

"He is exactly like all the rest. I've had him
watched. I know exactly where he lives and where
he comes from. His brothers are drunken sots, mill

workers the lot of them. One is so far behind on his rent that he's facing eviction. His mother lives in virtual squalor with two bedraggled adolescent girls who will be on the streets before another year's out, like as not."

"I won't listen to this, Papa. You don't know what you're saying. Michael works two jobs just to help out at home and put himself through the university. He doesn't drink any more than you do, and he's—" She blanched when he stepped close enough to strike her, but she stood her ground.

Her father lowered his voice to a menacing whisper. "If he's so much as touched you—"

Her mother burst into the room and forced her way between them. "Alexander, please!"

"Stay out of this, Virginia. I'll have no daughter of mine being courted by an Irishman."

"I hardly think—" her mother tried again.

"It's all over town by now, if Ophelia Clemmens has the same mouth she's always had." He turned on Beth. This time cold determination had replaced the fury in his eyes. "You, young lady, are eighteen. It's high time you were married and off my hands, and I intend to make arrangements to that effect today, before it's too late and no decent man will have you." He had stormed out of the house, leaving her mother shaken and Beth determined to find a way to have Michael before it was too late.

A sound at the front door shook her from her reverie. Beth shrugged out of her green serge as she wished she could shrug off the past. From the armoire near the door she withdrew a paint-

stained dress of faded peach cashmere and threw
it on, hastily working up the shirtwaist buttons as
she headed for the landing.

"I'm coming, Charlie," she called, hurrying down
the narrow stairs. The last button was closed by
the time she reached the door and pulled it open.

The past rushed in with the frigid air that
swirled around her. Beth stood paralyzed in the
open doorway.

Her lips moved, but she made no sound.

Michael.

The sight of him filled the doorway and her
heart with dread. He was taller than she remembered, broader, a man—no longer a rangy twenty-
two-year-old. He was stunningly dressed in black;
the lapels of his elegant cashmere coat were ebony
velvet. She took it all in at a glance, but her gaze
was quickly arrested by his hooded, piercing blue
eyes. They seemed to look over and then through
her.

Finally he moved, folded a scrap of paper in his
hand, and put it into his coat pocket.

Finally she spoke. "Michael." The sound was no
more than a croak. She had to clear her throat and
try again. "Please. Come in."

As he stepped over the threshold, Michael
Shaughnessey knew true gut-tightening fear for
the first time in his life. He doffed his hat and held
on to it, wondering whether she would ask him to
stay or usher him out as quickly as she could
before her husband found him there. He watched
her hesitate for a moment before she closed the
door and stood nervously by with her hands
pressed against her waist.

Reaction to the sight of her raced through him like a shock of ice water. Except for the fact that she was thinner than before, Beth looked exactly the same. Her brown eyes were just as rich and warm, her lips still as inviting. She wore her thick, shining hair in a simple upswept style, wound in a knot anchored to the crown of her head. Her gown was faded and covered with oil stains and paint. The smell of turpentine hung on the air.

She was staring at him as if waiting for him to justify his presence in her home. Michael reminded himself that it was she who had all the explaining to do. He waited for her to speak.

"May I take your coat?" she asked.

With slow, measured motions and without comment, he unbuttoned and shrugged off the coat, then passed it to her, along with his hat. She hung them both on the hall tree.

They spoke at once.

"Would you like some coffee?" she offered.

"Is your husband home?" he asked.

He watched her gaze drop to the floor. She pressed her palms together, wet her lips, and answered with a shake of her head. "He's not here," she said.

Michael knew that if he didn't put distance between them he would be hard pressed not to reach out and shake her. How could she stand there and treat him as politely as one might treat a virtual stranger or some drummer calling with his wares?

"Then I'll take that coffee," he said bluntly.

As she hurried away, he watched her cross the room. He had expected her to be living in high style. Instead, she was wearing a stained dress that was fit for a rag bag and living in a small wood-frame house much in need of refurbishing.

He quickly perused the room when she disappeared behind the kitchen door. The ceiling needed a good sanding and a coat of paint. The striped floral wallpaper was water-stained where the window frames leaked. The carpet set before the fireplace was so threadbare the pattern was nearly indistinguishable. It was freezing cold in the room. The smell of turpentine lingered on the air.

After he peeled off his gloves, the price of which would have paid for new draperies in a parlor this size, he slapped them with irritation against his thigh. Perhaps her husband was a skinflint, but what of her father? Did the illustrious Alexander Waverly, owner of one of the foremost banks in Boston, condone the way his precious daughter lived? Did he know?

He slowly sidestepped the settee and chairs grouped close to the fireplace and studied the photographs arranged in scrolled silver frames on a drum table nearby. He lifted the closest and studied the face of an older, heavy-jowled, bald man who sported wide muttonchops and a swooping mustache.

It was not Alexander Waverly. Father-in-law, he decided, as he set it down. Beside it was a photograph of Beth as a child. She was smiling brightly into the camera, her dark hair done up in a huge bow, a nautical look about the sailor dress she wore. He started to pick it up, then stopped when he heard her moving about the kitchen.

Behind the kitchen door, Beth waited anxiously for the coffee to boil. Tempted to open the door and peek out to see what Michael Shaughnessey was doing in her parlor, she busied herself instead with arranging and rearranging two cups, a creamer, and a sugar bowl on a doily-covered tray.

The clock in the stairwell chimed three. The sound startled her. What of Charlie? She couldn't believe he had walked Emma to the Fieldings' and had actually gone on home without stopping by to check on her. He always kept his word. What would she do if he arrived while Michael was here? What would she do if he didn't? How could she explain one to the other? And what of her lie? When Michael had asked if her husband was home she had merely said no, hoping he would leave if he believed Stuart Brown might appear at any moment.

She pumped some chilly water into a dishpan and dipped in both hands, then patted her cheeks to cool them. They were hot to the touch. Her hands were shaking. Her knees felt like jellied consommé. She thought she might laugh and cry at the same time.

Get hold of yourself, Beth.

The coffee was done; the rich, heady smell filled the warm kitchen. She quickly filled two cups and then found a bottle of milk in the icebox and used a bit to fill the creamer. Two deep breaths helped to ensure that she would not dump the tray before she reached the parlor. Beth pushed open the kitchen door with her hip, exited the room, and came up short when she nearly ran into Michael, who was standing in front of the sideboard in the dining room. He was studying her paintings intently.

His eyes flashed her way when she entered. "You're *the* B. Brown?" The reason for the stained dress was more than obvious to him now, as well as the lingering scent of turpentine and oil. Michael's brow knit in concentration. He watched her hesitate to answer.

She shrugged, but not before she set the tray down. "Yes." It was hard to hide her wariness. "Why?"

"I own a department store in Denver. I've stocked your holiday cards for three years now. They're very popular."

Her surprise was more than evident. "Denver?" *So close.*

"In fact, we're awaiting a shipment of valentines from Whitney. From the looks of these, it seems they'll be late this year."

"They'll be on time. I have until midweek to see that they're finished and on the train to Boston."

Both of them thought of a long-ago valentine.

Neither made a move toward the coffee.

He turned away and walked into the parlor, unable to stand the frightened, doe-eyed look on her face. Why should she appear so long-suffering, he wondered, when it was he who had been left behind?

With the length of the dining room and the parlor doors between them, Michael felt more in control. "The West is a great leveler. No one cares where a man's from—only where he's going."

"It looks as though you've done well for yourself." She looked down at her miserable gown and wished she had not changed so quickly. With the house in such disrepair, what must he think?

He tried to make his voice sound offhand and casual. "I have everything I want."

The coffee entirely forgotten now, Beth left the dining room and joined him in the parlor. There was not a sound in the house except for the low crackling fire and the slow-ticking clock hanging in the stairwell. He decided to be blunt and to the point, then get out. "When will your husband be home?"

She fidgeted with the sleeve of her gown, glanced toward the frosted front window, and acted as if she hadn't understood his question. Just when he was about to ask again, she blurted out, "He's dead."

"Dead." He couldn't believe it. Part of his apprehension fled.

"For three years now."

He glanced around again. Had the man left her with nothing, then? "You live here alone?"

"I—"

Before she could answer, there was a quick knock at the front door and then it swung open. Charles was head and shoulders inside when he began, "Sorry that took so long. I had to attend a tea party at Fieldings'. Dolls and gumdrops—"

Michael pinned the smiling blond man with a cold, silent stare. Then, ignoring him completely, he slowly turned his frigid gaze back to Beth. She looked from one to the other before she spoke up. "Charles, this is . . . an old friend from Boston. Michael Shaughnessey, this is Charles Massey."

Both men nodded, staring each other down like

stags about to do battle over a doe. Beth felt the blood rush to her toes and willed herself not to faint. Michael was standing rigid, one hand balled into a fist. The expression in his hooded eyes demanded an explanation more clearly than words.

She owed him none. She quickly met Charles's unaccustomed silence with a pleading look.

Charles answered the call. "How long will you be in Telluride, Mr. Shaughnessey?"

Michael didn't take his eyes off Beth. "I have unfinished business here. I'll leave when it's over."

Beth felt a shiver of dread course along her spine and wished she had taken more initiative, wished she'd asked him point-blank why he had come. He was speaking to her again.

"May I call on you tomorrow, Mrs. Brown?"

The look on Michael's face told her that he would accept only one answer. "Of course." Even as she gave it, her mind raced ahead. She would have to send Emma to stay with the neighbors again. "Two o'clock would be fine."

He bowed, like a courtly stranger. "I'll see you then."

She should have moved forward when he did to collect his coat and hat and bid him good-bye, as good manners dictated. Her legs felt like lead. She didn't move.

"I'll see myself out." Grabbing his things, he shrugged into the coat and was out the door before she or even Charles could move to open it for him.

Charles turned on her as soon as Michael crossed the porch and moved down the walk. "Who *was* that?"

"I told you." She hesitated. "An old friend from Boston."

"You've never mentioned him before." He followed her as she turned away and walked back into the dining room.

"Coffee?" Beth picked up one of the cups. It was still warm.

"Beth?"

She put the cup down again. "I guess there was no reason to mention him."

"Does he have anything to do with the way you were acting at the hotel?"

"No. No, I—"

"You look about to collapse again." He was at her side in a second, pulling out a chair for her, easing her down with his hand on her elbow. "If that man upsets you, say the word and—"

"No!" She had protested too quickly, and she knew it when Charles began to study her more intently.

"This is nothing I can't handle. Michael is an old friend of my cousin's," she added quickly.

With one hand on the back of her chair, he hunkered down beside her. "I've known you since you came to Telluride. I've been a friend of yours and Stuart's since Emma was a year old. In all that time I've never heard you mention your family nor have I asked about them, because Stuart told me once that they were a forbidden subject. Now you stand there looking as white as a sheet and tell me a friend of your cousin's has shown up on your doorstep. What do you expect me to believe?"

She knotted her fingers in her lap and said softly, "I expect you to believe me. Michael was a bit shocked to hear of Stuart's death, that's all. I'm sure tomorrow's visit will clear things up and he'll go back home."

To Denver. Oh, God, so close.

He took her hands in his and began to chafe them. "You're freezing."

She couldn't meet his gaze and so looked at the sideboard covered with unfinished paintings. Innocent blue-eyed cherubs frolicked through ribbons and blossoms; one drifted in a rowboat on placid waters. She had so much yet to do. She didn't need this disruption in her life.

Beth pulled her wits together. Forcing a smile to her lips, she squeezed Charles's hands to reassure him that she was fine. "You are a dear. Now," she said with finality before she let go, "I have to get back to work. Emma will be home before I know it."

"You're sure you're fine?"

She blinked, as if he had just said something so very absurd she could hardly comprehend it. "Of course."

He stood up, straightened his coat, and reached out for one of the cups of coffee. After draining it, he set the cup down and headed for the door.

"Charles?"

He turned around, his hand on the doorknob.

"Would you mind picking up Emma tomorrow around one-thirty so that Michael can state his business without interruption?" She could see that his smile was forced.

He watched her closely for a moment and then nodded. "Of course. I'll be here with bells on." Then, with a brief salute, he waved good-bye.

When the door closed, Beth sank back onto the chair and stared into space.

There were few people in the hotel dining room. Michael paid them no mind as he pulled the gold watch from his vest pocket and checked the time. One o'clock. He fought back a nervous twinge in his stomach, snapped the lid closed, and pocketed his watch. The waiter came by, offering a second glass of heady Burgundy, an accompaniment to the midday meal. Michael waved him away. He wanted his wits about him when he faced Beth again.

Yesterday had been a fiasco. The moment she had opened the door, all rational thought had flown. Now, as he looked back over their meeting, he realized he had been pompous and arrogant. Downright cold, if he was to be honest with himself. But hit with one shock after another, he could hardly blame himself. To have found her at all was a surprise. To find her widowed was something he had never contemplated.

Then there was Charles Massey. What was he to Beth? What part did he play in her life. Friend? Confidant? Lover? She'd offered no explanation for the man who walked confidently into her home as if he belonged there.

Michael leaned back and tried to relax a moment more. Beth's house was just down the street, so there was no need to hurry. The place itself was nothing like what he'd expected. Instead of a stately manor like the one in which she was raised, her home was small, a two-story wood-frame structure adorned with millwork and faded blue and yellow paint. The rooms inside had been just as surprising. Although there was a quiet charm about the place, it sported threadbare carpets, faded wall hangings, and peeling paint. For years he had assumed Beth had left him to marry for money. If so, where was the evidence of wealth?

Beth Waverly, the woman he had not been able to forget, the woman he had come to purge himself of, was exactly as he remembered her— and yet she had changed. No matter what her humble circumstances might suggest, she was now Beth Brown, an artist known nationwide for her delightful greeting-card paintings. Had she always possessed such talent? She had never even mentioned it when they both lived in Boston. Had desperate straits forced her to take up an occupation to make a living, or was she truly content with her art and her quiet, modest home?

If so, the carefully constructed image of her that he had perpetuated over the years was false.

Why, then, had she run from him? He needed to know now more than ever.

Michael heard the regulator clock in the lobby chime two and pushed away from the table. Musing had made him late.

She was determined not to let him catch her off guard this time. Beth plumped a fringed velvet pillow, propped it into the corner of the settee, and glanced at the clock in the stairwell. He was late. She walked to the front window and peered out at another clear, cold day. Ice frosted the window-panes creating a kaleidoscope of colored sunlight that danced around the room. Maybe he wasn't coming after all.

Determined not to let the wild jumble of nerves brought on by Michael Shaughnessey's appearance take over completely, Beth smoothed the skirt of her green serge and went into the dining room to look over her latest painting. Charles had made no comment when he came to collect Emma, but she could tell he was aware that she had donned her best dress to meet Michael. Her friend had been polite and even jovial in front of Emma, but a shadow in his eyes marred his usually sparkling smile. She knew he wanted an explanation, but he was too much of a gentleman to ask for one.

Standing in front of the sideboard, she lifted her latest work. Before a forest glade, a smiling cherub with pastel pink wings wore a quiver of arrows. An oval of gold surrounded the scene like a halo, and in perfectly lettered script below the rendering she had printed a verse: "If ever a heart were faithful and true, it's the very heart I'm offering you."

If he saw it, would Michael recognize the verse from that long-ago valentine?

Faithful and true.

Michael had offered her his heart. She had given him hers. Did the Michael Shaughnessey she had encountered yesterday—the man with the cold, cynical stare—know that he still held her heart in his hands?

At the sound of three demanding knocks at the door, she set down the painting and turned it toward the wall. Beth took a deep breath, ran her hands over her waistband and tugged her skirt

into place. Promising herself that she would have
the upper hand today, she went to answer the
door.

"Hello, Michael."

"Beth."

She stared up at him a moment too long.

"May I come in?" he asked.

Beth stepped aside and opened the door wider.
"Please do." She took a deep breath and closed the
door to shut out the cold. "Michael, I—"

He cut her off. "I'm surprised Massey isn't
here."

She frowned. "Why would you say that?"

He shrugged. "He didn't look very pleased
when I asked to see you again today."

"It's no business of Charles's who I see." She
had to brush by him to move into the room.

"Isn't it?"

Beth abruptly turned to face him. "No, it is not."

He was still standing near the door, hat in
hand, his coat open, a woolen scarf hanging loose
around his neck. His eyes were bright blue, his
ebony hair slicked back off his forehead. As always, his skin was radiantly alive with the glow of
the outdoors and life. She felt so pale beside him.

Gathering her courage, she ignored her duties as
a hostess and did not ask him to remove his coat
and sit down. "What are you doing here, Michael?
What do you want?" To herself she added, How
did you find me?

She watched him tighten his hold on the hat
until his knuckles went white.

His voice was so low and so ominously even that
she could barely make out the words when he

said, "I came to ask you why you left Boston. Why you walked out on me and our life together and disappeared without a trace."

Although she had suspected what was coming, she wasn't prepared for the bluntness of his questions—nor was she ready to give him the truth.

His gaze bored into her. She looked away.

"I'm waiting," he said.

"Can't we sit down and discuss this like two rational beings?"

He shook his head. "I don't know. Can we? Are you willing to discuss it at all?"

"Give me your coat." She held out her hand, and he shrugged the heavy dark wool off. After handing her the coat, hat, and scarf, Michael took a place on the edge of the settee.

Beth tried to pull an explanation together as she hung his things on the mirrored hall tree. When she caught a glimpse of her own reflection, she was haunted by her eyes. Brown, shadowed, worried—they were the eyes of a woman about to evade the truth.

"Would you care for some cof—"

Impatiently, he cut her off again. "Nothing."

She sat down in the wing chair opposite him. Stuart's chair. It gave her no courage. She met his gaze again.

"How did you find me?"

"Over the holidays your cousin Randal came through Denver. I asked him where you were. He said he guessed that after all these years it wouldn't matter if I knew." He shifted uncomfortably, like a man used to more accommodating surroundings. "I had to know why you disappeared right after—"

The stricken look on her face must have stopped him, for he ended with "After what happened."

"My parents found out about . . . about my visit to your room."

He tensed visibly. "How?"

Beth pressed her splayed fingers against her skirt and willed them not to tremble. "I told them," she said softly.

"Why?"

Surprised at how well she was able to fight back tears, she looked up at him again. He was still sitting on the edge of the small settee looking as if he were ready to launch himself at her. "My father found out about our meetings in the park when one of my mother's friends saw us the last time we met. My father was enraged. He hired someone to find out about you, about your family."

"My family?" Michael felt his stomach turn. He wished he had Alexander Waverly in front of him now. "He told you, I assume, about my drunken brother and about my mother living in a tenement and you ran like a scared rabbit."

"Their circumstances made no difference to me— you know that, Michael. Father threatened to have me engaged by the end of the week to put a halt to any rumors that might have started. So I did run. Right into your arms. I thought that if I . . . if we . . ." She wanted so much for him to understand. "I hoped that if we made love, it would be too late, and there would be nothing he could do."

"Obviously you thought wrong."

Beth stood and walked over to the mantel.

Michael watched in silence. She turned to face him again, knowing she owed him at least this much. "Yes, I thought wrong. My father locked me in my room. He found a man who owed him money, a man willing to take on soiled goods in exchange for having his name and credit cleared at the bank. Stuart Brown was from an old family of high standing in Boston. He had lost his fortune through a combination of bad investments and three grown sons who had drained his business dry."

"Grown sons?"

"Stuart was fifty-one when we married."

Unable to conceive of an eighteen-year-old in the arms of a man almost old enough to be her grandfather, Michael stood up, crossed the room, and stared out the window. While his back was to her, Beth dropped her face into her hands and rubbed her forehead. Before he turned around, she resumed her calm pose near the mantel.

"And now Brown's dead. What of this Charles Massey?"

"What about him?"

Michael left the window and stepped closer. "What is he to you?"

Beth bristled with righteous indignation. "I told you what you wanted to know. I owe no further explanations as to my circumstances or my personal life."

In two strides he was towering over her. Unable to stop himself, Michael grabbed her upper arms and held her away from him so that he could study her upturned face. "Well?" He demanded an answer.

The very scent of him was familiar. Up close she could see the tiny lines the years had etched around his eyes. His big hands were warm and powerful, and even though he held her tightly, she sensed he was tempering his strength. "You've changed," she whispered.

"If I have it's because of you."

Beth shook her head and fought back tears again. "I'm sorry, Michael. I was only eighteen. I was powerless to prevent the marriage."

Michael stared down into doe-brown eyes brimming with unshed tears. Knowing she was right, and that in those days he was as powerless as she, he hated Alexander Waverly all the more. He had gone to the Waverly mansion after their clandestine meeting and had been dismissed by an insistent servant who told him Miss Waverly had departed that morning and would not be returning to Boston anytime in the near future.

Now he could see her fighting for control. The sight of her trembling lips and the fact that he was holding her so close did little for his own self-discipline.

"It's over, Michael," she said unconvincingly. "The past is over and done."

"Is it? Is it, Beth? Have you forgotten so completely? Can you tell me that a day ever goes by when you don't think of me? Did you ever stop to think of what I was going through?"

She put her hands against the silk vest beneath his open suit coat and pushed. "Let me go, Michael."

For half a second, he thought about doing as she asked, but he had waited too long, dreamed of this moment too often, to simply let her go. He kissed her instead, pulling her into his arms, holding her tight so that she would not struggle.

Beth knew the instant his lips touched hers that she had no will to seek release. Instead, she clung to him as a woman might cling to her shawl on a blustery day. His kiss was far from tender. It bespoke his determination to brand her as his for all time, no matter what the future held in store.

Beth found herself falling deeper under the spell of his caress and, deep within, knew she had to fight to regain control of her emotions. She drew upon her inner strength and finally broke the kiss.

Barely able to utter a sound, she took a step back and discovered she was trapped between Michael and the andirons. "Please go."

He hated the shocked look on her face as he watched her try to back away. Still, he felt no remorse for what he had done. Her response only proved what he had already suspected: Somewhere within her heart her love for him waited to be rekindled like the glowing embers of a fire. "You don't mean that."

"I do. Someone else is involved now. Our lives have taken different paths. We can't turn back."

Why was there panic in her eyes even as her lips reddened from his kiss? What was she afraid of? What had she to hide?

"Once you begged me to make love to you. Now it's my turn. You owe me that much." He reached out and took the hand she tried to hide in the folds of her skirts. "Come upstairs with me, Beth. Now, just this once. Then say the word and I'll walk out of your life forever."

"How can you even ask me that?" Even as she said the words, she couldn't help reacting to the feel of his fingers as his thumb stroked the back of her hand. She wanted to melt into his arms again, to give in to his request and lead him up the stairs. It was what she had dreamed of during all the long, lonely years she had lain awake thinking of Michael while she listened to Stuart snoring down the hall.

He was urging her on, trying to persuade her to grant his plea. "You're like a drug I can't shake. At least let me purge myself of you."

Beth wondered if such an act might truly be the end of her own dilemma. Would making love to Michael here and now end the aching nights she spent tortured by his memory? Could she then forget him and marry Charles with a clear mind and heart?

For a moment she was tempted. Would it be a final leave-taking? A bittersweet ending to their young love?

Her conscience screamed no. There was Emma to think of, not to mention her good name in the community should anyone find out. There would only be new memories to add to labored nights once he was gone. No. Firm in her conviction, Beth straightened and met his gaze full on.

"Absolutely not. Two wrongs don't make a right. Please go, Michael, and go now."

He let go of her hand, but didn't step away. "I'm rich now, Beth. Even your father couldn't object." As soon as the words were out, he regretted them. Even though it had been his intent earlier, he hated to think he had actually stooped to flaunting his wealth in her face.

"I haven't seen or had contact with my family since the day I married Stuart Brown." If Michael was shocked, he didn't let it show. She continued. "I don't care how much money you have. I never did."

He ran his hand through his hair and then tugged on his lapels, straightening his coat across his broad shoulders. "I know that now. I'm sorry I ever doubted you."

He was going. Incredibly, she felt relief and panic at the same time. It was truly over. Michael Shaughnessey was about to turn and walk out of her home and her life for the last time. There would be no going back.

Halfway across the room, he paused beside the table laden with framed photographs. Her breath caught and held when he lifted the picture of Emma and stared down at it for a moment. "Your beauty was evident even as a child."

The sepia-toned likeness did not reveal the true color of Emma's smiling eyes or her shining ebony hair. Beth said nothing.

As Michael crossed the room he felt as if the soles of his shoes were leaden. He learned what he had come to know, but took no satisfaction in the truth. She had not left him of her own volition, but the barrier between them was just as insurmountable. Perhaps she was right; too much time had passed. Married to one man for years, she now had Charles Massey at her beck and call. There was no longer a place in her life for Michael Shaughnessey.

He put on his coat, threw his scarf around his neck, and picked up his hat. Turning back to her, he found her still standing beside the mantel, her lips set in a resolute line.

Michael opened the door, then paused on the threshold. "Good-bye, Beth."

She didn't say a word.

He closed the door and was gone.

Beth waited until the sound of his footsteps faded away. Then, like a sleepwalker, she moved through the parlor and up the stairs. When she reached the sunny front bedroom, she drew the draperies without looking beyond the snow-encrusted branches of the tree out front.

Stretching out on the quilted coverlet, Beth cradled her face in the crook of her arm and let the tears come at last.

It's over.

All the way down the Colorado Avenue, Michael's mind repeated the sentence that had haunted him since yesterday when he had seen Beth Waverly and realized that he had lost her to the swift currents of time and tide. It was over at last.

Carefully avoiding a deep mudhole filled with icy slush, he crossed the busy main street, intent on walking off his frustrated energy until it was time to board the train back to Denver. Just past the bank on the corner, he paused at the intersection and waited for a wagon pulled by a team of mules to rumble by before he crossed again. Two buildings away he saw Charles Massey step onto the sidewalk and turn to lock the door behind him.

Michael kept walking. Curiosity forced him to

confront the man who held Beth's favor. "Morning, Massey."

Charles Massey didn't try to feign a smile. "Shaughnessey."

Michael looked at the empty store. "Yours?"

"One of them. I own five properties here on Colorado Avenue. This one's for rent."

"May I see it?"

Charles looked at him suspiciously. "For what reason?"

Michael shrugged. Was that worry he saw behind Massey's eyes? Perhaps the man's claim on Beth's heart was not quite secure. "You never know. I might be interested in setting up another store here in Telluride. I hear the mines are almost played out, but it seems to be a stable enough town."

Although his expression revealed doubt, Massey slipped the key into the lock again and let the door swing inward. "What business are you in?"

Michael stepped inside with Charles close on his heels. "I own Allgoods, the largest department store in Denver. I've been thinking of branching out."

Massey closed the door. The high-ceilinged room was long and narrow, with plank flooring. The front windows reached almost from floor to ceiling and flooded the room with light. With the stove standing unlit, the place was nearly as cold inside as out.

Michael looked around, knowing full well he had no intention of renting the place. He watched Massey—tall, blond, handsome. Except in size and physique, Massey was his opposite. Was this the man Beth loved now? He gave all the appearance of success. There was an air of confidence about him. Michael thought that if he had to choose a man for Beth, Charles Massey would certainly be adequate.

Charles glanced out the front window and then turned to Michael. "Stuart Brown was a friend of mine," he began slowly. "I've known him and Beth since they moved here from Boston."

Arrested by Charles's cool, challenging tone, Michael gave him his full attention. "Go on."

"I don't know what you're doing here, but I know she was upset after your visit yesterday. Since I've asked her to marry me, I've made it my personal responsibility to be certain you don't do so again."

So, beneath the cool determination he'd seen, Beth was upset after she turned him away. Michael peeled off one glove and then the other and saw Massey stiffen. Michael said, "She wasn't upset when I left her. In fact, she seemed quite composed." Distant, cold, and unyielding.

"Beth came downstairs when we got home, and I could tell she'd been crying. She tried to tell me she'd been thinking of Stuart, but I didn't believe a word of it. Stuart's been dead for three years, and I can't recall her ever shedding a tear. So I figure her distress could only be your doing, Shaughnessey."

Michael didn't know what to think. Had the confrontation reduced Beth to tears? Had she perhaps felt as bereft, as miserable, as he?

"I love Beth and Emma," Massey was saying.

"Because I do, I'd like to ask you as a gentleman to stay away from them."

Them? A warning bell went off inside him.

"Emma?"

Charles Massey frowned. "Yes. Emma Brown. Beth's daughter."

Beth's daughter? Michael worked his gloves through his hands and knew instinctively that something was wrong. He'd seen no child, nor had Beth mentioned any. Perhaps the girl was older, one of Stuart Brown's children by a former wife. Unwilling to show any sign of weakness that would give Massey an advantage over him, Michael hid his shock and changed the subject.

"What's the rent here?" He gave the room another quick once-over.

"Ten dollars a month."

"Pretty steep," Michael commented.

"There aren't any other empty buildings on Colorado." Charles moved toward the door, opened it, and waited for Michael to step outside. "Shaughnessey . . ."

Michael didn't like the tone he heard in Massey's voice. "What?"

"I hope you'll take me seriously. Leave Beth alone."

Michael pulled on his gloves. A stage rolled by, spraying mud up onto the edge of the sidewalk. Down the way, a man on horseback called out to a barber sweeping off his walk. Michael smiled at Charles Massey and tipped his hat. "I'll do as I damn well see fit, Massey. Your warning doesn't scare me a bit."

Before Charles could say another word, Michael stalked off toward the Sheridan Hotel.

Beth hugged her parcel of completed paintings close and watched Emma weave her way down the snow-covered path toward the Rio Grande Southern Railroad station. Not even her child's antics could lift her spirits. Sending Michael away yesterday was the hardest thing she had ever done. Then Charles had returned with Emma and demanded to know why she'd been crying. During an intense exchange, she had remained adamant, refusing to let on that Michael was the cause of her pain. She had even gone so far as to lie and tell him that she was crying because she missed Stuart. Guilt assailed her. Stuart had never asked for more than she could give, and their years of marriage had been celibate. Beth had missed him but hadn't deeply mourned his passing, and that fact made her lie ever harder to bear.

The streets were quiet. It was almost three in the afternoon. Except for a few wagons and horses tied at hitching rails up and down the avenue, there was little sign of activity. Michael had kept his word and had not returned. She supposed he had left for Denver on the early-morning train.

Would her heart ever heal?

"Emma!" She called out to the child scampering ahead. "Wait for Mama."

"Hurry up, poky." Emma laughed. Her dark curls bobbing beneath a pert hat caught the bright sunlight and created an almost visible halo. The smile she flashed in Beth's direction was all too dear. Her heart squeezed tight at the sight of it.

She was almost to the platform when she spied a familiar figure in a long black greatcoat and beaver hat moving from the opposite direction, carrying a dark satchel. Panicked, Beth looked right and left, then at Emma, who was already climbing the platform steps. She was trapped. There was no place to go.

Michael saw her a second later. He forced himself to move on, gripped his bag tighter, and kept walking toward her. They reached the stairs at the same time.

"Beth." He nodded curtly.

"You're leaving," she said.

"That's right."

He shifted so a man could walk past and mount the stairs.

Beth hugged her package tighter.

Neither moved as they drank in the sight of each other the way thirsty soil might soak up water. Each memorized the sight for a lifetime.

"Mama!"

The sound startled Beth so that she visibly jumped. Emma, she thought. Oh God. Emma and Michael together. She had the sinking feeling that somehow, no matter what she did to keep it from happening, this moment was inevitable.

Michael felt a wave of heat immediately followed by icy cold rush through his veins as he stared over at the pixielike child hopping from foot to foot on the platform. She was bundled up in a tweed coat and a loopy hand-knitted scarf. Her little black hat was tied with a satin bow. Curiosity filled the Irish blue eyes that sparkled up at him, as deep and clear as his own.

The palms of his hands began to sweat. He had to clear his throat before he could speak. "Your daughter?"

Beth felt trapped, but there was nowhere to run. "Yes."

"She looks like one of your cherubs."

No words came to her. Watching him closely, Beth waited. He knows, she thought. *He knows*.

Emma bounced down the stairs with a worried frown on her brow. She took Beth's hand and held on tight, pressing a shoulder into her mother's side. "Who's that man, Mama?" she whispered.

Michael couldn't take his eyes off the little girl clinging to Beth's hand. "Massey told me you had a daughter, but I never—"

Beth cut him off sharply. "I have to see that these get on the train. Excuse us."

Too stunned to act, Michael watched them climb the wooden steps to the platform hand in hand and noticed that the little girl was still smiling at him over her shoulder as Beth dragged her toward the shipping window.

Slow, simmering anger, unlike any he had ever known, replaced Michael's initial shock. The coach he had elected not to take from the hotel stood near the platform awaiting arriving passengers. Michael approached the driver, slipped a coin out of his pocket, and tossed it to the man. "The name's Shaughnessey. Take this bag back to the hotel for me," he instructed. "I've changed my mind about leaving today."

Beth tried to smile as she handed her parcel of carefully packed artwork over to the shipping clerk. With shaking fingers, she withdrew the coin needed for the freight charge and handed it over. Harvey Little, the same clerk who had taken care of all the packages she sent to the Whitney Company, tried his best to engage her in conversation.

"More paintings? What's the occasion?"

"What?" Beth didn't think she could put two lucid words together. She wanted to look over her shoulder to see if Michael was watching her from across the platform, but was afraid he might be, so she kept her gaze forward.

"Holiday pictures? Christmas is over." Harvey was still smiling, slowly stamping the package paid and testing the strength of the strings she'd tied so carefully.

"Valentines," she managed.

"That's right. Comin' up next month, ain't it? Gotta get one for the missus."

He handed her a receipt. Beth mumbled her thanks and turned around.

She nearly ran smack into Michael Shaughnessey.

"Ow!" Emma tried to pull her hand out of Beth's punishing grip. "Mama. Ow."

Beth eased up. "Don't whine, Emma."

Michael smiled down at Emma, but his gaze cooled when it met Beth's again. "Obviously we need to talk."

Not here. Not now. "I don't think this is the time or place," she said.

Looking for an ally, Michael spoke to the child who was studying him so intently. "Let's all get out of the cold. How about if I take you two to the hotel for tea?"

"No," Beth said.

"Yes!" Emma squealed. Then, turning to her

mother she begged, "Please, Mama. Their tea cakes are so delicious."

Beth wanted to strangle him.

Michael only shrugged.

"Where's your bag?" Beth asked.

"I've changed my mind about leaving today." He indicated the stairs. "After you, ladies."

Emma led the way. The two adults silently followed, their minds in turmoil.

"Do you have a big house?" Emma asked around a tea sandwich.

"Don't talk with your mouth full," her mother admonished.

The scene at the table in the dining room of the Sheridan was reminiscent of their Sunday dinner with Charles, but today Beth's heart seemed to skip every other beat in its crazy, headlong race. Her mouth was dry despite the tea, her cheeks flushed. Every time Michael sent an accusing glare her way, she wanted the floor to open up and swallow her, chair and all.

He was doing his best to keep Emma entertained as he plied her with goodies and asked one question after another. And Emma, who didn't know a stranger, kept up her end of the conversation while Beth waited for an opening to suggest they leave.

"I have a very big house," Michael was saying, "with lots and lots of rooms."

"Do you live there alone?" Emma took another bite of a sweet cake and smiled prettily as she chewed.

Michael glanced over at Beth before he answered. "All alone, except for the servants. And the horses, of course."

"Do you have any ponies?"

He shook his head. "No, I've never had a need for one, but I certainly have enough room for one in the stables."

Feeling a threat behind his innocent words, Beth picked up her bag and draped the drawstrings around her fingers. "Finish up now, Emma. We've kept Mr. Shaughnessey long enough."

"I have all the time in the world," he said. "Besides, I intend to walk you home and finish our discussion there."

"I was certain you would. That's why I would like to get this over with," she said.

He leaned toward her. "I don't know why you look so worried, Beth. After all, you've had seven years to come up with some sort of explanation."

"I'm six years old," Emma piped up.

Michael leaned back with a smug, self-satisfied smile. "I know. You told me. Now, while you finish that last little bit of cake, Emma, why don't you tell me about some of your friends?"

"Tell Mrs. Fielding you can only stay an hour," Beth called from her front porch where she stood watching Emma make her way alone to the neighbors' house down the street. She waited until Emma disappeared into the Fieldings' and then lingered on the porch a moment more, collecting her thoughts, building her defense. Then she walked inside.

Michael crouched beside the fireplace in the

parlor stoking the glowing embers with wood. He didn't look up until she closed the door.

"She's mine, isn't she?"

Beth took off her coat and hung it beside his on the hall tree in the corner. She could lie again, but she had lived a lie for so long that now she wanted to be through with it. "Yes."

"Did you know you were carrying my child before you married Stuart Brown?" The room was icy cold. He shoved his hands into his pockets.

Beth rubbed her hands up and down her sleeves. "No."

Michael knew in his heart that Emma Brown was his. Her eyes exactly mirrored his own; so did her midnight hair. Still, he asked, "Then how can you be certain?"

Beth came alive with anger. "I know because I was married to Stuart in name only. He married me to pay off his debts. He didn't love me and knew I didn't love him. He was kind to me and to Emma and never told anyone she wasn't his own. You're the only one I ever slept with."

Michael roughly returned the poker to its stand. "Why in the hell didn't you let me know? Your marriage could have been annulled. That girl should know her real father."

She dared step closer, her anger and fear driving her. "Let you know? At least I had a roof over my head and a way to see that Emma had enough." She made a broad gesture to indicate the room. "Stuart wasn't rich, but you can't live on dreams alone, Michael. I learned that the hard way. All you had back then was a head full of dreams and enough money to buy an education. Where would we be if I had run back to you with Emma—living in a room like the one you had while you attended the university? Or would the need to provide for a wife and child have driven you back to the mills?"

"You might have given me a chance, Beth. Good God, she's my flesh and blood."

She could see that he was struggling by the way his hands were shaking. It was hard for her to cope with the hurt and accusation in his tone. How could she make him understand? "My life was already in ruins because of my stupid plan. It wasn't your fault. I didn't want to ruin your life as well as my own."

"How noble of you," he spat.

"Michael, don't. Don't hate me any more than you already did."

He turned away, afraid of standing too close, afraid of what he might do. Michael wandered through the small parlor, entered the dining room, and then paused beside the sideboard.

Beth watched him lift the one painting she had decided not to send off to Whitney, the one of the archer cherub exactly like Emma with the treasured verse from their Valentine's Day together inscribed below it. She covered her mouth with her hands and closed her eyes while he stared down at the painting.

When she opened them again, he was moving toward her.

"You didn't forget," he said softly.

"I've never forgotten a single moment of the time we spent together," she whispered truthfully. "Not one second."

" 'If ever a heart were faithful and true . . .' " he began.

" 'It's the very heart I'm offering you,' " she finished.

Still furious but shaken, he carefully set the painting on the mantel. He tried to keep his voice smooth, controlled. "I have to get back to Denver, to the store. . . ."

Numb, she nodded, knowing there would be more. Emma had taken to him instantly. He had even carried the child back to the house on his shoulders. Michael was rich now. She knew first-hand the power that wealth could buy. She didn't care if he never forgave her, but if he tried to take Emma—

"I want my daughter in my life," he was saying. "I'll be back as soon as I can to arrange things."

"She's mine, Michael. You can't take her from me."

"She's ours. You've kept her to yourself for six long years."

Defiantly she squared her shoulders and said, "I'll run. I'll take Emma and run as far as—"

He reached out, took her by the arms, and gave her a firm shake. She jerked away.

"Listen to me, Beth Brown. Two days ago you told me it was too late for us. That may well be, but it's not too late for me to know my daughter. I don't intend to take her away from you, but I will see that I have a stake in her life. You can have Massey if that's what you want—"

"I—"

"—but we're telling Emma who her real father is

before this goes on much longer. I'll have it no other way."

"Michael, please . . . how can I explain this to her now? She's only a child. She won't understand."

Michael turned away to collect his things. He held his tongue until he was dressed for the outdoors again. In the open doorway he said, "I'll be back in two weeks at the most. I don't care how you decide to work this out—that's your problem. But if you're not here, if I find out you've taken Emma away, I'll hunt you down to the ends of the earth."

With that, he slammed the door so hard its oval window almost shattered.

Beth hurried past the stately brick courthouse on her way to Charles's house. Her pace, between a walk and a trot, had her perspiring beneath her heavy coat. She turned a corner, hurried past three other houses, and then ran up the icy walk. When she crossed the porch, it was all she could do to keep herself from pounding on the door.

Charles's housekeeper answered, a widow whose husband had died in one of the mines and left her with six mouths to feed. Beth knew her from the ladies' group at church. "Hello, Hannah. Is Charles home?"

With a curious look, Hannah Cornish ushered her in. "He's up in the study lookin' over some papers. You can wait in the parlor while I go get him." She left Beth pacing the room only to return an instant later. "I forgot to ask, you want some tea or somethin'?"

"Nothing, thank you." How could she think of eating or drinking anything with such a feeling of impending doom hanging over her?

Her feet trod the thick Persian carpet. Charles's home was everything hers was not—large, comfortably appointed, elegantly decorated. She had heard he even had indoor plumbing. There was a piano in the corner window. Beth opened her coat and slipped it off, dropping it on the tufted piano stool.

Charles walked in, his face aglow. "Beth! What a surprise." He extended both hands, and she grabbed them. "Nothing wrong, I hope?"

Her chin trembled and she hated herself for her weakness. "Everything."

Immediately, his expression clouded, his anger apparent. "It's Michael Shaughnessey again, isn't it? What has he done to you?" Charles dropped her hands and started toward the door. "Don't worry. I'll find him and —"

"Charles, stop! I came to talk."

Obviously angry, he came back to her side and led her to the settee. Unlike hers, it was long, plump, and perfectly upholstered. There were no cozy pillows adorning the corners.

Seated, she turned to him. "There's no simple way to tell you this, Charlie." She took a deep breath and blurted, "Michael is Emma's father."

His reaction was immediate. "What? How?"

With more calm and self-assurance than she would have imagined ever possessing under such circumstances, she told the tale from the very beginning—their introduction at the dance, the stolen hours in the park, Michael's willingness to face her father, and the fear that had forced her to keep the two away from each other. With sketchy but honest details, she told him of her visit to Michael's room and how she had badgered him to make love to her. She spared nothing in the telling, nor her father's anger, the sudden engagement and wedding, or the truth about her life with Stuart Brown.

It was then Charles spoke up. He shook his head. "I never suspected. Stuart never said anything."

"He was wonderful to me," Beth said. "He understood—at least that's what he told me—that the circumstances surrounding our marriage were unique. The one thing we had in common was a hatred of my father. Stuart knew I didn't love him, but he still respected me, Charles. And he loved Emma."

"Who wouldn't?" A sadness had taken over Charles's usually open expression. "What will you do now?"

A feeling of hopelessness overwhelmed her. So much had happened in so little time. "That's why I came to you. What should I do?"

"Do you still love him?"

"Who?"

"Shaughnessey, of course."

"He hates me now."

"Not necessarily. He's received a great shock. He's probably angry—"

"Definitely angry."

"—and hurt. Not only did he lose you, but in losing you he lost Emma as well. Now he's found you only to learn that you've kept all knowledge of his only child from him."

Beth wadded her skirt in her hands and then smoothed it out. A long lock of hair had slipped out of the bun atop her head as she hurried to his house, but in her haste she had ignored it. Charles reached out, lifted the strand, and carefully pushed it back into the topknot.

"You haven't answered my first question, Beth. Do you still love Michael Shaughnessey?"

She knew her answer would hurt this kind and gentle man, but she was through with lies and deception. "God help me, I still do."

He was very quiet for a long moment while he held her hands and seemed to be making a silent decision. "Tell him."

"You didn't see his face when he left." She shivered at the thought.

"Why would any man bother to seek you out after seven long years if he didn't still love you?"

She glanced out the window and back again. "Do you think so?"

There was a tender, bittersweet look in Charles's eyes as he said, "I don't see how he couldn't love you, Beth Brown. I know it's going to take me quite a while to get over you."

"Oh, Charlie." She reached out and hugged him close. "I'm so sorry. I never meant to hurt you. I never meant to hurt anyone." The tears she'd held so long began to flow. He pulled her close and smoothed his hand up and down her spine.

"Shh. At least I know now I haven't lost my touch. You've been in love with him all along, haven't you?"

"Uh . . . huh." She sobbed against his shoulder.

He tried to pull away. "Here, look up now." Charles whipped a spanking clean handkerchief from his pocket and wiped her tears. "You'll have to blow your own nose; I don't do that well." He handed the kerchief over to her.

She blew her nose, wadded the cloth, and dabbed at her eyes again. "Here I go crying buckets all over you. What will Hannah think?"

"Who cares? Feeling better now?"

"Thank you, Charles."

"Give it time, honey. When Shaughnessey comes back he'll have had time to think things through. See how he's feeling then. And above all, be honest with him."

"I wish I'd been honest with you, Charlie. I've wasted your time."

"Not at all." He smiled again. "I was giving up this spring, remember?"

She nodded.

"Do I still get my valentine?"

Beth stood up and shook out her skirt. "Of course." She knew she was about to cry again, but drummed up enough courage to see her through. "Emma and I will start making them in a few days."

"Good." He waited while she slipped into her coat and then walked her to the door. "That will keep your hands occupied while you wait to hear from him again."

On tiptoe, Beth pressed a kiss to Charles's cheek. "Thanks for being such a good friend,

Charlie. I hope you'll still come to see us as often as you can."

"Bet on it."

She stepped outside into the cold. Charles walked her to the edge of the porch.

"Bye, Beth."

"Bye, Charlie." She waved.

Halfway down the block she paused to look back. He was still watching.

"Does this look pretty, Mama?"

Beth bent over Emma, who was kneeling on a dining room chair so that she could more easily reach the snippets of ribbon, cutouts of paper flowers, and pieces of lace scattered about the tabletop. She looked at the over-decorated valentine her daughter had created and smiled to herself. There wasn't room on the gaudy paper heart for one more item. Beth's artistic eye rebelled at the massive jumble of decorations matted with glue, but she let it be. It was Emma's own design, and there was love in every detail of it.

"I think it's very pretty. Very different. Who is that one for?"

Emma held the valentine at arm's length and concentrated. "I think . . . I think Mr. Massey."

"A good choice. Charles will like it."

"What do you think about Mr. Higgins the milkman? Should I make him one? He's always so nice and cheerful in the morning."

"Did you make him one last year?"

"I didn't, but I was younger then and got tired. We have enough pretty things left."

Beth nodded sagely. "We certainly do. Go

ahead, then. I think he'd like one backed in blue satin."

As Beth snipped and glued her own creations, one for Charles, one for her neighbor Marjorie Fielding, one for Mr. Owen, the butcher with a cockney accent who often brightened her day with a smile and a compliment, she felt more at peace with herself than she had in three weeks. It was already February third, and there had been no sign of Michael Shaughnessey.

It had taken her a week to get over feeling anxious every time she heard a footfall on the porch. One week passed into two, and her trepidation had mounted. Now she had actually begun to relax and sleep the night through without awakening in fear that Michael might return at any moment and try to take Emma from her.

Late-afternoon shadows dimmed the remaining daylight in the room. Beth pushed away from the table and lit the gas lamps. It was so cold in the parlor that she shivered and put another log on the fire.

"Would you like some hot cocoa, Emma?" she asked as she passed through the dining room again on her way to fix herself a cup.

"Yes, please." Emma didn't bother to look up.

Beth poured milk from a bottle on the windowsill into a small pan and set it on the stove. She smiled as she listened to the sound of her daughter singing to herself as she worked. Emma had grown so much in the last few months that it was time to devote herself to altering her daughter's wardrobe so that winter dresses might last until spring.

The knock on the door was short and sharp. Something in the impatient sound alarmed Beth just as she reached for the tin of cocoa. She let go abruptly, and it fell with a clatter, rebounding off the edge of the kitchen cupboard onto the floor.

"Emma! Wait!" Grabbing up the tin and tossing it back on the cabinet, she started for the door. Her heart was lodged in her throat, her hands suddenly clammy. It was probably only Charles. *Please, don't let it be Michael.*

She pushed through the swinging door but was too late, for as she looked down the length of the long dining room table and through the parlor beyond, she saw Emma dwarfed by the man standing in the open doorway.

Instinctively Beth had known it would be him.

Michael cradled a bouquet of roses in one arm while in the other he held a long package tied with a huge satin bow. Even from a distance, she could see that he had somehow changed.

Beth could do nothing but watch as Emma piped a joyful greeting. "Oh, come in, Mr. Shaughnessey! We're just making valentines. Do you want one?"

Michael looked not at Emma but down the length of the rooms. "I'd like two," he said.

Emma spun around. "Mama? Are you going to make a valentine for Mr. Shaughnessey? I am."

As Emma raced back to the dining table to begin a new valentine immediately, Michael was left standing in the open doorway. He stepped through and, still burdened, closed the door with the toe of his boot. With the flowers and the box in his arms, Michael walked through the parlor and stopped at the opposite end of the table from Beth. Between them their daughter climbed back up on a chair and stared down at the eight-foot table of clutter.

Michael was smiling. "Are you, Beth?"

The smile, which made him appear so much like the man who had once loved her, caught Beth off guard. "Am I what?"

"Going to make me a valentine?"

"I—"

"Perhaps you'll take a bribe?"

"Bribe?"

He looked for a place to set the box and put it across the arms of the chair at the head of the table where he stood. He held out the flowers to her. "These are for you."

Without taking her eyes off his face, she walked the length of the table and reached out for the perfect blood-red roses. He laid them in her arms as one might a newborn child.

Her mouth suddenly gone dry, Beth licked her lips. "Thank you."

"I was afraid they wouldn't make it all the way from Denver on the train. They've come from a hothouse in California."

She had to get away from the warm glow in his rich blue eyes. "I'll get a vase."

Inside the kitchen, Beth pulled the roses close and inhaled their heady scent. The buds were just about to open. She laid them on the cabinet and then rummaged through the pantry until she found a tall footed vase. Lake a madwoman, she raced to prime the pump in the kitchen sink and then worked the pump handle up and down until the vase was three-quarters full. After tearing the green waxed paper off the bouquet, she jammed the roses in the vase and carried it back into the dining room.

The scene that greeted her was far too serene for the way she was feeling inside. Michael had removed his heavy outerwear and was sitting in a chair he'd pulled up beside Emma's. Seeing their dark heads bent so close together as they concentrated over Emma's valentine brought tears to her eyes. With her tears came a jarring realization: There was no way she could keep them apart any longer.

Michael seemed content to ignore her as he worked with Emma, and it gave Beth ample time to study him. The harsh lines she'd noticed around his eyes, the tautness of his lips, had eased over the weeks they had been apart. He smiled readily and often as he and Emma exchanged ideas on what colors they liked paired together. When he did glance her way, Beth felt the warmth of the quick smile he sent her to the tips of her toes.

She set the flowers on the sideboard, then looked up to find him watching her intently and forced herself to think of something to say. "How long will you be in Telluride?"

Half expecting him to change—to make a caustic remark like "Are you anxious to see me gone?"— she was surprised but not relieved when he merely said, "I'm not sure."

"Do you like this green ribbon with the purple?" Emma asked him.

"Not really, darlin'. How about the pink and the purple?" He suddenly frowned and asked Beth, "Is something burning?"

"The milk!"

Beth raced back into the kitchen, grabbed the pot handle without thinking and yelped, "Ouch!" The pot clattered on the stove, and what was left of the scorched milk sloshed out across the stove top. "Damnation!" she whispered under her breath before she stuck her scorched fingers in her mouth.

The door swung wide, and Michael strode into the small room. "Here, let's run some water on that." He led her to the sink and pumped chilly water over her fingers as he held her wrist. "Better?"

He was standing so close she could feel the scratchy wool of his thick suit jacket and smell the heady scent of his toilet water. It reminded her of rum and sea spray combined. He bent over her hand, and she watched him through lowered lashes, wondering why he was not showing signs of the hatred she'd last seen in his eyes.

"Do you have any butter?"

"In the icebox."

He let go after plunging her fingers into the dishpan of cold water beneath the pump and hurried over to the wooden icebox near the back door. In a moment he was back, the butter dish in his hand.

"Really, Michael, I'm fine. You don't have to—"

"I want to," he insisted as he opened and closed drawers looking for the silverware. The third drawer contained a jumble of paint and brushes, just like the other two. Exasperated, he sighed and shook his head. "Do you have anything to cut butter with?" He picked up one of her brushes. "I guess I could brush it on."

She found herself smiling.

He smiled in return and opened another drawer. "Found it."

Knife in hand, Michael returned to her side and scraped off a blade full of butter. He slipped it onto his own fingers, and then, as if he were holding a robin's egg, he gently cupped Beth's reddened fingers in his palm and with the other hand, began to spread the butter over them.

She looked up into his eyes and found him studying her closely. His fingers continued to sensuously ply her tender skin with the cool butter. She was melting as fast as the creamy yellow substance he worked into one finger at a time.

He cleared his throat. She watched his thick midnight lashes sweep down over his eyes and up again. "Better?" he whispered.

She nodded. They were a mere breath apart. He felt warm, solid, and giving and very much like the old Michael of her memories. It was a feeling she had not experienced in a very long time.

"I've had a lot of time to think, and plenty to think about since the day I left here," he began.

She waited for his anger to surface, waited to hear his demand to take Emma with him, if not forever, at least for a time to make up for the lost years. Instead, he continued to hold her injured hand and watch her closely.

"I thought about many things, Beth—the past, you and me, and Emma. When I got back I went straight to Allgoods. I walked through the aisles, between the displays and the glass-fronted cases, and realized I had worked very hard and long for very little."

"Allgoods is one of the biggest stores west of the Mississippi," she said in his defense.

"That evening the same thing occurred to me when I got back to my house. I guess you could call the place a mansion, but it has certainly never been a home. It's the sort of place I imagined you'd be living in with your Mr. Brown."

"Michael, I—"

"I sat alone in the dark for quite a time, thinking about all I'd dreamed of and what I'd finally achieved, and a grand thought came to me."

For some reason, her heart felt lighter, and with each and every beat, long-enduring hope gained strength. "What was it?"

"Just that I did it all because of you, Beth. I fought and scraped, begged, borrowed, and slaved until I had it all. I wanted to prove to you that I could be as rich as your father, richer than Stuart Brown. Rich enough to throw it in your face someday and let you know what a great mistake you'd made in choosing him over me. But then I came to Telluride and found out that none of what I'd believed about you was true." He paused and brought the palm of her hand to his lips and kissed it gently. "And I found Emma."

"And now?" Her body was all too aware of his warm breath on her fingers.

He let go of her hand and held her at arm's length. "I hope it's not too late to ask you to forgive me for the way I acted the other day. When I saw Emma, when I realized what you had done, all I could think of was having her. But I know that even then my life would still be incomplete without you. I know about Massey, and I know you think it's too late for the two of us to start over, but I'll swear to you now on the staff of Saint Patrick that I'm not willing to throw away a second chance with you. I'm going to do my damnedest to persuade you to marry me, Beth Brown, and I'm not leaving town until you say yes."

The kitchen was almost dark now. The smell of scorched milk permeated the cold air. Beth caressed his features with her gaze, his eyes, his lips, the dimple that creased his cheek. The time she had dreamed of for so very long was at hand, and yet she found it hard to believe. She wanted nothing more than to be Michael's wife, now and forever.

"Yes, Michael," she barely managed to whisper.

He went on as if he hadn't heard. "I know you're fond of Massey, and believe me, darlin', I can see why. He—"

Beth tried again, louder this time. "Michael, I said yes."

"There's no use in arguing with me." He paused, cocked his head, and asked slowly, "What did you just say?"

"I said yes, I'll marry you. Yes, I still love you. Yes. Yes. Yes!"

Without another word, he grabbed her in a fierce, rib-crushing hug and held her tight. Then just as abruptly, he raised his head and pressed his lips to hers. Savoring the sensation of his warm mouth moving over hers, Beth welcomed him back into her life and her arms, opened her lips to his kiss, and reveled in the exchange. He cupped her face in his hands and deepened the kiss, tempting her with his tongue. They were lost in the moment, lost in each other, when the swinging door suddenly opened and Emma said, "What are you doing in the dark?"

Michael was the first to pull away. With one arm about Beth's waist, he stepped back and smiled at the small silhouette framed in the doorway. "I'm kissing your mother, Emma. Now shut the door and go get that big box on the chair while I light the lamp."

The door closed in less than a second, and Michael commenced kissing Beth again until it reopened. "I've got the box. Why isn't the light on yet?"

Michael's voice came out of the darkness. "We've decided we'd better come into the dining room with you, haven't we, darlin'?"

"Yes," Beth agreed. "I think it's time we found out what's in that box, don't you, Emma?"

Hand in hand, as if afraid to lose each other again, they followed her into the parlor.

"Damn!" Michael whispered under his breath. "Why is it always so blasted cold in here?" Emma sat in front of the fire with the box across her lap.

"I have to pay someone to chop wood. It's expensive," Beth started to explain as Michael piled two more logs on the low fire.

He frowned down into the flames and watched them lick the dry wood. He hated a cold house. It reminded him of the freezing rooms he had grown up in. In a tight voice he told her, "You won't have to worry about that anymore, will you?"

She shook her head. "No, I guess I won't."

"May I open it now, or is this for Mama?"

Michael grabbed Beth's hand and tugged her over to the settee. Not content with letting her sit beside him, he pulled her down on his lap with a teasing wink. "The flowers were for your mother. This is just for you."

"Open it, muffin," Beth encouraged.

Emma tore off the bow and tossed the lid aside. Beneath a mound of tissues lay a beautifully gowned and coiffed doll with a bisque head and hands.

"Oh, Michael, it's beautiful." Beth slipped an arm about his neck.

"She looks like me, Mama. She has black hair and blue glass eyes." Emma ran her small fingers over the doll's ruffled gown and then gave them her most serious expression. "Timmy's not touching this even once."

Michael looked stern. "Timmy?"

Beth laughed. "Terrible Timmy Fielding. Our neighbor. He's Emma's little friend."

Michael grumbled, "She's too young for boyfriends."

Emma responded immediately. "Poo! Boyfriends? Oh, poo, Mr. Shaughnessey!" She watched the two of them intently for a moment and then slowly stood up, carrying her new doll with her. When she reached the settee she stared at them for a moment, then asked, "Mama, what are you doing on Mr. Shaughnessey's lap?"

Beth turned bright red and started to scoot off, but Michael held her tight.

"Would you like to sit here with us, Emma? There's room for three," he offered.

Emma scrambled up next to Michael and held her doll on her lap. Michael draped his free arm over her shoulders. They sat for a time in companionable silence, Michael and Beth staring into each other's eyes while Emma inspected her new doll's underclothing. Finally she looked at Beth and Michael again and sighed a long sigh.

"Does this mean you aren't going to marry Mr. Massey after all, Mama?"

They answered together.

"No, she's not," he said.

"No, I'm not," she said.

Emma sighed again, a dramatic, long-suffering sigh that neither adult missed.

"Something wrong, Emma?" Michael asked.

Beth had a feeling she knew what was coming.

"Then I guess this means I'm not getting another papa after all." She cast a sideways glance at Michael and shrugged.

"Oh, yes, you are Miss Emma," he told her. "You're getting the very best kind."

"And what kind is that?" Beth wanted to know.

"The *real* kind," he told them. Then he took Emma's hand in his and said, "I'm going to be your papa from now on."

"You are?" Emma set the doll aside and got to her knees beside them. She studied her mother closely to be sure she had heard correctly.

"Me," Michael assured her.

"It's true," Beth added.

Still not ready to believe her good fortune, Emma pressed them. "When?"

Michael turned to Beth. "When?"

"Is eleven days too soon?"

He leaned close and whispered to Beth, "I think that might be too long if you intend to squirm around on my lap every night until then." Then, aloud, "Why eleven days?"

"In eleven days it's Valentine's day!" Emma shouted. "I'll have a real papa on Valentine's Day!"

"And I'll have you," Michael whispered to Beth.

She looked up into his shining eyes and returned his smile. "And I'll have you, too."

HEART ON HIS SLEEVE

by

Jodi Thomas

Dear Reader,

When my editor, Gail Fortune at Berkley, contacted me about writing a story for Valentine's Day, I did what I always do at the beginning of every story. I talked it over with my husband. He told me about an old custom brought to the colonies from Europe. During a party, each unmarried man drew a paper heart from a box and pinned it to his sleeve. The girl named on the heart became his sweetheart for the evening. That is where the term, "heart on his sleeve" came from.

Since my editor had suggested opening the story with a Valentine's Day dance, I did. But I chose the two people who least wanted to attend: the stranger and the town's old maid. As always, my characters took over and "wrote" the story from that point on.

I named my heroine Amanda after the sweet little eight-year-old daughter of a close friend. Amanda Jones is full of mischief and, I predict, will have many a young man wearing his heart on his sleeve in a few years.

Valentine's Day has always been very special to me, maybe because I've been happily married to my first love for twenty-one years.

I hope you enjoy "Heart on His Sleeve."

—JODI THOMAS

Chapter One

Clint Matthews hated the thought of attending a Valentine's Day dance, but the boss was going and Clint had been hired to protect Colonel Winters with his gun and his life if necessary. So he'd dressed in his funeral best and ridden the ten miles to town beside the colonel's buggy. It was ridiculous; the entire county was about to explode into a range war, but all anyone could talk about tonight was Miss Peach's annual party.

Clint swung from his horse, crammed his hat low against the wind and headed into Miss Peach's house with the others. He had a feeling he'd count the hours until this night was over. His only hope lay in the north wind that promised a storm and, he hoped, an early end to the festivities.

"You'll have to leave your spurs and guns at the door," a plump lady of about fifty said to Clint as he stepped inside. She was little more than half his height, but she gave the impression of looking down at him. Her white lace dress and thin reddish-gray hair left no doubt that this was the hostess, Miss Peach.

Clint glanced at the colonel for instructions. He wouldn't be much use as a bodyguard with his gun belt hanging on a hook by the door. If Don Lawson and his gang showed up, Clint would need a revolver. Lawson was more likely to be at the saloon gambling, but a man couldn't be too careful. When Lawson wasn't drinking or womanizing, he was stirring up trouble.

The colonel nodded slightly before drawing Miss Peach's attention. Clint silently slipped his Colt inside his right boot. If trouble came a'dancing, Clint was ready.

The weight of the gun was uncomfortable, but he figured all he had to do was walk slowly around the room for a few hours and keep an eye on the colonel. He certainly had no interest in participating in the party. He'd given up trying to be sociable. Some folks hated him, most respected him because of his gun, but they all kept their distance and that was just the way he wanted it.

Clint gazed slowly around the room. Miss Peach's home was a long ranch house with a dance floor bigger than most dance halls he'd seen. Everything was decorated in red and white, her favorite colors. A small group of musicians in the corner sounded as if they were practicing rather than playing. But then, this was the panhandle of Texas, not Dallas. She was lucky to have found four men who knew the same tune.

The number of guests indicated that no one in Quail Springs had turned down the invitation. Children ran about unattended while young couples danced. In one corner, several older women were circled up tighter than a wagon train. Their husbands were huddled near the windows smoking their cigars and pipes. From time to time both groups' voices drowned out the band.

A large crystal bowl rested on a pedestal in the center of the room. Clint watched young men select red heart-shaped papers from the bowl and read the name written inside. Some smiled, some frowned, and some quietly slipped the paper back into the bowl and made another selection. As each man walked away he pinned the paper heart to the sleeve of his shirt. Finally there was only one heart left in the bowl, and no young man remained to pick it up.

"Mr. Matthews." Miss Peach waddled toward him, her eyes gleaming with purpose. "I wonder if I might talk with you a moment?"

Clint saw the colonel conversing with a group of the town's matrons. He seemed in no danger, so Clint gave his attention to Miss Peach.

"I'm trying to decide if a handsome man like you would be married." She placed her hand on his sleeve.

"No, I'm not, ma'am," Clint answered without encouraging her to continue. Many a woman had called him handsome, but that was before the last four years had chiseled a hardness into his strong jawline and darkened his eyes to a steely blue.

When he didn't elaborate, Miss Peach continued her quest. "And how old might you be, sir?"

Clint raised one dark eyebrow. "Old enough to know I want to remain unbranded."

Miss Peach laughed and swatted his arm as though he'd just said something unbelievable. She didn't bother to look up into his deadly serious eyes. "Well, Mr. Matthews, I have a problem. You see, I put the names of all my young female guests into this bowl." She pulled him to the center of the room like a wrangler dragging a yearling calf. "It seems I miscounted, and there is one sweet young thing left. Now, Mr. Matthews, what kind of Valentine's Day party would we have without every girl having an escort?"

Clint fought the urge to say just how little he cared about her problem. He knew what was coming. If she'd been a man he would have shrugged her hand off his arm and told her in no uncertain terms what she could do with the last paper heart in her bowl. But by now they were in the center of the room with everyone watching them.

"Now, don't worry." Miss Peach patted his arm. "I talked with the colonel, and he thinks it's a grand idea if you relax for an evening."

Clint glanced over to Colonel Winters and found the old man smiling sheepishly at him.

The little woman pulled the remaining paper from the bowl and unfolded it. "Oh, my, my," she whispered with the same reverence she used when discussing incurable diseases.

Clint stood still as she pinned the paper heart on his sleeve. He was not a man who allowed himself to be manipulated, but Miss Peach couldn't see the anger in his eyes.

"Your sweetheart for the evening is Miss Amanda Hamilton. She's a fine woman. A fine woman. Everyone in this town respects her."

He thought of reminding Miss Peach that Amanda Hamilton was the last name in the bowl. Not exactly the pick of the litter. Closing his eyes, Clint swore to himself. Not only did he hate parties and crowds, but now he had to spend an entire evening talking to the least popular and probably the homeliest girl in town.

Miss Peach patted him with something akin to sympathy. "She's not here yet. Maybe she won't show up." The little lady then looked guilty about her own uncharitable thoughts. "She's a fine woman. A fine woman."

"You said that before," Clint reminded her.

"Oh, did I?" Miss Peach was looking around for an escape. "Well, now, don't you worry, Mr. Matthews, when she comes I'll introduce you. She wasn't able to attend my party last year, but I made her promise to come this time."

"Great," Clint mumbled, suspecting she was not only the homeliest old maid in town, but also a leftover from years past.

He remembered noticing one of the cowhands spiking the punch when they came in. Suddenly he was very thirsty.

Clink drank and watched the dancers. The evening wore on, and he began to relax. He leaned his long, thin frame against a corner and studied the folks of this little town. They looked nice enough, but he'd learned a long time ago that folks in their Sunday best acted a great deal different than the same people fighting for a cause. Some of the same men who'd burned his house in Kansas, causing his wife's death, had shown up at the funeral the next day wearing their mourning clothes. If he'd known who they were at the funeral, he'd have shot them during the service.

It was far better not to get involved with people, he'd decided. Stay on the outside. If they don't

matter to you, they can't hurt you. He'd been hurt
enough times to have learned this lesson well.

"Mr. Matthews," Miss Peach called from the
foyer. "Oh, Mr. Matthews."

Clint pushed himself away from the wall and
looked into the hallway. Miss Peach was coming
through the door with another victim in tow. This
time her prey was a tall woman Clint guessed to be
in her mid-twenties. Her brown hair was twisted
into a tight knot at the nape of her neck, and her
clothes were tailored more like a schoolmarm's
uniform than a party dress. The box-shaped jacket
made her look heavy from shoulder to waist. She
stood out like a tall cornstalk in a flower bed of
pastel colors.

As she neared, the woman looked straight at
him. She had icy gray eyes, and there was no
softness in her carriage.

"Mr. Matthews," Miss Peach began, "I know
you want to meet your sweetheart for the evening.
May I present Miss Amanda Hamilton? She's a fine
woman, a fine woman. Runs the town's newspaper all by herself and does a grand job."

Clint knew he was supposed to shake hands or
say something, but all he could do was stare at the
person before him. He'd expected some dumpy
little half-wit who giggled and babbled while she
brushed crumbs off her dress. Amanda Hamilton,
if she didn't break from her rigid stance, was
indeed, as Miss Peach almost said, a fine-looking
woman.

"I'm sorry I'm late," she said with no hint of
honesty in her voice. "I had to finish the edition
that goes out tomorrow."

"Oh, that's quite all right, dear. I'm just so glad you could come." Miss Peach was a southern lady who knew how to pretend even when those around her didn't. "Mr. Matthews has been patiently waiting for you. Now you two get acquainted while I replenish the refreshments. What with all the dancing, everyone is drinking more punch than I counted on."

She wandered off, leaving Clint and Amanda staring at each other. He couldn't stop looking at her eyes. They were the color of the endless sky on a cloudy day. Blue—no, gray. Dear Lord, he thought, a man could get lost forever in those eyes.

"Would—would you like to sit down?" Clint stammered like a boy at his first party.

"Thanks." Amanda moved to a pair of chairs in one corner of the room. For several minutes she watched the dancers, studying them more than enjoying them.

Clint folded himself into the chair beside her and wondered if she even knew he was there. She seemed interested in everyone but him. He liked being alone, but he wasn't too fond of being ignored.

"Can I get you some punch?" He tried to break the ice that had formed around her.

"'*May* I,'" she corrected him. "And yes, you may."

Clint walked away mumbling, "Hell, lady, you *may* want to get it yourself next time."

When he returned she thanked him for the drink, then resumed her observation of the dancers without even trying to start a conversation.

He leaned back and watched her. She wasn't bad
looking, but she was as cold as a January frost.
Everything about her told him she had no more
interest in socializing than he did. Even her shoes
were the black lace-up winter boots rather than
the soft satin-topped dancing shoes most of the
younger women wore. If he decided to stay in
town, he might try to learn more about her—not
because he was interested in her socially, of
course, but just out of curiosity.

Finally he could stand the silence no longer.
"Would you like to dance, Miss Amanda?" With a
Colt crammed into his boot, the last thing he
wanted to do was dance, but he could hardly
spend the evening not saying a word.

"No, thank you," she answered without looking
at him.

Anger had a way of twisting in Clint even faster
than his finger could pull a trigger. "All right. Why
don't we just sit here and ignore each other for a
while longer?"

Amanda looked at him for the first time. Their
eyes met and held as if waiting for the other to
draw. He could see sparks of gold flash in the
depths of her eyes like lightning through thunder-
clouds.

Slowly she turned until she was facing him. Her
face softened slightly. "I'm sorry, Mr . . . ?"

"Matthews. Clint Matthews."

"I'm sorry, Mr. Matthews. Maybe I should explain. You see, I know I was the last name drawn
from Miss Peach's famous bowl and you got saddled with me for the evening."

Clint raised an eyebrow. If there was one thing

he admired it was honesty. "Are you a mind reader or a reporter?"

To his amazement Amanda smiled briefly. "It doesn't take a mind reader to know what happened before I got here. You see, Mr. Matthews, I'm the least preferred of all the single women in town."

He didn't interrupt or argue.

"First," she continued, appreciating his silence, "I'm taller than over half the men in this room, and no man wants to spend the evening looking up. Second, I'm educated, and that in a woman is worse than the pox."

For the first time in many months Clint laughed. Really laughed. When he was able, he said, "And I'm the innocent stranger who got harnessed with you tonight."

Amanda lifted her head. "Well, you're no prize, either. I know you're the colonel's hired gun, and I doubt that any woman in this room was pining to have her name pinned to your sleeve tonight."

Clint nodded as he continued to chuckle, only now Amanda joined him. Several folks glanced their way, deciding the spinster and the gunman must have had too much punch.

"Truce." Clint held up his hand. "Since we'll be together for the next few hours, let's try not to kill each other."

"Not that anyone in the room would care," Amanda said.

"Not that anyone would care," Clint agreed.

"Then, Mr. Matthews, I'd like to dance." Amanda stood and smiled when he unfolded his tall frame. "It's been a long time since I've danced without a man's head on my shoulder."

Clint pulled her into his arms, enjoying the way he could look her in the eye as they danced. Her slender body moved against him, naturally swaying with his long steps. They danced three reels before he realized the Colt in his boot had worn the hide off his leg.

Chapter Two

"Would you mind stepping outside for a minute?" Clint tried not to limp in pain.

Amanda looked at him as if he'd asked something improper. After a moment she slowly nodded.

They crossed the dance floor and foyer. She didn't hesitate as he opened the front door for her. The long wide porch was perfect for strolling in the shadows, but the weather wasn't cooperating this starless night. The cold wind cut a chilling blast through their bones, and the air was heavy with promised rain.

Clint slipped the gun out of his boot and put it in his holster. "Thanks," he said, smiling at the sudden lack of pain against his leg. "I'm not sure I could have danced another round."

He couldn't see Amanda's eyes in the darkness,

but he could hear the sudden fire in her words. "You carry a gun in your boot!"

"Yeah." Clint couldn't believe she was surprised. If the truth were known there were probably several men here tonight with weapons tucked out of sight. But they'd had the sense to bring something smaller than a Colt. "In case there's trouble it's always best to have a weapon handy."

Amanda turned her back to him and hugged her jacket tightly around her. "I don't like guns. Just being around them makes me nervous. Didn't you ever hear that the pen is mightier than the sword?"

"Sure, lady, but ink never stopped a bullet."

"And bullets never solved a problem." She studied his shadowy outline, forgetting the cold wind. "Did you know that several farmers have started carrying weapons just because the colonel hired you?"

"I'm not here to start trouble."

"But you'll be here to finish it if there's a fight. You'll end it by killing someone." She couldn't have said the words in the light, but in the darkness she felt somehow protected. While they were dancing, it had been easy to forget what he did for a living. Now, in the shadows, she was reminded of his reason for coming to her town.

"Look, lady, don't be mad at me. I didn't start this fight." Clint hated it when folks assumed that trouble followed him everywhere just because he was fast with a gun. "I walked into this nest of hate. It didn't come packed in my bags."

Amanda turned her face toward the windows. He was right. The hate in Quail Springs had been building for months. Farmers needed to fence the land to protect their crops, and cattlemen like Colonel Winters needed space for their herds to roam. But right or not, Clint Matthews could only mean more trouble in a town that already had enough.

"Tell me, Mr. Matthews"—she couldn't stop questioning; digging out facts was in her blood from three generations of newspapermen—"how many men have you killed?" Already the headline for this interview was forming in her mind.

Clint pulled out a thin cigar and lit it before answering. He'd been asked the same questions in every town he'd ridden into for four years. "Not counting the men who needed killing . . . none."

"And how do you define a man who needs killing?"

"Someone pointing a gun at me," Clint answered simply. When she didn't comment, he added, "Look, Miss Hamilton, I don't keep score. This isn't a game; it's my job. I'm not hired to kill people. I'm hired to keep folks alive."

"Like Colonel Winters?"

"Like Colonel Winters," he echoed.

She leaned closer to him in the shadows. "And what if the colonel is doing something wrong?"

"That's for the law to decide, not me."

Amanda stomped her foot in frustration. "Damn, I hate this conflict!"

Clint wanted to change the subject. "I don't think young ladies are supposed to curse. What if I told Miss Peach? She'd stop saying what a fine woman you are."

Amanda couldn't hide the smile that crept over

her lips. "Guess I'd better stop. I'd hate to lower my standing as the least eligible old maid in town."

Clint found this topic much safer than the last. "You know, you're not a bad looking woman. Height's not always a drawback. If you'd curb that tongue a bit, you could move right up to the top ten."

"I don't remember asking for your advice," Amanda answered. "And I can do without your back-handed compliments. If I can't speak my mind in front of a man, he's not worth talking to. I will not pretend to be stupid just so I can be married and bedded and pregnant for the rest of my life."

Maybe this wasn't a safe topic after all, Clint thought. Maybe they should go back to talking about the men he'd killed. Describing death seemed to upset her less than talking about her marital status. "Look, lady, I was only trying to help."

"First, Mr. Matthews"—she pushed her finger into his chest—"I don't need your help. Second, stop referring to me as 'lady,' and third, you've done enough for my reputation by asking me to step out here on the porch with you. Everyone at the party will think you brought me out here to kiss me."

She was so close he could feel her breath against his cheek. "Is that what you thought?"

Amanda didn't want to admit her thoughts. She'd enjoyed dancing with him. His hands had felt good around her waist. Formal, not too inti-mate, but comforting. For a moment she could almost believe she was like every other girl in the room and had a sweetheart for the evening. Not that she wanted to be like everyone else, but sometimes it got a little lonely never being asked to dance, except by the older men who had been friends of her father.

"That's exactly what I thought, but that was before I knew you stepped out only to rearrange your arsenal."

His voice came slow and low. "You thought that and you agreed to step out with me? You surprise me, Miss Hamilton."

She was thankful he couldn't see her face turning as red as the paper heart he wore on his sleeve. For once in her life she could think of nothing to say. If she said yes, she would be admitting she wanted to be kissed, and if she said no, she would be lying, which she never did. Suddenly she wished the north wind were ten degrees colder. Maybe it would freeze the fire in her cheeks.

Clint moved sideways into the complete blackness beside the window. "Miss Hamilton, step over here out of the light and I'll make the rumors true."

She moved her hands into the pockets of her short jacket and remained still. "Who said I wanted to kiss you? Maybe I just wanted folks to talk. First, I—"

His arm reached out into the pale light and pulled her into the blackness. In an instant she moved from the freezing cold into his warm arms. After turning her so that his back blocked the wind, he pulled her against him. "Stop counting everything, Amanda. Some things just have to be felt." His lips brushed along her cheek until he found her mouth.

"I don't think—"

"Shut up, Amanda," he whispered as his mouth covered hers with more gentleness than she'd thought a gunslinger could possess.

His kiss deepened, and she no longer felt the cold. Closing her eyes, she gave herself fully. All her life she'd wondered what it would be like to be kissed like this, but she'd given up hope of ever having it happen to her. The kiss spoke of passion and reverence, power and strength, but not domination.

Slowly she removed her hands from her pockets and slid them up his chest to his hair. His thick black hair was softer than she'd thought it would be and it felt wonderful between her fingers.

As her mouth opened in pleasure, his kiss changed slightly, causing a flame to shoot through her like fire through dry sagebrush. His fingers shoved her jacket aside, and he wrapped his hands wide around her waist, pulling her closer to him. She didn't withdraw, but allowed him to press her against his chest.

His hands twisted in her hair, sending pins flying and allowing the brown velvet locks to tumble past her waist. While his palms cradled her head, his lips left her mouth and moved to the lace at her neckline. Very softly he kissed the tender skin at her throat, then returned to her lips as if starving for the taste of her mouth. His fingers moved over her blouse, pulling at the material as he kissed her.

She could feel the warmth of his touch even

through her tightly laced corset. His fingers were strong and bold with a need to touch her.

He grew more urgent, demanding more as she felt his heart pound against her own. A storm was raging inside her, a storm she wasn't sure she ever wanted to stop. Dancing with him had made her feel like a part of life and not an observer, but kissing him made her feel like a woman.

The front door suddenly popped open, jarring them back to reality. Clint pulled her deeper into the shadows. His arms remained around her, protecting, sheltering her. A young couple moved to their waiting buggy, but their giggling left no doubt that they'd recognized the two tall shadows in the corner of the porch.

When they were once more alone, Clint stood away from her. "I'm sorry." He said the words as if they caused him great pain. As if he'd never said them to anyone before in his life.

Amanda was embarrassed by what she'd allowed him to do. She wasn't foolish or naive enough to think that he'd taken any more than she'd freely given, but his apology made her furious. "I've never been kissed like that before." She hurried toward the door, pinning her hair up in haste. "And I'm not sorry, but it will be a cold day in hell before I allow you to touch me again."

Clint opened his mouth to explain he was sorry only that he caused her embarrassment, but she was like a windmill in full spin.

"Good night, Mr. Matthews." She slammed the door and was gone.

Clint slapped his palm against the porch post and swore. He couldn't believe he'd kissed her.

Always, his first rule had been not to get involved. He called himself every name he could think of.

It took him several minutes to cool off enough to return to the dance. When he reentered the foyer, Amanda was saying good night to Miss Peach and Colonel Winters. Clint stood for a moment staring at her, wondering how a woman who held herself so tightly in check could feel so right in a man's arms.

"Thank you for inviting me, but I must get home. Mr. Matthews and I just checked the weather, and I'm afraid I'd best hurry in order to walk back before the rain starts."

"I wish you could stay longer, but I'm so glad you came." Miss Peach glanced toward Clint. "I'm sure Mr. Matthews wouldn't mind seeing you home."

Clint wanted to scream. No, not another moment alone with this woman. Her righteousness was as tightly bound as her bust line. But he simply nodded once.

"That won't be necessary." Amanda's voice could have cut glass.

Miss Peach looked at the colonel with pleading eyes, and the old man melted as he had for thirty years. His words were issued as an order to Clint, but his eyes never left Miss Peach's face. "Take my buggy and see Miss Hamilton home. I'll be here when you get back." His voice softened. "It wouldn't be proper for a lady to walk alone this late. She might run into Lawson and his gang of drinking buddies."

Miss Peach smiled and put her hand on the colonel's.

Clint grabbed his coat and left to fetch the buggy. He decided he'd simply get this over with, then see that his and Amanda Hamilton's paths never crossed again. He'd always hated her type of woman. He hoped she never married, for if she did, she'd make some poor man's life a living hell.

When he returned to the house, Amanda was gone. She was a half block down the street before he caught up with her.

"Get in!" he ordered with more anger in his voice than he'd intended.

"Go to hell."

"Look, lady"—Clint steered close to her—"I'm going to see you home if I have to hog-tie you and throw you in this buggy. So get in!"

Amanda continued to walk. "I can't think of a man I dislike more than I do you, Mr. Matthews."

Suddenly Clint laughed. Something about this woman brought all of his emotions to the surface. "Do all your evenings with gentlemen end like this, lady?"

"First, stop calling me 'lady,' and second, you are certainly no gentleman." She pulled her cape hood low as rain began to splatter her face.

Clint jumped down from the buggy and was standing in front of her before she could step aside. "Why?" he asked. "Because I kissed you the way you were meant to be kissed?"

Amanda tried to walk around him, but he grabbed her arm in a firm grip. "Answer me, Amanda." His breath was warm against her cold face.

The truth was the only thing that came to her mind, and she always spoke her mind. "I've never been kissed like that. I've never been treated like this. Let go of my arm." Her chin rose slightly as he released her. "And don't you dare apologize. I want only your word that you'll never try to kiss me again."

"Will you get in the buggy if I promise? We can't just stand here and get soaked."

Amanda nodded and allowed him to help her up into the seat.

A hundred thoughts were racing through Clint's mind. He needed time to think. Without a word he picked up the reins and slapped the horses into action. At this moment he'd have shot himself in the leg rather than touch this woman again. He suspected she felt the same way. Kissing her on the porch was the dumbest thing he'd ever done. What made it worse was he wasn't a bit sorry.

He drove a short piece before Amanda pointed. "Up there," she said simply. "I live above the newspaper office."

Clint stopped the horses and helped her down.

He walked her silently to the door of the office. "Good night, Miss Hamilton," he said very formally.

"Good night, Mr. Matthews." Her voice was as cold as the north wind again. "Thank you for seeing me home."

She went inside and closed the door before he had time to say another word. The click of the lock seemed to put a period to an evening that had awakened feelings in Clint he thought he'd buried long ago with his wife. Feelings he didn't ever want to feel again.

He shoved his hat lower to shield his face from

the rain and headed toward the buggy as a light came on in what seemed to be her office. Just as he stepped up to the buckboard, he heard the shattering of glass and a startled scream. The light flickered and vanished, leaving only darkness inside the newspaper office and dread in Clint's heart.

Chapter Three

With one mighty push of his shoulder, Clint broke the lock. In an instant he'd pulled his Colt and stepped inside the darkened office. The smell of ink and paper filled the air mixed with the rank odor of kerosene.

"Amanda?" Clint moved slowly, allowing his eyes to adjust to the blackness.

From the shadows deep inside the shop he could hear soft thuds, like someone rolling across the floor.

Without moving his gun hand, he reached into his vest pocket and pulled out a match. Holding it away from his body, not wanting to present a sudden target in the darkness, Clint struck it against his thumbnail. The sulfur flared and light spread across the room for an instant. Shattered fragments of glass from a broken lamp littered the floor in front of him. Clearly, someone had frantically jerked every drawer open. Papers and type trays were scattered everywhere.

He heard a moan of pain and feet scuffling. Clint blew out the match and tossed it out the front door before moving toward the sound.

Raising his weapon, he felt his way between the high worktables. He could hear breathing, but he couldn't tell how many others besides Amanda were in the darkness.

Someone shoved against his shoulder, almost knocking him down. Clint twirled and grabbed a second form running past him. Suddenly arms and legs were hitting him from all directions. He fought to control the attack before launching a war of his own. A back door opened somewhere in the blackness, allowing a weak beam of moonlight to powder the room.

"Let me go!" Amanda screamed. "Let me go!"

Clint jerked her body against his, no longer aware of the blows she was delivering from all directions. "Stop!" he yelled as he ducked her assaults. "Amanda, it's me."

She froze for a moment, then swung her fist again in anger, not fright, clipping him hard on the chin. He released her and stepped back.

"Are you crazy, lady? I came to help."

"Help!" She stormed at him again, and for the first time in his life the gunfighter backed down. "I was getting the better of the intruder before you came in and *helped*. If you'd stayed out of it, I'd have him now and not just a wide-open back door."

Clint wondered briefly if anyone in town would

bother to charge him if he plugged her right now. "I thought you were hurt."

"I am, but I can still take care of myself." Her voice was almost normal now, but her breath was coming in short gasps. "There's a lamp on the table behind you. We'd better get some light in here. You seem to be making a habit of attacking me in the dark."

Clint grumbled and lit the lamp. When he turned, he was unprepared for the sight before him. Amanda was leaning back against one of the tables. Her hair tumbled around her in soft brown curls. The top three buttons of her blouse were ripped away, and the sleeve of her jacket had been torn completely off at the shoulder. Her face was turned toward the light, but her eyes were closed. Tears inched down her cheeks even as she fought to stop them.

Clint stood staring at the most beautiful woman he'd ever seen. He wanted to comfort her, but he wasn't sure what to say. All he could think about was how lovely she looked with her cheeks all red and her hair down. Somehow he knew that putting those thoughts into words would have little calming effect on her.

He moved close beside her. "Are you hurt?" He tried to make the words soft and caring, but his voice was rusty.

She nodded without opening her eyes and lifted her arm. A long red line oozed from her elbow to her palm. "I cut it on the glass on the floor."

She stared at the blood now dripping onto her skirt. "I'm going to faint," she said as her eyes rolled back and she fell toward him.

Clint caught her just before her head hit the floor. He lifted her gently in his arms and carried her up the stairs. As he walked into a tiny one-room apartment, he wondered for a moment if Amanda lived alone. The last thing he wanted to encounter was an elderly mother and father. Then he dismissed the thought. Anyone upstairs would have to be deaf not to have heard the fight.

He maneuvered his way around several trunks by moonlight. After laying her on a bed, he felt around for a lamp, but his fingers brushed the cold metal of a gun. He couldn't help but smile. So, Miss Self-Assured did believe in the effectiveness of guns after all.

Forcing himself not to comment aloud, he found a lamp and lit it, then moved to the washstand and poured a basin of cold water. Sitting on her bed, he cleaned the wound and wrapped it with a clean towel. The cut was not deep and looked like little more than a scratch when the bleeding stopped.

Amanda moaned and rolled on her side toward him. Clint studied her in the pale flickering light. Even now, after all the things she'd said to him, he had to fight the urge to kiss her. He wanted nothing less than to stretch out beside her. It seemed a lifetime since he'd lain beside a woman. The one kiss they'd shared had meant more to him than the attentions of all the women he'd known in bars from El Paso to Galveston.

She slowly opened her eyes. For a moment she looked up at him as if he were a dream that would fade. Her fingers tightened slightly against the wool of his pant leg. The action meant nothing to her, but something twisted around his heart.

"You're going to be fine." He pushed a strand of hair from her face. "I cleaned the cut and wrapped it. In a few days you won't even know it was there."

Amanda sat up and looked at her arm. "Thank you," she mumbled. "I'm not afraid of much, but the sight of blood always makes my head spin."

"Is that why you hate guns?" Clint felt suddenly awkward sitting on the edge of her bed. He stood and paced the tiny room. If he didn't put some distance between them, he'd have her in his arms again.

"Among other reasons," Amanda answered as she examined the damage to her clothes.

"Then why do you keep a huge old Paterson by your bed?" He watched pain suddenly fill her eyes and wished he hadn't asked.

"It was my father's," she whispered. "I've kept everything of his and Mother's." She pointed to the trunks. "Besides, he died with that gun in his hand."

"He died in a gunfight?" Clint asked as he wondered why that should surprise him. Gunshot wounds were a common cause of death in Texas, and he'd done his share to increase the rate.

Amanda's nervous laughter had no humor in it. "My father fired a gun only a few times in his life. The thing wasn't even loaded when he pulled it from his drawer downstairs. But the angry reader didn't know that. He emptied his gun into my father without even noticing me standing a few feet away."

Clint leaned against the window frame. "How old were you?"

"Ten," Amanda answered. "My mother and I published the paper after that, until she died last year."

Clint could imagine what it had been like for her as a little girl to watch her father die. Judging by the trunks, he could tell she was not a person who let go easily.

"I'm sorry," he mumbled, realizing he'd said those words twice to her in one night.

Amanda eased off the bed. "It was a long time ago. I don't dwell on it."

"Are these your parents' trunks?" Clint called her lie. When she nodded, he knew the truth.

Steely blue eyes watched stormy gray. He couldn't call her bluff, for he knew that even though his trunks were invisible, he also lived surrounded by the past.

Finally she looked away, pulled a shawl from the wardrobe and moved toward the door. "I'd best go clean up the glass."

Clint had no choice but to follow her downstairs. He repaired the lock he'd jerked from its door plate while she swept up the glass and mopped the floor. As he replaced the tools on a shelf, he asked, "Aren't you going to check to see what was stolen?"

Amanda hesitated but didn't meet his gaze. "I don't think anything is missing."

Clint had lived most of his life in trouble spots, and he'd learned to recognize when someone was hiding the truth. "You're lying," he said.

Her head shot up, and the fire was back in her eyes. "I'm in the habit of telling the truth, Mr. Matthews."

"Then what are you hiding? You know what he was looking for, don't you?"

Amanda opened her mouth to lie, then hesitated. She could tell him the truth without really telling him anything. "Yes. I know what he wanted. He thought I'd be stupid enough to write down the farmers' meeting place." Frustrated, she continued, "You can tell Colonel Winters that his man found nothing and did not succeed in killing me."

Clint laughed. "What makes you think the colonel had anything to do with this? And from what I heard, you were trying to kill the intruder, not the other way around."

He raked his fingers through his hair. "Why would the colonel send me to escort you home if he'd sent someone to ransack your place? And how would you know about the meeting place unless you were planning to go to the meeting?"

Amanda's face was a mask. "I'll tell you no more."

He moved to stand only inches from her. "You've got to tell me. Maybe I can stop the fight if I know where the farmers are meeting!" He was yelling now as if she were half a block away.

"No!"

"Maybe you should trust me."

"I'll never trust a man like you."

Clint fought the urge to pull her to him and prove her a liar. "You're not planning to go."

"I'm not in the habit of taking orders from gunfighters."

"If there is such a meeting, there could be

trouble. A woman would have no place anywhere near there."

"I run a paper. I print the truth, and I have to see it to print it."

"You're not going!"

Amanda raised her head slightly. "You can't stop me."

Clint stepped to the door. "At least report the break-in to the sheriff."

She moved behind him, ready to lock the door as soon as he passed. "There has been no sheriff since that gambler Don Lawson came to town a month ago."

Clint's fist clenched and relaxed before he finally gained enough control to say "Good night, Miss Hamilton."

She pulled her shawl close around her. "Goodbye, Mr. Matthews."

After locking the door, Amanda climbed the staircase slowly. She'd never felt quite so alone as she did tonight. Her cheeks still burned with anger from the argument they'd had, and she could not push the memory of his kiss from her mind. She kept recalling the way he'd talked to her at the dance, the way he'd kissed her in the shadows, the way he'd left, slamming the door as though he never wanted to see her again.

She'd never attended the Valentine's Day party before, because she feared the pain of being the one woman not chosen. But tonight she had taken the risk. She'd been held and kissed as if she were really Clint's valentine, but she'd also been hurt, just as she'd feared.

With a sudden longing, she ran to one of the trunks where her parents' things were stored. After searching through several boxes of old letters, she found a single homemade valentine her father had given to her mother when they were young. Yellowed and worn, the folds sliced the paper in half, but the love was still there.

Amanda crushed the card to her, trying to remember her parents' love. A love they'd shared with her. She fought down a sob. They were gone, and even keeping all their belongings close around her couldn't bring them back. She'd been wrong even to dream that Clint cared. Nothing, no one, would ever mean as much to him as this old valentine meant to her.

Undressing slowly, she allowed tears to fall unguarded. The bruises on her body from fighting the intruder were nothing compared to the bruises Clint had left on her heart. How could he have kissed her as no man had ever dared, then walked away without a word?

She climbed into bed and pulled the quilts over her. As she touched her bandaged arm, she thought of what a puzzle he was. So tender one moment, so cold the next. He was not a man she could trust. But he had done one thing that no other man had ever done for Amanda Hamilton. He had made her feel like a woman.

She closed her eyes and wished it were another time, another place. As the tears flowed, she knew there would never be a place or time for her and Clint. His gun was a part of him, and her hatred of violence would never change. She had to do her part to stop this range war, just as he thought he had to do his job.

Frustrated, she pushed the tears from her cheek and reached for her father's gun. With a tug she removed the note stuffed inside the barrel. As she memorized the directions to the farmers' meeting place, she set her mind to the task she must do, no matter what the danger or how many men like Clint Matthews tried to stop her.

Chapter Four

Clint went back to the dance and waited outside in the cold until the colonel finally decided it was time to go home. He rode back to the ranch beside the buggy, thankful that the old man wasn't in a talkative mood.

By the time they were halfway to the ranch, Clint had decided that getting mixed up with Amanda Hamilton was like playing with fire in the middle of a dry prairie. She was headstrong, stubborn, and short-tempered. She was also the only woman he'd wanted to hold in his arms all night since his wife died. But he had a feeling that if trouble didn't come looking for Amanda, she would go to find it. The last thing he needed in his life was a woman like her.

It was almost dawn when the colonel's buggy

pulled through the gate of the ranch. Clint could relax now. Here the colonel was safe. He walked to the bunkhouse without saying a word to anyone and collapsed onto his bunk, not bothering to remove his gun. Even though it took him some time to fall asleep, he didn't open his eyes. He didn't want to rehash the party with the returning cowhands. They kept their distance, and he liked it that way.

In what seemed like only minutes, someone kicked at the toe of his boot. "Matthews, the colonel wants to see you about somethin' over at the house."

Clint sat up, instantly wide awake. He glanced at the windows and noted the sun was already high. Within five minutes he was standing in the colonel's study with a cup of steaming coffee in his hand.

"Matthews"—the colonel rose from behind a massive desk and walked toward Clint—"I got a job I need you to do. I found out from a friend of mine that the farmers are planning a big meeting tomorrow night. There's a few troublemakers, like that gambler, Lawson, who'd like to make this a war." He lit a cigar as fat as his finger. "Now, son, I'm not afraid of a fight. I fought Indians for this land, and I can sure as hell fight sodbusters, but only as a last resort."

Clint took a deep breath. He'd guessed the colonel was a reasonable man, but until this moment he hadn't been sure. Reason seemed to die when men fought over land. Clint decided to test him further. "Someone broke into Miss Hamilton's place last night looking for the location of that meeting." He was relieved by the colonel's surprised reaction.

"Damn fool. There were plenty of men spreading that information at Miss Peach's party." The old man took a puff of his cigar and smiled to himself. "Speaking of Miss Peach, I'm kind of fond of that little woman. She doesn't approve of all this trouble between the farmers and the ranchers. She'd like to see something settled, and so would I."

Clint grinned. He'd never have guessed the old man would be influenced by a woman. "What do you want me to do?" he asked, happy that for once he might not have to pull his gun to settle a fight.

"I want you to ride into town and get a room. Spend the night. Then go to the farmers' meeting tomorrow and listen to what's got the burr under their saddles this week and what they plan to do about it. I'm willing to make allowances, but I'm not backing down like some pup and allowing them to fence off my water."

"Why not send one of your men?" Clint could think of several ranch hands who could do the job.

"Because there might be trouble. My boys are good, but there are a few in town, like Lawson, who might shoot first and ask questions later. If that happens I want you to be the one asking the questions."

"I understand." Clint set his cup down and started toward the door. Several things needed doing before he'd feel right leaving the colonel. "I want to talk to a few of the hands before I load up."

The colonel's brow wrinkled. "Another thing, Matthews. I want you to see to it that that Hamil-

ton woman is nowhere near the meeting. We'll tell
her about the deal when it's settled. If there's
trouble I don't want to read about it in the paper."

"Right." Clint nodded once and left the room,
wondering how on earth he could keep Amanda
away from the meeting when she already knew
about it.

It was after midnight when Amanda blew out
her lamp and snuggled down under the covers.
She knew she needed rest, but the memory of
Clint's kiss haunted her again tonight as it had last
night. As she drifted in and out of sleep, dreams
became reality and reality dreams.

Slowly she opened her eyes to the pale shadowy
light of her apartment. Clint's tall slender outline
was silhouetted against the window. His hat was
low, shadowing his face, but there was no mistak-
ing his familiar stance. Like a man sure of himself,
but unsure of his surroundings, she thought. A
tiny light from his thin cigar moved with his hand.
The aroma of aged tobacco drifted across the air in
thin white clouds.

He turned toward her, slowly unbuttoned his
coat and removed his hat. His always angry eyes
looked tired, ready to rest from his world. He
lowered his gaze from her face to the swell of her
breasts above the camisole she slept in. Carelessly
he tossed his coat and hat over a rocking chair.

As he moved toward her, he whispered in a
voice as low as faraway thunder, "Lord, lady,
you're something to behold. I told myself a thousand times I wouldn't come here tonight, but I
knew I'd never sleep until I saw you."

Amanda smiled and closed her eyes, enjoying the dream. She stretched her arms above the covers, loving the way his words warmed her. When she opened her eyes, her dream was nearer, more real. Timidly she touched the hard outline of his shoulders. His cheek was cold as it brushed against her face.

The memory of their one kiss blended with her dream as his mouth brushed hers. For a moment she was too peaceful and happy in her fantasy to respond. His arms pulled her up against the wall of his chest as his mouth roamed over her face. Her nearness was warming his skin, making the dream seem real.

"A dream," she managed to whisper before he silenced her with another kiss. The memory of their kiss at the party paled in comparison to this. His lips seemed to demand her very soul in return for the pleasure they brought her. It was too early to think of what she should do. All Amanda wanted was to snuggle deeper into his arms and enjoy the unexpected happiness he brought her.

When his lips left her mouth and trailed to her ear, he whispered, "All I've been able to think of since the party was how much I wanted to hold you again." He pulled her tightly against him in a hug as though his need to hold her was far more than physical. "You feel so right in my arms." He allowed his hands to slide to her waist and up over her back. "You taste like Heaven. Something this right could never be a dream."

Then he was kissing her again with a passion driven by years of starvation. His lips were hard and demanding as his hands molded her close to him, drawing her from her dream to the real world of his need. His hunger set a fire deep inside her that spread over Amanda like a fever she thought must surely be fatal.

When she was younger she might have been shocked by his boldness. But for the moment she wanted only to enjoy. She was old enough to accept and young enough to respond. She didn't want to think; she only wanted to be alive and in his arms.

Hesitantly, she brushed her fingers along his shoulders enjoying the feel of his powerful body, loving the way her soft touch tightened his muscles until they felt like carved wood beneath her fingers. His hair was thick and longer than that of the businessmen in town. He smelled of the outdoors—wind, morning frost, campfires, and horses.

Her fingers plowed into his hair and pulled his face closer as her body pushed against his. As his kiss grew wilder, his hands slowed to a loving touch. He warmed her body with tender caresses as his fingers touched her where no other man had dared.

"I knew you'd feel like perfection without that damn corset binding you," he whispered into her ear as his hands spread wide just beneath her breasts.

Without logic or reason, she accepted his nearness. She was in a reality far better than any dream. When his hand brushed her breast, she moaned with pleasure, opening her mouth as he deepened his kiss.

For a long moment there was no time other than

now and no place but each other's arms. His kiss turned gentle as he remembered how to care.

She moaned softly and moved within his arms. His fingers covered her breast, loving the softness that filled his hand. She didn't have to tell him this was the first time for her; he could feel her trembling.

He hesitated, knowing that if he went further, there would be no stopping until the journey was complete. "Amanda," he whispered as he collected his last ounce of willpower and removed his hand from her breast. "I hadn't meant to . . ."

Sanity returned to her mind as well. She pulled away from his arms and rolled across the bed. In an instant she was on her feet and reaching for her robe along with her last scrap of pride. "Don't you dare apologize for kissing me again, Mr. Matthews." Her fingers shook slightly as she turned up the lamp. "Or I swear I'll load that Paterson and shoot you myself. I don't get many such kisses, and I'll be damned if I'll repent my sins while I'm still warm from the act."

Clint laughed. He'd expected her to be angry because he'd broken into her room and taken liberties he knew he had no right to take. But not Amanda. His entire body ached to hold her again.

"I wouldn't dream of being sorry for kissing you. In fact"—he moved toward her—"I wouldn't mind repeating the crime."

Amanda backed to the windows. "No!" Kissing him because she thought he was part of a dream was one thing. Kissing him wide awake in the light was another. "I'm not used to having men break into my home in the middle of the night. What do you want?"

Thinking he'd like to tell her what he wanted—or better yet, show her, Clint smiled. But now was not the time. "I came to tell you not to go to the farmers' meeting tomorrow."

"We've been over this before. What makes you think you have that right?"

"It's not my order; it's the colonel's." Clint lowered his voice. "But I agree. There might be trouble. It's no place for a lady."

"I'm a newspaperwoman first. If there's a story I'll go."

"You're not going. If I have to tie you up and lock you in one of these trunks, I will." He looked around her tiny apartment as if deciding which trunk would best suit his purpose.

"You'd do that?" Her question tested the steel in his gaze.

"I'll do what I have to to keep you from getting hurt."

Amanda cocked her head slightly as if weighing his words. Finally she nodded, giving up the battle. "If I don't go, I want a complete account of what happened."

Clint couldn't believe the woman had sense enough to know when to give up. Most women would have argued and cried and begged, but not Amanda. She simply proposed a bargain. He couldn't help but admire her good sense. "Deal," he answered.

"One more thing." Amanda crossed her arms. "The next time you come to call, try knocking. I'm having a new lock installed at dawn."

Clint knew he was being dismissed. He also knew if he stayed one minute longer he'd have to hold her again. The woman was an addiction. His palms were already warm with the need to touch her. He saluted and grabbed his coat. "Sometime I'll come to call when I can stay longer. I'd like to finish that discussion we were having as you woke up."

"I'm not some easy girl to be won with a few kisses, Mr. Matthews."

"That you're not, Miss Hamilton. You are every inch a woman." His knowing smile brought color to her face. "When this trouble's over I plan on coming by to prove that point."

"When this trouble's over, you may find the door bolted."

There was no softness in her words or her stance, and Clint wondered if this could possibly be the same woman he'd held in his arms only minutes before.

"I'll take that chance," he said and disappeared through the doorway as silently as he'd entered.

All day he couldn't get her from his mind. The last thing he wanted was to get involved with a woman, especially one as hot-tempered as Amanda, but there was no halfway point with her. One moment he wanted to take her to his bed and make love to her until they were both too exhausted to move, and the next moment he was fighting to keep from choking that pretty neck of hers.

With his mood as dark as the heavy clouds, Clint rode out to the meeting site. Because he didn't know the country as well as the locals, he wanted to get there plenty early and study the lay of the land. Then he planned to relax until the meeting was well under way before revealing himself.

The location was perfect for his plan. A small box canyon opened out onto flat land. Once the meeting started, no one could ride within a mile of the place without being seen. Before dark Clint stationed himself behind the rocks in the canyon where he was out of sight but probably close enough to hear everything being said. If the meeting turned ugly and the crowd became a mob, he'd stay low until everyone left.

While the sun set, Clint relaxed and watched as men started arriving. Most were farmers riding the plow horses they'd worked all day. A few looked as if they'd been drinking, but most were sober. The first men built a campfire out of dried mesquite. The others congregated around the fire in small groups, as if waiting for a leader.

Just after dark a thin man in black rode in with several men in his wake. The group parted to allow him into the center.

Clint studied the man closely, guessing him to be Don Lawson. His clothes weren't those of a farmer, and his gun was slung too low to mark him as anything but a gunfighter.

Carefully, Clint leaned against the rock in front of him so that he could hear what was being said. He kept his movements steady, not even wanting to disturb a pebble and give away his location.

Without warning, a shoulder brushed his in the darkness. He'd thought he was alone. The sudden contact made his skin feel as if it had jumped two feet away, leaving his bones and muscles behind to fend for themselves.

As he reached for his gun, a soft voice whispered, "Hello, Mr. Matthews. Glad you could make it." Her fingers patted his arm as if he were some old codger who'd managed to hobble up the church steps before the service was over.

Murderous thoughts flashed through his mind as he tried to stare through the darkness and look into her bottomless gray eyes.

Chapter Five

Amanda wished she could have seen the expression on Clint's face. From her perch at the top of the canyon, she'd watched him set up his hiding place. In the walls of the shallow gorges in these parts were caves and winding paths that led to the narrow valley in the center. She'd simply waited until dark and followed a path down to the rock where he hid.

She'd learned a long time ago not to argue when a man told her what to do. It was better to wait until he dropped his guard and then ambush him.

"Anything happening that I should report yet?" she whispered a few inches behind him.

Anger made his eyes flash brighter than the campfire. Amanda had the feeling he might have grabbed her and shaken her senseless if thirty men hadn't stood a few yards away.

"Quiet," he managed to whisper between clenched teeth.

As casually as a woman accompanying her beau to a Sunday picnic, Amanda looped her arm through his and watched the meeting. "I'll be happy to fill you in on the background of any of the men out there. I've known most of them all my life."

As she slid her cold fingers from his elbow to his hand, Clint's arm muscles tightened. "Do you mind if I borrow your jacket?" she asked.

For a moment she thought he might refuse or tell her to go freeze to death somewhere else. With forced slowness, he lifted his jacket from the rock beside him and draped it over her shoulders.

"Thanks," Amanda whispered.

His hands lingered on her shoulders. She could see just enough of his face in the firelight to know he was still angry, but his hands were gentle as they smoothed the jacket over her.

Finally, reluctantly, he lowered his hands and glanced back at the men near the fire. "I've figured out what I need to know. The farmers don't want trouble any more than the colonel does, but the gambler, Lawson, is stirring them up. He's taken every opportunity to remind them that the land is legally theirs and they can fence it off if they want to."

Suddenly an old farmer named Pap Lloyd started shouting at Lawson. Clint pulled Amanda lower behind the rock as they listened. But Pap Lloyd's slow-talking reason was no match for

Lawson's lightning tongue and itchy gun hand. One by one the men began to side with Lawson.

Amanda leaned closer to Clint. "Lawson arrived a while back. He reminds me of a weed in the garden. You don't see it coming; you just look around one day and there it is." She was so near she could almost feel his cheek blocking her breath. His taut muscles told her he felt the same way. "If I could figure out what Lawson has to gain from all this, I'd print it. He doesn't even own any land that I know of, and I'll bet his hands have never steadied a plow."

Clint considered clipping her with a right jab just under her chin to keep her quiet. The noise would be minimal, and he'd be gentlemanly enough to help her to the ground. Maybe she'd stay unconscious until the meeting was over. Holding his right fist tightly to resist temptation, he mumbled, "I've known circus barkers who were quieter than you!"

"I have as much right to be here as you do," she answered, moving a bit closer, knowing that her nearness bothered him far more than any danger they were in.

Damn, he thought, but she felt good against his side. Every time she leaned toward him to whisper in his ear, he felt the soft roundness of her breast against his arm. The gentle fullness kept brushing against him as the midnight scent of her seemed to surround him.

Lawson suddenly started yelling at Pap Lloyd, forcing their attention to the campfire. Clint knew it was time to move away from Amanda and try to stop this argument before it became a war.

"Stay here," he ordered as he moved forward, not noticing the defiant lift of her chin as he advanced toward the group.

She watched him walk into the circle of firelight. For a moment no one seemed to notice him. Then one by one all the men grew silent and stared at the stranger among them.

"I didn't come to cause trouble." Clint raised his hands away from his guns. "The colonel wants you men to know that he'd like this feud to end. He's willing to meet you halfway."

Clint looked at Pap Lloyd. Reason would come from his corner if he was strong enough to block Lawson's influence.

"We're not interested!" shouted Lawson. "Since when does a peacemaker come wearing matching Colts?"

Pap Lloyd moved between Lawson and Clint, scratching his whiskery chin. "We'll hear the gunman out."

Lawson glanced around for support, but everyone was nodding in agreement with the old man.

Taking a deep breath, Clint lowered his arms a few inches. "The colonel would like a few of you to meet with him and some of the other ranchers."

"We ain't settling this on his ranch!" Lawson yelled. "The colonel will have to stop being so high and mighty if he wants to talk!"

Clint stared at the old man, ignoring Lawson completely. "On neutral ground. How about Miss Peach's place? It's the biggest house in town."

"Or at my office," Amanda remarked as she stepped into the light.

"Damn," Lloyd mumbled, "if there ain't more

folks behind these rocks than ghosts under tomb-
stones."

"One too many if you ask me," Clint agreed.

"Why not my office? Everyone knows the paper
doesn't take sides." Amanda smiled at Lloyd and
the other farmers, but ignored Clint completely.
"You can meet and decide what to do, and the next
day everyone can read about your decision in the
paper."

"Don't listen to her!" Lawson shouted. His
hands were jerking slightly as if itching to be
scratched by his gun handle. "She was with the
gunman. She's on the ranchers' side. They'd
like nothing better than to keep Texas range country for another hundred years."

Amanda stormed toward Lawson. "How dare
you make such a claim!"

Lawson jumped nervously. A log in the fire
popped and the sound echoed off the canyon walls
like rapid fire from a gun.

In a second Clint watched Lawson jerk his gun
free of its holster. Clint had no time to hesitate. He
could either draw his weapon or grab Amanda and
whisk her out of harm's way.

He grabbed her, but his swift movement panicked Lawson. The gambler swung his weapon
slightly to the left and fired.

Amanda turned as Clint's fingers dug into her
arm. In one moment she saw his body take the
impact of the bullet, which knocked him backward
into the darkness. She saw the pain in his eyes
before he fell. Pain, but not surprise. Blood splattered crimson across his chest as his fingers pulled

her with him for a moment before releasing her, as he crumbled to the ground.

Horses stomped as men mounted and rode, but Amanda didn't hear their shouts and confusion. The only sound that reached her mind was the silent scream that ripped her heart apart.

Closing her eyes, she knelt among the panicked riders and fought to keep the total blackness away. "Clint," she whispered. "Don't leave me."

Someone pushed her gently aside.

"Get him into the light!" Pap Lloyd shouted as men lifted Clint.

Clint gritted his teeth to keep from screaming as fire raged through his insides. Time seemed to drift by, first fast, then slow.

Lloyd had lived through battles with both Indians and Yankees. He knew what to do. Within minutes Clint's chest was wrapped with someone's shirt and tied so tightly he could barely breathe. "We'll get you to my farm, boy," the old man said. "I'll get that bullet out before infection sets in."

Clint relaxed back into someone's arms as the men pulled up a wagon. Feeling the soft roundness of her breast against his cheek, Clint had no doubt who was holding him. He looked up into Amanda's tear-filled eyes. Her face was white and her mouth slightly open in shock.

"Don't faint on me, lady," he whispered.

She gulped back her sobs. "You're not going to die on me, are you?"

"Nope." Clint smiled through the pain. "I'm going to live long enough to torture you to death slowly. I should have known better than to get mixed up with a woman like you."

"A woman like me?"

"Yeah, a woman who never listens."

"Stop acting as if I'm the one who shot you."

Clint wanted to tell her a few things—like how it was all her fault and how he'd do it all again to save her. He wanted to hold her once more before he died and convince her she was worth dying for. He wanted to tell her she was the only person he wanted nearer to him than ten feet . . . but his mind faded to black.

She pulled him close and rocked him softly to her in fear and grief. With men running and shouting around her, all she could think about was how much she wanted to press her lips against his and feel his warm breath against her cheek. He could yell at her all he wanted to if he'd just stay alive.

Hesitantly she moved her fingers down his arm and touched his blood-covered hand. There was no returning grip in his strong fingers, only stillness. Shaking, she looked at his chest, daring the wound to frighten her. For one moment she watched the blood seep through the makeshift bandage, and then, as her heart cried out in sorrow, she fainted.

Chapter Six

"You're real lucky, son," Pap Lloyd mumbled as he wrapped the wound. "A few inches over to the left and I'da had to take out your heart to stop the bleeding."

Clint swallowed another mouthful of whiskey. He'd never thought of himself as lucky, and as for a heart, he wasn't sure he needed one. He hadn't heard his own beating since he left Kansas. "I plan to live long enough to strangle the town's only reporter," he answered between drinks.

The old man chuckled. "You wouldn't be the first man who wanted to do that. Miss Hamilton does have a way of testing a man's patience." Lloyd leaned closer. "But, son, you saved her life, and folks around here value Amanda Hamilton."

"Don't remind me of my mistake," Clint whispered as he fought the fire raging in his chest with another drink. "I'll not listen."

"You got it bad for her, don't you, son?" Lloyd's laughter sounded like hiccups. "I knew a Yank once who was a lot like you. If he'd been God Almighty there wouldn't have been no use prayin', for he was never listening."

Pap Lloyd kept wrapping Clint's chest and talking as if his words brought some comfort. "I had to bury that Yank years ago. Couldn't resist chiseling on his stone, 'You should have heeded my warning.'" Lloyd laughed so hard his teeth rattled.

Clint didn't see the humor. "You got something to tell me, old man?"

Lloyd closed his lips tightly, making them disappear from his weathered face. "No, son, I'll just wait for the marble."

Clint decided the old man was as crazy as Amanda. He took another drink and nodded off again.

It was long past noon when Amanda noticed Clint stirring. He lightly touched first his wound, then his head, and she smiled, certain that both were giving him pain.

Moving to the side of the cot Pap Lloyd had set up in his kitchen, she said, "There's no fresh blood. Pap says that's a good sign. The bullet went through a muscle in your side, missing a lung by a hair."

Clint rose slightly and flinched in pain. "I've been hurt worse and walked away. I'll survive.

"Is that coffee I smell?" Clint forced his eyes to focus on the room. "I'd even settle for water," he whispered. "My mouth feels as if it's been used to process cotton."

Amanda handed him a mug Pap had left by the bed. "Pap says for you to drink this first. Then you can have some coffee. I've been keeping it hot for you."

Clint took a swallow and fought to keep from spitting it out. "What . . . ?"

"Something Pap made up out of roots. He laced

it with some of that whiskey you liked so much last night when he was fixing you up."

After taking another drink, Clint swore and then said, "The old guy must hate me."

Amanda laughed and took her first deep breath since the night before. If he was in good enough shape to swear, he'd live. "Pap's the reason you're still alive. I heard the other farmers say if they'd taken you all the way into town for help, you'd be feeding worms right now."

Clint leaned back. He wasn't sure he cared one way or the other. He'd learned to live waiting for the bullet he knew would someday end his life. A gunfighter who did not value other people's lives was dangerous enough, but a gunfighter who didn't even value his own life was far more frightening, for he was already dead inside. Clint Matthews had been dead inside. Until this town. Until Amanda.

He felt her cool hand running gently over his face. She was so close that the familiar fragrance of her drifted around him almost in a caress. She reminded him of the warm, welcoming odor found in print shops that made only the finest of books. She smelled of print, ink, paper, and woman. Warm, loving, passionate woman.

"I almost died when you were shot. In one flash of fire I realized how much you mean to me," she whispered as her hand continued to caress his face. "But I can't live with your guns." She had to tell him how important he was to her. She couldn't run the risk of watching another bullet cut him down. He had to see his life the way she saw it.

Clint didn't open his eyes as her words settled

into his mind, heavier than any lead from a gun. Despite all her brave talk, she had a gentle spirit. The vision of her face, pale and afraid, floated inside his mind. He'd crush her if he tried to love her. Every time he strapped on his holster, she'd relive not only last night but her father's death as well. She could never live with his way of life and he knew no other way. He had to stop her now, before she fell in love.

"It would never work between us." He couldn't bring himself to look at her, and he felt like a coward for his weakness. "I make my living with my guns, and you hate them." The time for dreams was over. It was time for reality to set in.

She leaned forward and rested her cheek against his. "No one's ever made me feel as you have." Her lips moved lightly to brush his in a bittersweet final kiss. "There must be a way." Tears spilled down her cheeks.

Clint knew there was a way, the only way for a man like him with a woman like her. He had to love her enough to let her go. He had to make her hate him.

"I've made many an old maid feel special." He tried to smile, but the knife he used to cut her also dug into his soul. A woman like her could handle hate but not heartbreak. He had to push the blade deeper until her need to survive overruled her need for him. "You were nothing more to me than a diversion, lady. A delightful diversion. Do you think a woman could really mean anything to me? If any woman could have rooted me, it would have happened long before now. I'll forget you as soon as I'm in the next county and in another lady's bed."

She didn't want to believe him. All her life she'd waited to feel this way about a man, and she couldn't let him destroy her dream. "You have a fever." She knew her words made sense, but she had to push logic back. "You need rest."

Clint's laughter was cruel. "This fever will cool as fast as the fever I had for you."

"But . . ."

He moved his hand up to her breast. "You do fill a man's hand nicely, but so does the handle of my Colt and, believe me, it's a great deal more reliable."

He saw the spark of anger in her eyes and knew he'd won. Let her hate him. Hell, most people hated him on sight. Let her push him away so that she could sweep up the scraps of her dignity and piece her life back together.

She shoved his hand away and stood. "Goodbye, Mr. Matthews." There were a thousand things she wanted to shout at him, but she kept her lips tightly closed, holding on to her pride by a hair. She'd see him dead before she'd admit how much she cared for him.

Feeling a sudden urge to run, she grabbed Clint's jacket from the back of a kitchen chair and stormed out of the room with all the dignity of a good woman leaving a low-down nothing of a man.

Which was exactly what Clint felt like.

Amanda saddled her horse and started into town. She knew she'd have to ride fast to make it by nightfall, but she couldn't bear to look at Clint Matthews even once more. Her dream that some-one, even a drifter like him, might care for her was shattered. She had to get away, back to her own life, where everything could be organized into tiny boxes inside her print trays.

Leaning forward, she let the wind dry her tears. How was it possible that the only man to stir her blood had a heart the size of a bullet? Even now, in all her anger and hate, she could still feel his lips pressing against hers as he gently touched her body. She could still hear him saying her name as though it were a prayer. How could such a man have won her love?

Time seemed to whirl past, as did her thoughts. She was in town before she realized it. She rode to the livery and handed her horse over to the stableboy. If he saw the tears in her eyes, he made no comment.

Amanda walked the short distance to her office unaware of the people she passed. When she bumped into a stranger, she looked at him in disbelief as he tipped his hat and walked on. Couldn't he see the pain in her eyes? Couldn't he tell her heart was shattering?

Following the single light she'd left burning in her apartment, she climbed the stairs and col-lapsed on her bed. All the trunks and stacks of her belongings seemed to huddle around, comforting her, but things were no comfort when she longed for a pair of strong arms to hold her. Wrapping the leather coat around her, she wept. He was gone from her life as quickly as he'd come. Like a shooting star, he had burned brightly for only a moment.

Now she was condemned to live the rest of her life alone.

By the time the tears finally stopped, the moon had risen and started its journey across the night sky. Slowly Amanda crawled from her bed, feeling completely exhausted.

As she removed the warm leather jacket, she realized it belonged to Clint. He'd put it on her at the meeting.

No more tears came. "I've cried all I'm going to for that worthless man," she whispered, not noticing her fingers folding the coat lovingly despite her vow.

A tiny white spot of material poked from the breast pocket. Curious, she lifted the material from its hiding place. The cloth looked old and fragile, as though it had been washed many times to keep it spotless, then folded carefully. The lace handkerchief was delicate, reflecting a fine dainty hand at sewing.

Amanda moved over to the light and noticed a tiny name embroidered in one corner: Angeline Matthews. Was she his mother, his sister . . . or wife?

Very slowly, she unfolded what she knew must be Clint's most treasured possession, since he carried it wrapped in this polished linen, next to his heart.

In the center of the handkerchief was a heart made of red paper. Amanda turned it over and read her own name on the back. As she lifted it into the light, she realized it was the paper valentine he'd pinned on his sleeve at Miss Peach's party. The last heart in the bowl. Her heart.

In one shattering moment she realized what she meant to Clint. She hadn't been only one of many; she'd been cherished. With a sudden determination, she ran to the washstand and splashed water on her face. She had work to do.

Chapter Seven

After another two days with Pap Lloyd, Clint had taken all the doctoring he could endure. The old man was as good as most country doctors, but his bedside manner would have driven a cattleman to raise sheep. When Pap's youngest boy, Andrew, rode in with the news that Colonel Winters wanted to meet with the farmers in town on Sunday, Clint saw his chance to escape.

He talked Andrew into saddling his horse and helping him mount while Pap and the other farmers were discussing the meeting with the colonel. Clint knew that, with any luck, he'd be in town by the time the old man missed him.

The night was cold, and Clint missed his leather coat. Andrew had wrapped a bedroll around him, but it didn't stop the Texas wind from chilling him to the bone. He wrapped the reins around the saddle horn and prayed his horse would find the way, for pain was already starting to blur his mind. He knew he needed another day of rest, but he had to see Amanda. Clint had to know his words hadn't broken her, that she'd survived and gone on with her life. He'd buried one woman he loved; he couldn't stand thinking that he might have crushed another's spirit. Enough things had died in his life.

The horse somehow found not only the town but the livery. Clint let the boy help him down and managed to lift his saddlebags over one shoulder. An old grandfather clock was chiming midnight when he opened the door of the town's only hotel. By now he could feel the heat of a fever. He knew the lobby was always well lit, but the lights looked like pinholes on a black wall.

Clint moved toward the brightest light.

"Evenin', Mr. Matthews," someone in the darkness spoke. "We're mighty glad to have you back with us."

Clint nodded slightly and felt his entire brain slosh back and forth. The action caused the room to lighten and he noticed several men sitting at a table playing checkers. They all nodded and smiled at him warmly, and Clint knew he'd crossed from reality into nightmare. Folks always made a habit of not noticing him. He closed his eyes and gave himself over to sleep, unaware that he was standing in front of the main desk.

In what seemed only moments, he blinked away sunlight. As he looked around, he recognized the hotel room he'd used once before, white cotton curtains, oak bed, Indian rug on one wall. Slowly Clint remembered the night before. He remembered riding into town and stabling his horse, but he couldn't recall climbing the stairs or getting into bed. Looking down at his chest he noticed a clean white dressing.

The rattling of the doorknob made him reach for his holster, which was hanging from the bedpost beside his pillow. As he pulled his Colt from the leather, he relaxed at the sight of a young doctor he'd met at Miss Peach's party.

"Don't shoot me." The doctor smiled. "I'm not finished treating you yet."

Clint lowered his gun and relaxed.

The doctor handed him a cup of water that tasted thick with medicine. "You're doing fine, but I can't believe Pap would send you into town without at least another day's rest."

Clint drank the water. "He didn't know. I kind of snuck out when he wasn't on guard."

The young man laughed. "Well, like the old guy or not, he did a fine job of fixing you up." He reached down and collected his bag. "There's not much I can do except tell you to rest for a few days, get plenty to eat, and don't take any more long rides. The powder in that water should help you sleep most of today, and I left three more doses if you have any trouble sleeping at night."

Clint nodded. "What do I owe you, Doc?"

The man waved his hand. "Nothing," he insisted. "Saving Miss Hamilton's life was payment enough. I'm proud I could be of some small service to you."

Clint looked at the doctor more closely, wondering where he'd gotten his information. Another thought struck Clint's mind. "You real partial to Miss Hamilton, Doc?"

The young man nodded without hesitation. "Yes, sir. We all are in Quail Springs."

Clint wanted more. "And you in particular?"

The doc winked. "I know what you're thinking, and she is a fine woman—that's a fact—but my wife and three young ones might object to me being too partial to her."

Clint's hopes sank. So much for trying to play matchmaker. Besides, if a battle-scarred bear like him couldn't handle Amanda, what made him think some country doctor who was shorter than she was would have a chance.

As the doc turned to leave, he added, "Get some rest. By dinnertime you should feel like walking next door for a steak."

Clint closed his eyes and took the doc's advice. When he awoke at sunset, he felt weak but on the mend. He dressed slowly and ventured downstairs.

It was Saturday night, and the stores on the main street had taken on an almost festive atmosphere. Ranchers and farmers had come to town to trade and also to attend the big meeting. Some would stay with friends in town, but most just pitched tents and set up camp wherever they could.

As Clint stepped out of the hotel a man was waiting to enter. "Howdy, Mr. Matthews. Mighty glad to see you up and about."

Clint raised an eyebrow, trying to place the man in his memory. The gentleman disappeared into the hotel, and Clint started down the plank walk to the restaurant. To his amazement, all the old men lining the walk turned away from their checker games and smiled up at him. One brave soul stood and removed a battered Confederate cap. "Evening, Mr. Matthews."

Clint stared hard, trying to place the man. Nothing. Maybe he'd lost his memory because of the fever. It wouldn't be inconceivable for two men to know his name—lots of folks knew him on sight—but for people to speak to him like friends was another matter.

Extending his hand, Clint asked, "Do I know you from somewhere?"

The old reb's smile never left his face. "No, sir. I don't believe I've ever had the honor. Name's E. P. Taylor and this here is my friend, Mike Scott."

To Clint's surprise, the men stood one by one, removing their hats and extending their wrinkled hands. Clint felt like a sinner fresh from his baptism in the river, being welcomed into the fold. By the time he'd shaken their hands, he decided they must have him mixed up with someone else.

But when he entered the restaurant the same thing happened. Every man, woman, and child in the place looked up at him and smiled. When he did a short salute they all waved as if their hands were tied to the same string.

The waitress showed him to a table and hurried to bring him the house's only offering, a steak with a side of potatoes and onions cooked in butter. Clint ate like a man who'd been starved. Toward the end of the meal he finally stopped looking up to see if folks were still smiling at him. He knew they were.

After the waitress had poured his third cup of coffee she said, "I went to Kansas once when I was a kid." She waited, holding the hot coffee, for him to answer.

Clint figured locoweed must have gotten into the water supply and driven everyone in this town completely crazy, but he wasn't about to insult anyone holding a pot of steaming coffee. "Oh?" He swallowed a scalding mouthful. "What part of Kansas?"

"Down near Wichita," she answered. "Not near Salina, where you're from."

Suddenly her rambling had direction. Trying to sound casual he asked, "How do you know where I'm from?" He doubted even the colonel knew that.

The waitress shrugged. "Read it in the paper."

Clint set his cup down very slowly. "You wouldn't happen to have a copy of that paper, would you?"

Within a minute she was back with the issue, and within ten minutes Clint was standing in Amanda's office, so angry she could feel the nerves in his body jerking uncontrollably.

He heard her coming down the stairs and guessed he'd caused enough racket to wake the dead.

She passed by the front door and set the lantern down. "You broke my lock again!"

Clint turned slowly, steeling himself against the beauty he knew he would see. But no shield could have protected him. She looked so wonderful in her white nightgown with her hair falling all around her shoulders and her bare feet trying to curl under the hem of the gown. She might not be other men's idea of beauty, but she was his and always would be.

"Is this a weekly ritual you have? Come over and break down my door?" She stood there talking as if she'd done nothing wrong, as if everything was his fault. "Did it ever occur to you that locks are there for some reason?"

"I should have let that gambler kill you the other night and saved myself the trouble."

As usual, Amanda didn't have sense enough to be afraid of him. "What are *you* so angry about? If it's about your coat, I'll give it back."

"It's not my coat." She was so close he could smell her. All fresh-washed cotton and Amanda.

Clint shook his head slightly and breathed out heavily, trying to expel the fragrance of her from his nose and his mind. "I'm here about this damn article in your paper."

Amanda moved behind her desk as though preparing to conduct business. "And what is your complaint?"

Clint fought the urge to shout at her. He tossed the paper between them. "My complaint is that you told every damn thing about my life on the front page of your paper!"

"The past is something we all must live with."

"But not on the front page. I buried that part of my life." His gaze was so full of anger it was almost a physical barrier between them.

Amanda straightened slightly. "Was any of the information false?"

For the first time since the shooting, Clint's head hurt even more than his chest. He didn't want to answer. He didn't want to think about his past, much less see it splattered across the paper.

Amanda turned the article so that she could read it. "Let me see. What might be false? Were you born in Kansas?"

Clint collapsed in the chair across from her without answering. He put his elbows on the table, folded his hands, and rested his head on them without a word as she continued.

"You volunteered for the army at sixteen when the war broke out. After Vicksburg, you served with Grant in Tennessee, retiring as a much decorated captain. You came home with a new bride to find Kansas in turmoil. Six months after the war, your wife and unborn child were killed by outlaws who raided your farm and burned your house." Amanda looked up, "Stop me when I hit a lie, Mr. Matthews."

Clint felt as though he were drowning. Angeline's memory was only a haze hidden in the past. She'd been so young, not even twenty when they married. He'd thought she'd outgrow her helplessness and fear of guns. But the night their farm was raided by outlaws she hadn't even tried to fight. She'd let them take her life and all he loved without even firing a shot. He'd never talked about the day Angeline died. He'd buried her and ridden away to find her killers. It had taken him almost a year, but he'd tracked them down one by one and made sure his face was the last thing they ever saw. By the time he completed his vengeance, his heart had hardened to granite and the wall he'd built around himself had never crumbled . . . until now.

"You are known as a gunfighter with honor. You have never shot a bystander or a man under eighteen, even when the boys try to call you out." Amanda smiled at her research. She'd had to wire every lawman she knew in three states to collect her information. "You saved my life almost at the cost of your own." Her words slowed as she realized how much she must have meant to him for him not to reach for his gun when Lawson pulled his weapon. By saving her, he'd gone against the instinct that had kept him alive all of his adult life.

He was silent for so long that she wasn't sure he'd heard her. Finally he lowered his hands and pulled the hard invisible mask he always wore into place. "And the last paragraph?"

Amanda looked down at the article. "Oh, the last few sentences. Well, I figured you'd never let Lawson get away with shooting you, so you'd want to even the score."

"If I do, and I'm not saying I do, the last thing I'd want would be to have the news printed in the paper."

With deadly calm Clint stood and walked out of her office. If he stayed, he knew she'd want to talk about his life, and that was a subject he refused to discuss.

Amanda watched him leave, her heart breaking. There was so much she wanted to say to him. It didn't matter to her if he never talked of the past, if he would only open up to the future. More than anything in the world she wanted to hold him. As she pressed her face against the window pane, she knew he was walking out of her life forever.

Tears blurred her vision as he crossed the now quiet street to the hotel. A lone shadow of a man stepped from between two buildings and slowly followed Clint. But as the man in black neared the hotel doors, he ducked between the buildings once more. Amanda knew the black shadow with a gun slung low on his thigh was Don Lawson.

Chapter Eight

Amanda watched the man she loved disappear into the hotel. For the first time in her life she regretted what she'd printed. She'd cut Clint Matthews open and dissected him for the whole town to see. He was a very private man, content in his denial of the past. She'd made him face all that had happened. Just because she kept trunks full of relics from her past didn't mean he should do so.

She ran up the stairs to her bedroom window where she could see the hotel more clearly. As she watched for any sign of trouble, she lifted the valentine from the table. Had she misread the reason he'd kept the paper heart? Had he told her the truth when he said she meant nothing to him? Was she making a fool of herself for a man who cared nothing for her?

A flicker came on in one of the second-floor rooms at the hotel. She knew it was Clint's room, for he'd never stop to visit in the lobby with the group of men who made the room their permanent meeting hall. He was a loner; maybe he always would be. Her heart went out to him for she, maybe more than anyone in town, knew what it was like to be alone.

As she stared at the single light, a black shadow moved silently from window to window along the second-floor balcony. The man in black stopped beside Clint's window and crouched low as if waiting for the light to go out.

Amanda jumped back, realizing what was about to happen. The gambler Lawson planned to murder Clint in his sleep. Everyone would talk about it tomorrow, but without a sheriff to investigate, no one would do anything.

In sudden panic, Amanda ran to an old trunk in the corner. She pulled out a pair of pants and a shirt from among her father's things. With the precision of a warrior preparing for battle, she dressed, adding her own boots and Clint's jacket. When she turned to the mirror, she was surprised at just how much like a man she looked. For once her height was an advantage.

She tucked her hair under a wide-brimmed hat, then picked up the old Paterson revolver. Amanda hesitated for the first time, wondering if she was rushing into something she couldn't handle. She didn't even know how to load the gun, much less fire it, and what made her think Clint needed or even wanted her help?

Then she saw the paper heart lying on top of his wife's handkerchief, and she knew what she had to do. Somehow this gunfighter had drawn her real heart from the bowl that night. She might be the only woman in town no one wanted to love, but this strong, silent man had kept the paper heart like a treasure, and he'd saved her life. What more proof of his affection did she need?

Amanda's hand shook as she strapped on the gun belt. "You're no pick of the litter, either, Clint Matthews," she murmured. "But I know you love me. I've just got to keep you alive long enough for you to realize it."

She moved out the door of her office and silently crossed the street. Within minutes she was at the back stairs of the hotel and climbing onto the balcony just as Lawson must have done.

Clint gulped down a triple dose of the doctor's sleeping mixture, knowing it would take far more than a little medicine to allow him to rest. He turned down his light and tried to relax. Lawson's bullet had been minor compared to the way Amanda's news story had ripped through his heart. He wished old man Lloyd *had* taken his heart out. It had never been anything but a bother.

Relaxing against his pillows, he closed his eyes and tried to remember one time in his life when there'd been beauty in his world. The only thought that came to mind was the other morning when he'd awakened Amanda. He tried harder to remember as the medicine began to work. Suddenly Clint realized he'd grown into manhood fighting a war and somehow had never stopped fighting. He'd watched others go home and leave the war behind, but when he'd tried to unstrap his gun belt there had only been a short rest between battles.

A breeze ruffled the curtains at Clint's open window as he drifted into sleep. His last conscious thought was that he wanted his war to end, he wanted to sleep with Amanda in his arms.

"Matthews!" A voice suddenly invaded Clint's sleep. "Matthews, wake up!"

Clint seemed to be wading through a giant field of wheat that had grown above his head. He knew someone was calling him, but he couldn't find direction or light.

Without warning the cold steel barrel of a pistol slammed against the side of his face, and Clint came fully awake. He rolled from the bed and reached for his Colt. But the gun was gone and his hands were bound with steel.

"You don't think I'd leave the gun within your reach, do you, Matthews?" Even in the shadowy light Don Lawson's frame was easily recognizable. "I knew the sheriff's wrist irons would come in handy."

Clint straightened, showing no fear of the snake before him. He pulled his fists as far apart as the cuffs would allow, not caring that the metal cut into his skin.

"Matthews, you've been a bother to me since you hit town," the gambler said. "I had a nice little war fixing to start up, and you keep getting in my way."

Clint's gaze searched the room for a weapon as he said calmly, "What's this town to you, Lawson? You have no ties here, no land."

"Oh, but I will when the farmers and ranchers

start killing each other off." The gambler laughed as if he'd made a fool out of everyone. "I've been looking for a town like this for years to settle down in. Someplace where, for a few hundred dollars, I can live like a king. Can't see myself homesteading and building a place, but I could step in and run a ranch like the colonel's. In fact Colonel Winters would already be dead if you hadn't rode in."

"You'd never get away with it." Clint moved slightly toward the washstand.

Lawson laughed. "Who's to stop me once the colonel's gone? Old man Lloyd and that pesky newspaperwoman are the only two with backbone in this town."

Clint continued to move toward the stand as he pieced together the gambler's plan. "So if you could start a war, no one would notice a few extra bullets flying toward the colonel, Lloyd, and Amanda."

Lawson shook his head. "I don't plan on killing the woman, just scaring her away. You know how women are—ransack their place a few times and they pack up like a mother cat moving kittens."

"And then there's me." Clint was almost within reach of the stand and the porcelain pitcher. He shook his head slightly trying to clear the effects from the large dose of sleeping powder he'd taken.

"Then there's you," Lawson answered.

As Clint's bound hands reached for the pitcher, Lawson's gun flew through the air and struck Clint's already bruised face. The blow cut his cheek and knocked him off balance.

"Don't try anything, Matthews, or I'll shoot you right here in town and not out on the road like I'm planning." Lawson laughed. "No one would do anything anyway."

"I might," came Amanda's shaky voice from the window.

Both men turned to watch as she crawled into the room, the huge old Paterson revolver pointed directly at the gambler.

"Drop the gun, Lawson," she said. "I'm mighty nervous, and if this old thing goes off it'll blow a hole in you as deep as a well."

Clint saw his chance in the moment the gambler hesitated. He slammed both fists into Lawson's side. Lawson fired as both men hit the floor.

They rolled in the darkness, both trying to gain control of the pistol. Finally, with one mighty jerk, Clint pulled the weapon out of Lawson's hand and flung it wildly across the room. Amanda ran to the corner and stood guard over the gun.

Suddenly the room was full of men from the lobby. Like children all wanting the same toy, they wrestled Lawson between them. One found the handcuff keys, removed the cuffs from Clint's wrists, and clamped them around Lawson's. Someone shouted to take the gambler to jail, and they all shuffled out of the room with their prize. No one seemed to notice Amanda standing in the corner.

She looked at Clint in disbelief. He rose slowly from the floor and moved to the washstand. "You can put down that cannon you call a gun now."

Realizing she was still holding her weapon, she slowly returned it to the holster.

Clint grabbed a towel and wiped the blood from his cheek before he faced Amanda. "How'd you

know he was here?" Clint's hard face softened
with a hint of a smile. "Or were you just breaking
into my room?"

"I saw him from my window. He was waiting on
the balcony outside your room, so I followed."

"Why'd you wait so long before coming in?" he
asked as he watched her closely.

Amanda pushed her hat back, allowing a few
strands of her hair to tumble out. "I wanted to hear
the whole story, but when he hit you . . ."

Clint turned to face her. A crimson line marked
his cheek just under his eye, but there was no
blood. Silently he opened his arms. She moved
into them eagerly, like a child running to safety.

For a long while he just held her, loving the way
she felt next to him. All his wounds would heal, if
only he could hold her to him. "Would you really
have shot him, Amanda?" he whispered as his
hands moved beneath the leather coat to mold her
closer against him.

"Yes," she answered. "If I could have figured
out how to put some bullets in this old gun."

His arms tightened around her as he kissed her
cheek. They could hear the mob returning from
the jail across the street and knew their time
together was ending.

"You'd better go out the way you came."

Amanda couldn't let go. "I don't think anyone
recognized me."

"Not before, but they will now as they rehash
everything. If they find you in my room, Miss
Peach will never call you a fine woman again." He
pressed his lips against hers in a promise of more,
far more, to come.

As men thundered up the stairs, Amanda broke the kiss and slipped back out the window. As she ran down the stairs and across the street, she didn't see him lean against the frame, fighting to stay awake.

Hurrying back to her room she removed her father's clothes. She knew as soon as Clint was finished talking with the men, he'd be over. For once in her life nothing mattered but being in his arms. They could work out all the problems if only he would hold her tonight.

But the night passed slowly, and Clint never came. She waited excitedly, hopefully, and finally longingly, but he never came. By dawn all of Amanda's old feelings about herself had returned. She dressed, tightly laced and corseted, for the meeting. She would bind her heart and her feelings deep inside, and no one would ever hurt her again.

Picking up her notepad and Clint's jacket, Amanda walked out of her apartment determined not to let her pain show.

Chapter Nine

By the time Amanda arrived, most of the men had already assembled for the meeting in Miss Peach's parlor. Clint was standing by the colonel. He looked up when she entered, but she didn't meet his eyes. How could she? What would she say to him? He hadn't even thanked her for saving his life.

The jacket on her arm gave her direction. She marched toward him. When he tried to speak, she stared at his shirt and interrupted, "Thanks for the use of your coat."

"You're welcome," he answered in a voice low and slow with a hundred words left unsaid.

The meeting came to order, granting Amanda the escape she needed. She moved to the back and found a chair close to the door.

She tried to write down all that was said, but as the time passed she could feel Clint's gaze on her. The words he'd said to her at Pap Lloyd's house returned to drown out the real world. She knew he'd been hurt by her article. Had the hurt turned to hate?

Finally, when several men suggested Clint take the job of sheriff, Amanda could endure the meeting no longer. She stood and silently slipped from the crowded room, unnoticed except by one pair of clear blue eyes.

Holding her head high, Amanda marched back home. She kept her back rigid until she reached the safety of her room. Finally, as she turned the lock, she allowed herself to crumble. She curled into her rocker and let the tears silently fall. Clint Matthews had not only broken her heart, he'd made her act like a fool. Now he'd be living in town, and she'd have to face her feelings for him every time she saw his face.

Her quiet refuge was shattered by the sound of the door being kicked in. Moments later Amanda jumped up to face the gunfighter as he stormed into her room. From the black fury in his eyes it didn't look as if he'd come to thank her for saving his life. It didn't matter what he intended to say; she would never let him know how he'd shattered her quiet life.

The walls still vibrated with the force of his entry, but he stood silent before her. She could withstand his stare only a moment. "You have something to say to me."

He didn't move, but spread his legs wide apart and tucked his thumbs inside his gun belt. "You have something that belongs to me."

Amanda tried to show no fear, but her hands were trembling as she handed him the handkerchief that had been his wife's.

Clint took the thin white square and slowly folded it away in his pocket as if he were folding a part of his life away one last time. Turning his back to her, he moved toward the door.

She could feel her world splitting at the seams, but she would not beg for his love. He didn't want her, and she'd never want anyone else except him, but she'd survive. She had to.

Pausing at the doorway, he hung his coat on one of the pegs. Slowly, very slowly, he unbuckled his gun belt.

Amanda straightened slightly, trying to hold on to her last ounce of pride. "What do you think you're doing?"

"I'm here to ask for that heart back, not the handkerchief."

"But, Clint—"

"It's about time you called me by my first name."

Amanda panicked. She couldn't believe he wanted the valentine back. She couldn't reach under her pillow and retrieve the heart without looking like an absolute fool. Besides, it was hers. She would add it to her treasures so she could remember, always. The paper heart could mean nothing to him compared to how dearly she would treasure it.

"I don't remember what I did with it." She could feel her face redden as she lied. He'd know she kept it; she kept everything.

Clint moved closer. "For a fine, honest woman, you sure do your share of lying, lady."

Amanda straightened her back, realizing she'd developed the habit since meeting him. "It's only a paper heart."

"It means far more than that to me." He laid his gun belt over one of the trunks and moved nearer. "You said I could never touch you as long as I was wearing a gun."

Raising his hands slowly, he brushed her arms lightly with his fingers as if testing to see if she'd run. "I plan on touching you now, Mandy."

She could feel his breath against her warm cheeks as he whispered, low and filled with need. "As long as you've got that paper, you've got my heart and I can never leave. Now, are you going to give it back?"

Amanda closed her eyes and leaned closer to him until she could feel his heart pounding against her own. This moment was all she'd ever need to hoard away in her memory. It would shield her from loneliness for the rest of her life. His touch was all the feeling of belonging she'd longed for.

She moved into his embrace, praying he would hold her one last time.

But Clint's hands brushed her body with urgency born of years of withdrawal from love. His lips found hers in a desire that had been unsatisfied for too long.

His kiss was warm and loving, telling Amanda how much he needed her. As her mouth slowly opened to his teasing, she relaxed against him, loving the way his fingers slid over her body as though he were touching something he treasured.

His powerful hands suddenly moved over her hips and pulled her against him. When she gasped in surprise, his kiss turned hot with longing, riding the tide of her emotions from innocence to passion. He drew her into his fire with long, bold strokes over her body and kisses that made her forget to breathe. His actions told her he would not play a game of loving with her.

His fingers fumbled at the buttons of her blouse. Suddenly frustrated, he broke the kiss and demanded, "Are you going to give that heart back?"

"No," Amanda answered honestly and felt his hand jerk open the material of her blouse. Buttons flew from her throat to her waist.

In one swift motion he swept her into his arms and carried her the few feet to the bed. She was still bouncing on top of the covers when she felt the weight of his lean body press against her.

He shoved material aside so the morning light shone on her breasts. With a storm raging in his eyes, he studied her. Slowly, almost hesitantly, he lifted his hand and covered one of her velvet mounds. His fingers spread wide as his palm gently caressed her.

"Do you love me?" he whispered.

When she didn't answer, he increased the pressure of his hand and the pleasure he brought her. "Do you love me, Mandy?"

Closing her eyes, Amanda fought to keep from crying out in pleasure at his touch. Even the nickname she'd always hated sounded wonderful when he said it. She leaned her head back and arched her hips, loving his touch. His mouth brushed light kisses along her throat, and then he slowly moved down to the soft flesh between her breasts. She felt his name catch in her throat, half sigh, half adoration.

"Answer me," he whispered, his breath warm against her skin.

When his lips covered her breast with heated promise, she could no longer contain her cry of pleasure. "Yes!" she cried. "I love you."

She raised her arms above her head and rocked slowly back and forth against the cool sheets. His hands pulled away the rest of her clothes, tossing them to the floor to join his own.

Leaving her breasts, he moved once more to her mouth. As his kiss silenced her low moans, he lowered his body atop her. His weight pressed into her very soul, and they became one in a timeless place accessible only to lovers.

"I've broken down my last door to find you, Mandy," he whispered in her ear as his hands laced into her hair. "I want you forever in my arms and in my heart."

She stretched and locked her arms around his neck. "I come with a lot of luggage."

Clint laughed. "As long as you come to bed, sweetheart, you can keep the trunks wherever you like."

Amanda touched the face of the man she loved. "I have to save them. They have everything from my grandmother's china to my baby clothes." She had to make him understand how important each possession was to her.

"You can keep them all," Clint said as his stormy eyes turned dark with sudden need. "As long as you never let Miss Peach put your name in her bowl again." He kissed her nose lightly. "And as long as you'll promise to be my valentine today and every other day for the rest of our lives."

Though he'd once worn her heart on his sleeve, she now saw it held with reverence and love in his eyes.

Amanda answered him with a kiss that vowed . . . forever.

RIBBONS AND LACE

by

Colleen Quinn

Dear Reader,

Valentine's Day has always been one of my favorite holidays. It comes in the dead of winter (which in New Jersey is pretty dismal) and two months after the Christmas holidays. Its arrival is as welcome as the first snowdrop, and as eagerly anticipated.

As children we traded those little Valentine cutouts, hiding them in our desks until the appropriate moment, then passing them out as tokens of friendship and occasionally, admiration. Who can't remember at least one year when the boy we thought didn't know we were alive sent us a precious Valentine? Of course, he ignored us the very next day, but that's irrelevant. For one brief moment, holding the cheap tinsel card in our hand, the world became our Camelot.

Valentines have been with us for hundreds of years, but I feel they reached their peak during the Victorian era. The late 1800s was the time of the Industrial Revolution, when sex roles were called into question. It was a time of great change, when our president was the unstable Ulysses S. Grant, and the country was recovering from a bloody civil war. Queen Victoria's influence was much needed and embraced on both sides of the Atlantic, and the Valentine, with its lace and ribbons, was the embodiment of the era.

Valentines then, unlike today, were not only given on February 14, but were used as a method of courtship all year long. Men would order Valentines from the Valentine maker, and would send the love poems to the lady of his desires in an effort to win her favor. This could easily take months or years. The Valentines themselves were very ornate, and could cost up to thirty dollars, an immense sum in that time.

During the Victorian period in America, I discovered there was a woman who was very successful in running a business making Valentines, an unheard of feat for a female. Importing the finest materials from England, she wrote her own verse, produced her own cards, and sold them in her father's shop. The paper and lace confections were a hit, and she made a good deal of money in a time when many men struggled to earn a living in the sweatshops and labor yards.

I couldn't stop thinking about this remarkable woman, and the significance of her art. How did she feel about what she did? What did her neighbors think? Did the Valentine maker ever receive any cards of her own? Was she in love with a man? Was she ever asked to help court a woman by a man she loved?

Thus came the idea for "Ribbons and Lace." It is a Valentine for all women everywhere, especially women who have been overlooked by the history books but who have been quietly making their contribution all the same. They are all around us still, from the women who donate their time to clinics to the mothers who raise their children and sacrifice their own needs. Like a Victorian Valentine, they are a tribute to what it really means to love.

Happy Valentine's Day.

—COLLEEN QUINN

Chapter One

The first flakes of snow fell quietly on the rooftops of Philadelphia, cleansing the air of the eternal soot and lending a soft glimmer to the brick chimneys and glass windowpanes. Rich women strode away from the theater district, clutching their fur capes against the cold, while homeless Irishmen huddled above flaming barrels of coal, trying desperately to keep warm.

Clayton Girard sat in the back of his luxurious carriage and watched the snow fall. It was late; the gaslights threw halos over the dank wet streets, and the moon was obliterated by the thick clouds. Fingering the envelope he held in his hands, he glanced down, then opened it once more, marveling at the card inside.

It was beautiful. There was simply no other word for it. The card was embossed with the finest of paper lace, imported from England, and stamped on satin paper so smooth it tempted the finger to trace the lovely moire pattern. A nosegay of forget-me–nots, tastefully decorated with silver beads, adorned the center, while inside a poem of heartbreaking beauty was scrolled on a slip of parchment.

It was a valentine, of course. But not just any

valentine. This one was made by Victoria Wickersham, and a Wickersham original was not only
worth quite a bit of money, it was guaranteed to
win the heart of any woman, young or old.

An ironic smile curved Clayton's mouth as he
enfolded the card back inside the envelope and
placed it in the pocket of his greatcoat. If anyone
had told him a year ago that he would be on a
journey like this, he would have laughed first and
called the person crazy later. But now, one of the
most successful physicians in Philadelphia was on
an errand of love, and to the valentine maker he
was destined to go.

The carriage neared Second Street and he
glanced out, seeing the neat little row houses and
shops that hadn't changed much in the past de-
cade. Had it really been that long since he'd been
here? As he passed one identical home after another, each with its elegant Federalist windows,
green shutters, and white marble steps, he realized the area hadn't changed at all. It was as if time
stood still on this narrow street with its freshly
washed cobbles and red brick.

He could only wonder if the same was true for
Victoria. It had been so long since he'd last seen
her—ten years to be exact. He could still recall the
first time he'd met her at Friends School in the city.
She was eight years old and coming out of the
classroom when Danny Sevarino pelted her with
snowballs, making her drop her books all over
the school steps. Frightened and bewildered, she
shook the snow from her hair while the boys
hooted and jeered at her odd clothing and shy
manner. She looked up then, and something about

her expression devastated him. Without thinking, he hit Danny, then came to her rescue with a handkerchief, drying her off, making her laugh in spite of the snow ruining her precious books. Tears misted her eyes and she glanced up at him, rubbing them with the back of her hand.

"Why?"

He smiled at her, wiped the wetness from her face, and shrugged. "He wanted your attention. You are, after all, the prettiest girl in school."

It was true, but the look of disbelief she gave him, followed by one of profound gratitude, he would never forget. They became true friends then, climbed hills together, collected fireflies and white-winged moths, shared books and secrets, watched ships on Front Street. Although he didn't keep in touch when he went away to school, due to the rigors of medical college, he'd never forgotten her.

Victoria was a part of his past, a part that meant more than he would have thought possible. He needed her now, and he smiled as he realized the irony of that. He only wondered how she would feel toward him, if she'd feel angry or rejected, or if she would refuse to see him at all. In the next half hour he would have his answer, one way or another.

Victoria Wickersham yawned, then glanced at the cuckoo clock chiming above her. The little bird appeared, earning a smile from the weary young woman, cooing nine times before disappearing into its wooden nest.

Nine. No wonder she was so tired. Dispiritedly,

she jabbed a needle into the silk and lace valentine in her hand, securing another sequin so that the roses sparkled prettily in the center. A tabby cat stretched in the window of the shop, then curled up again and dozed in the lamplight, obviously used to his mistress's doings. After drawing the lamp closer, Victoria adjusted her spectacles and tried to concentrate.

It was two weeks to Valentine's Day. Fourteen days to finish several hundred of her creations, tokens of love that the Philadelphia gentlemen bought to present to their favored ladies. Wearily she glanced at the stacks of billets-doux, love poems that would be placed within the cards, and she was pleased that she'd managed to pen so many during the long winter. Now she merely had to add her own special touch to the valentines that would make them Wickersham originals.

Smiling in satisfaction at the good fire burning cheerfully, she glanced at the thick cotton curtains at the windows, the bowl of cream waiting for Leopold, her cat. There were chickens in the yard and bread on the shelf. Although their way of life didn't allow for extravagant clothes, it pleased Victoria to see her aunts at church on Sunday dressed in warm woolen capes and hats that won them glances of envy from the gentry. Valentines had proved very lucrative.

"Are you still working, dearie?"

Victoria smiled fondly at her aunt Esther, who always looked like a sugarplum fairy. Lamplight fell on her spun-silk hair, making it glisten, and her plump figure was swathed in a woolen shawl so thick that it could have stood on its own.

Slightly deaf and more than a little absentminded, Esther nevertheless retained a sweetness that was impossible to overlook. She had come from their home above the shop, and now her blue eyes appeared worried as she surveyed the mountain of paper, the bolts of lace, and the piles of poems that lay on the counter.

"I just want to finish a few more before I go to bed," Victoria assured her. When Esther's expression did not change, she tried another tactic. "You wouldn't want to disappoint the young ladies, would you?"

"No, I suppose not." Esther sighed softly, fingering a pink satin ribbon. "But you look so tired, dear. I was just saying to Aunt Emma that you work much too hard. You need to get out more, meet some handsome men! Why, at your age, I was the belle of the city."

"I imagine you were." Victoria smiled again. "Tell me about Jonathan again. Was he really so handsome?"

Esther preened, her face lighting up like a young girl's. "Yes, he was. As I recall, he was tall and dark. And kind. So kind. You can tell a lot about a man just from his eyes, dear, remember that. Jonathan's were the warmest blue I have ever seen, just like a lake at dawn. Did I ever tell you about the time he picked me violets . . ."

Victoria finished sewing the valentine while Esther spoke. Although she had heard the tales over and over since she was little, she never tired of them in spite of Aunt Emma's insistance that Aunt Esther's suitors were all in her head. The two women sat quietly in the lamplight, sharing the late hour as they had done so many times before. It was a conspiracy between them, an unspoken agreement that helped Victoria pass the time while working and Esther to relive her youth. A small price, Victoria thought, for what the elderly lady had given her.

"Now why don't I get you a glass of mulberry wine? Aunt Emma made it just last week."

Victoria shuddered. Emma's wine was really homemade gin, but neither lady would ever admit it. "No, I don't think so. Why don't you have mine? It seems to help your arthritis."

"Ah, it does that, dear. Thank you, you're so kind." Esther poured herself a glass from the decanter, then gave Victoria another worried look. "Are you sure you don't want anything? Hot tea, perhaps? There's a cup of milk . . ."

"No. I'll be fine. Good night, Aunt Esther."

Grinning, Victoria returned to her work. Aunt Esther would have been in serious trouble had it not been for the revenue from the cards. If one was poor and senile, one was mad, but when one had money, one was pleasantly eccentric. Victoria was grateful for the two elderly ladies who had taken her in when her parents died in a carriage accident. She had been only seven then, but she remembered the day as clearly as if it were yesterday. It was Aunt Esther who had told her the truth, Aunt Esther who had brought her back to the rambling row house on Second Street and told her she should never be afraid, for they would always take care of her.

After tucking back a stray dark hair that had fallen into her eyes, she placed her needle on the counter and reached for the packet of poems. Somewhere in the stack was the perfect sentiment for the pink and silver card. This one was for a newly launched debutante in the throes of her first love.

A painful ache began inside Victoria as she read through several poems, an ache so familiar that she scarcely recognized its existence. The tabby purred and leapt down from the sill, rubbing against her smock as she sifted through the love letters, reading words of devotion, longing, and love, words that had never been written to her.

There had been a man once—a boy, she amended mentally. As children they had been best friends, and she had somehow hoped that later the friendship would come to mean something more to him, as it did her. You're turning into a silly fool, she chided herself. Pretty soon she would be just like Aunt Esther, fabricating romances to substitute for the lack of love in her life. Yawning again as her glasses slipped down her nose, she decided on a poem and began pasting it into the card.

A moment later there was the sound of a carriage outside and then footsteps muffled by the snow. Glancing up in surprise, Victoria saw the door swing open and a man step into the shop.

"I'm sorry, sir, but we're closed."

He was dusted with snow, from the collar of his stiff greatcoat to the tips of his polished boots. A gentleman, Victoria thought, then quickly readjusted her glasses. He had his back to her as he stamped his feet, careful not to bring any slush into the room. Then as he turned in the lamplight, her heart pounded as if it were trying to escape from her chest.

"I know I've come late . . ." His voice trailed off, and a warm smile replaced his polite words. "Victoria."

"Clayton." Her voice was a whisper. Dear God, was he really here? Or had she lost her mind, dreaming of him so often? She glanced suspiciously at the decanter of wine on the sideboard, but aside from Aunt Esther's glass, it was still almost full.

"It's so good to see you again." He stepped closer, then took her hand. His skin was chilled from the snow, and he laughed at her startled expression, then let go of her hand and rubbed his palms together. "Sorry. It's freezing outside. I was just so glad to see you. I've heard about your shop."

Numbly she nodded, glancing awkwardly around the room and seeing it with new eyes. Lace hung everywhere, from every rafter to the windows and the door. Needles were jabbed haphazardly into the wall behind her, and silk threads of every imaginable color streamed from them like the tails of flaming arrows. The tabby cat, caught in a jumble of ribbons, tangled on the floor, while poems and books lay strewn about, invitingly open and enticing to the eye.

Aunt Emma deplored the clutter, saying she couldn't understand how anyone could work in this condition, but Victoria found it conducive to her imagination. And when the money began rolling in from the cards, even Aunt Emma had stopped lecturing.

"It's . . . a little untidy." Victoria blushed as amusement swept his features. He turned back to her and her breath stopped.

He was even more handsome than she remembered. The hair that had been a dark brown in school was now ebony and fell charmingly across his forehead. His eyes were a soft brown, and his mouth was compassionate, strong and firm. He'd fulfilled every promise she could ever have imagined, and she tried in vain to straighten her hair as she stepped self-consciously toward the stuffed chairs near the window.

"Please sit down. I'm sorry, I didn't even ask . . . Would you like some tea or something? I know it's cold."

He stared at her a moment, his smile genuinely kind. "Coffee, if you have it. I can't drink that wretched tea, though my family lives on it."

She laughed, a soft tinkling sound in the room. The tabby cat glanced up from the web of ribbons, then went back to wrestling as his mistress retreated to the kitchen to brew the coffee.

Her hands were shaking as she lit the stove and she was grateful he couldn't see her.

He was here, he was actually here. She wanted to smile, to laugh, to sing out loud, then she giggled at the ridiculousness of her thoughts. It was silly to feel so happy; she was sure Aunt Emma would think so, but she just couldn't help it. Clayton was back.

Her smile faded as she recalled his long silence, and doubt crept into her mind.

She was an orphaned child, adopted by the town's eccentric aunts. She'd been poor, ridiculed, and shy. He had been a member of one of Philadelphia's first families—rich, successful and popular.

How could she wonder why she hadn't heard from him?

The kettle boiled, and the coffee ran over the sides. Victoria grabbed the spewing pot and burned her hand. Letting out a shriek, she reached for a cloth and retrieved the pot. She poured the bitter liquid into a cup and set the pot well out of the way, then returned to the front room and handed him the coffee.

"I hope it's all right. It sort of . . . boiled over."

"I'm sure it's fine." He took a mouthful of the coffee and managed gallantly to hide his true reaction as the liquid stung his tongue. Placing the cup on the table beside him, he smiled. "It's wonderful. Just what I needed. You know, it's really good to see you again. I've thought about you a lot, and my sister told me how well you were doing with the shop. I'm so glad for you."

Why? Her mind shouted at him. Why didn't you ever write? But she smiled back at him, knowing she could never ask without risking their friendship. "I'm glad you came by, though it is late. . . ." She looked at him questioningly.

"I know. I'm sorry, but I needed to see you and spend some time with you. You see, my practice has been extremely busy."

Victoria nodded. Clayton had become a wonderful doctor, highly respected in the city. Some of his wealthier acquaintances derided him for treating the poor as well as the rich, but money, for Clayton, had never been a problem. He was a true physician in every sense of the word, and people from both the Main Line and the impoverished wards sought him out.

"This was the first chance I had to come by. I've been wanting to for so long. Please believe that."

Victoria's heart swelled. Could he have retained some feeling for her similar to what she felt for him? It seemed impossible, and yet there was something about the way he looked at her. She stared down at the floor littered with thread, not even daring to hope. "I did miss you," she admitted shyly.

"And I you. I was thinking about you on the way over here, what good friends we were in school. Do you think we could be that again? I promise not to drop out of sight now that I'm established. It was so important, those first couple of years, to concentrate on school, that I really didn't see anyone. But now . . ."

Her breath quickened. It was just too perfect. No one could feel this happy. All of the poems she'd ever written meant nothing; the rhymes, meaningless. It all culminated in this one moment, when she truly understood what it was to really care.

"Now?" At any moment she would be crying, and she couldn't do that. She wanted to savor this time, to remember it as perfect, unmarred by inappropriate emotions. He fished inside his coat and produced a newspaper clipping.

"I'm sure you must have read the notice in the *Ledger*." He handed her the slip, obviously unaware that Victoria never saw a newspaper. "I need your help."

Nodding, Victoria unfolded the paper. She

would do anything for him, anything at all. Adjusting her glasses, she saw a picture of a young woman. There was something familiar about the likeness, but at the moment she couldn't quite place the face.

"Elizabeth Chester," he said fondly. "I'm going to marry her, and I need you to help me court her."

Chapter Two

Numbly she stared at him, unable to believe what she'd just heard. Help him to court another woman? Surely she had misunderstood, it was just some dreadful miscommunication, but he continued in the same tone, not noticing her reaction.

"I know it sounds foolish, but I don't know the first thing about writing romantic letters or wooing a woman. I don't express myself well on paper—do you remember those horrible compositions I used to write for school? It just doesn't come easily to me. And as a valentine writer, I thought you might be able to assist me."

Anger and humiliation washed over her. He hadn't come back for her, hadn't even considered her in that light. He had come, as so many before him, simply for her writing skill, to let her pen the words that he could not. She meant nothing to him, nothing at all.

"I would be so grateful. I will pay you whatever sum you name."

Somehow she managed to find her voice. "When?" As he looked at her in confusion, she choked out the words. "When do you wish to be married?"

"I don't know yet," Clayton said thoughtfully. "But I want to propose on Valentine's Day. With Elizabeth, I don't want to wait."

Victoria nodded, finding that statement easy enough to believe. Elizabeth Chester was the much coddled daughter of the Main Line Chesters, who were one of Philadelphia's first families. Blond and outrageously beautiful, Elizabeth had been the shallowest person in school. She'd thought of nothing but her appearance, her dancing lessons, her dubious talent on the piano. Yet the boys had adored her; they'd taken one look into her huge gray eyes and were forever lost. Apparently Clayton wasn't above all that; he was the same as any other man who'd met her.

"What of your family?" Victoria tried to make sense of her emotions as she sorted through the story. "Do they approve?"

Clayton nodded. "My mother had some reservations, but Elizabeth is the perfect choice in so many ways. She has influence, and her family is well known. They've contributed quite a bit of money to the hospital and are well respected by the medical profession."

"But how do you feel about her?" When Clayton glanced at her curiously, Victoria continued quickly. "I need to know—if I am to accept your proposition, that is. I have to decide what approach to take."

"Ah." That seemed to satisfy him, and he smiled. "Elizabeth is . . . so beautiful. I have to admit I've never seen such a pretty woman. She's vivacious, fascinating . . . Well, you remember her from school. I consider myself very lucky."

Her heart sinking, Victoria nodded. "And does she return your feelings?"

He hesitated, then continued. "She is elusive. Elizabeth isn't like most women, blurting out her thoughts and emotions. But I am certain that my feelings are . . . reciprocated. I haven't been able to look at another woman since I saw her again recently."

"I see." Victoria couldn't take any more of this. She had to get away, to find some dark, quiet place where she could express all the rejection and disappointment she fought to keep hidden. Extending a hand to him, she shook his briskly in her best businesslike manner.

"Does this mean you accept?" Clayton asked hopefully, as he got to his feet.

"I have to think about it." When his face fell, she explained. "This is my busiest season, and I have to make certain I don't take on more than I can handle. I just want to look through my orders and see where we stand."

"I see." He picked up his coat and gave her a warm smile. "Is two days enough time? We can discuss the terms over lunch."

Victoria nodded, her heart breaking. She barely managed a civil reply as he turned toward the door. Then he stopped on his way out.

"I really did enjoy seeing you again. You mean a lot to me, Victoria. You remind me so much of . . . my sister." He smiled, then turned and left.

The door closed, and she crumbled behind it. Damn him! Who did he think he was, walking back into her life and making her feel like this? This was worse than any of the times the other children had laughed at her. No, Clayton Girard, with his kindness, had hurt her much more.

Memories rushed back to her, all that much more painful now. She recalled him at ten, admiring her crafts at a school fair and persuading his parents to buy up all of her sachets. Two years later he had secretly taught her how to play baseball on the grounds of his Main Line mansion, laughing at her fumbles and cheering her successes. At sixteen all of the girls had wanted him, but it was Victoria he'd asked to the dance. It was the only time he'd ever been angry at her, for she had to refuse. She couldn't tell him she had no dress, no shoes, and no gloves. So he'd taken Mary Ann Drexel instead, and Victoria had tried hard not to care.

Tears tumbled quickly, and she wrapped her arms around her knees, sitting in the chair he'd just vacated. Fury washed over her, but a saner voice protested and she remembered what he'd said. Elizabeth really was the perfect choice for a doctor's wife. She was beautiful, rich, well situated, and able to advance his career. She, Victoria Wickersham, was the spinster niece of the town crazy aunts, the valentine maker. Good Lord, she was out of her mind even to dream he would see her as anything else.

"Is two days enough time . . ."

Two days. She had to decide if she could do this, if she could put her own feelings aside and help him win Elizabeth's hand, no easy task in her estimation. It would take everything she had to do what he asked, but in reality, she cared about him too much not to want to help him.

She just didn't know if she had the heart for it.

"And I told Sally the lace maker that we really needed more pink for Valentine's Day. Pink is so . . . pink, don't you think, dear?" Esther asked.

Emma glanced at Victoria, who was seated at the kitchen table, buried in books. The morning light spilled into the room through the curtains, making sunny webs on the table and chairs. Normally Esther's prattle brought a fond smile to her niece's face, but today Victoria ignored her and scribbled figures, added columns, and frowned at the result.

Hurt, Esther huffed and poured herself another cup of tea. "One would have an opinion, at least. What do you think, Emma?"

"Hush." Emma sent Esther a sharp look, then glanced at the books. This was more than work. Something was definitely wrong. Victoria looked distraught today. There were signs of tears around her eyes, and her face, never hearty to begin with, looked as pale as English china.

Frowning, Emma remembered hearing a carriage late last night, and she'd distinctly heard a male voice in the shop. That wasn't so surprising, especially this time of year, but coupled with the appearance of her niece this morning, it seemed significant.

Emma sighed. Used to carrying burdens, this was just one more she would have to shoulder. Peering out from behind her spectacles, she tapped the page her niece was studying.

"This is the retirement fund you are trying to set up for the working women in the ward?"

Victoria looked up. "Yes. You know we have quite a few women doing piecework for us out of their homes. They badly need something for their old age. I want to get a better idea of how much cash we need. I was offered a lucrative business proposition last night. I hate to take on any more work right now, but the numbers aren't promising."

Emma nodded in agreement. "What you want to do is noble, but it will cost quite a bit. What kind of business deal are you talking about?"

Shrugging, Victoria put the ledger aside. "I have to help a man court a woman, write his sonnets and love letters. He says I can name my price."

Esther's plump face lit up. "Oh, that's wonderful, dear! And you're so good at that. Why, I recall that sweet old spinster you helped marry just by penning a few notes for her. What was her name?"

"Thackery," Emma answered. "Lizzie Thackery." She turned back to Victoria curiously. "Will you take the job?" There was a touch of understanding in her voice, and Victoria nodded.

"I need the money, and I think I'd be foolish to pass it up. As Aunt Esther says, it will be an easy task for me." Turning to her aunts with a smile, she indicated the clipping from the newspaper. "Now I just need you two to find out everything you can about Elizabeth Chester. Her likes, dislikes, colors she fancies. You know what I need."

Emma groaned, but for once held her tongue. "That should be easy—she's often mentioned in those horrid society papers. We'll get you the information you need. By the time we're done, you'll know enough about Elizabeth to write a penny dreadful."

Valentine's Day had always been her favorite day—until now, Victoria mused two days after Clayton's visit. Sifting through the pile of information that her aunts had bought, bribed, or legally obtained about Elizabeth Chester, her face grew grimmer.

Elizabeth had changed very little in the years since she'd finished school. None of her servants had nice things to say about her, and the other society girls had even worse comments. It wasn't as if Elizabeth was a terrible person. She just seemed thoughtless and self-centered, unaware of how easily she could hurt others.

Her favorite color was red, her best perfume came from France, daisies made her sneeze, and her feet were very large, a fact that she was sensitive about. She wore white shirtwaists from Wanamaker's and flexible skirt supporters from Warner's. She preferred feathers to flowers in her hats, lace gloves to mitts on her hands. She wore chenille in the summer and frizzed hairpieces in the winter. In short, Elizabeth was up on the latest fashion and devoted much of her time to her appearance.

Victoria sighed and picked up her pencil for the third time. He would be here at any moment. She had been unable to write a word that would make Elizabeth's heart flutter. Somehow she had to find a way—for everyone's sake.

"This way, Mr. Girard."

Victoria followed the headwaiter to a beautifully set table near the window of the City Tavern. One of the oldest restaurants in Philadelphia, it was simple and pretty, maintaining its colonial heritage. Fresh flowers graced the tables, and pewter gleamed on the snowy linen tablecloths.

Glancing around the room, Victoria drank in the sight of women dressed in the height of fashion, with their bustles and parasols, ostrich plumes and creweled satin bags. They looked like summer peonies, gowned in every color imaginable, from blue to gray to yellow and pink, and in every fabric *Godey's* had ever recommended.

And the gentlemen! They were equally elegant, carrying their black derbies and pearl-handled canes, many of them sporting waxed mustaches that curled intricately beneath their noses. Enjoying a port, they met with other men to discuss business, or with ladies to enjoy a leisurely lunch.

It had been so long since she'd been out that Victoria couldn't resist staring. Aunt Esther was right, she mused, drinking in the sights. She'd become a shut-in, almost as spinsterish as her aunts. She had missed so much, it seemed.

"Victoria?"

It took her a minute to realize that Clayton had repeated himself. Glancing up in embarrassment, she blushed and met his eyes.

"Do you want something to drink first? Tea, perhaps, or a glass of wine?"

"Tea, please."

"And I'd like a whiskey."

The waiter nodded and returned a moment later to place the drinks on the table and hand them menus.

Victoria sighed. "It's so nice here. But we really didn't have to come out in the snow. We could have talked at the shop."

Clayton smiled, and she was once more amazed at how warm his eyes could be. "I didn't want to discuss our business there. No offense, but I remember how Esther and Emma can be. Esther would be peeping around the doorframe trying to listen, and Emma wouldn't be able to resist stepping in and giving us advice. I didn't think it would be conducive to our work."

Victoria giggled, the sound surprisingly sweet. "They are trying at times, but I don't know what I'd do without them."

He stared at her, not realizing what he was doing until she lowered her eyes in confusion and dug into her case for her papers. He hadn't realized how much he'd missed her until this morning, when he thought about seeing her again. She really was pretty. Her hair was a beautiful brown, her eyes a clear blue. But the glasses she wore, coupled with her unfashionable hat and dress, detracted from her looks. She seemed blissfully unaware of her appearance as she hoisted out several books and sheets of notepaper, depositing them on the table just as the waiter appeared to ask for their order.

"I'm sorry, but I—really don't know," Victoria stammered, glancing at the menu. Most of the offerings were unfamiliar to her, and she scanned the list, not wanting to appear ignorant.

"Do you mind if I order for both of us?" Clayton said.

Victoria shook her head, relieved, and he told the waiter his choices.

"Excellent, sir. It will take but a moment."

The waiter disappeared, and Victoria scrambled for a pencil, obviously awkward and ill at ease. That troubled him, and Clayton placed his hand over hers, stilling her motions. She glanced up in confusion.

"We don't have to start right away, although I am deeply grateful that you've accepted my offer. Look, Victoria, we have a lot of catching up to do. Why don't we concentrate on that? We can worry about the work later. We have plenty of time."

She nodded, putting the pencil down, then glanced again at the crowded room. "I haven't been here since . . . I can't remember when."

Astonished, he indicated the street. "But you live less than three blocks away."

Shrugging, she sipped her tea. "We never had the money when I was little. You know that."

"But now?" He indicated her papers. "Everyone knows that Wickersham valentines are a huge success. Surely you indulge yourself in every little luxury, like an occasional lunch?"

"The debts were unbelievable at first," Victoria admitted, unaware that ladies never talked business with gentlemen. "Once they were settled, the house needed repair, Esther needed medical care, and I had to put some of the profits back into the business. I have several women working for me from their homes. I want to establish a pension fund for them. Do you know—" she leaned forward, her face alight with a passion that was completely unselfconscious—"that these women have no unions, no shop stewards, no job protection?"

Clayton nodded. "There are too many immigrants fighting for the same jobs. It creates the situation."

"But it's wrong!" Victoria flushed, then sat back slightly as the waiter brought a thick brown soup.

"I know. I treat their children. I was in one of the wards last week, and I found a whole family that had cholera. The conditions . . . aren't fit to be described."

"I can't just ignore it. I have to help. If it wasn't for the cards . . ."

He knew what she meant: There but for the grace of God. He glanced at her compassionately, not at all surprised. Victoria was always sympathetic to others, even when they hardly deserved it. "I remember that time you insisted we give a beggar our lunch."

"And he sold it for whiskey." Victoria smiled ruefully. "You told me so."

"But I didn't think less of you for it. If anything, I admired you more."

Something about his expression confused her

and made her feel weak. Stop it, she told herself sternly. He wants you to help him win Elizabeth's heart. Clayton doesn't think of you in any other way. Still, as she sipped the soup, she had to look away from him. He was too close, too handsome, and too charming.

"Do you remember when we used to swim in Wissahickon Creek? You used to get in trouble for getting so much mud in your clothes."

"Aunt Esther still thinks it was from the school sandbox," Victoria admitted. "I remember helping you with your homework, and Mr. Clark writing 'very' on mine and 'interesting' on yours."

Clayton laughed. "You should have disguised it better. Seems the Wickersham style was apparent even then."

The waiter brought fresh fish, two vegetables, fruit, and rolls. Clayton went on talking to her, and she began visibly to relax, enjoying the meal and his company. Some of the anger and humiliation had left her, and she became resigned to the thought that this man, the only man who'd ever meant anything to her, would never be hers.

Still, she could enjoy his company, as selfish as it seemed. Even if it was to benefit Elizabeth, she would be able to see him for the next two weeks and to share in a friendship that was as strong as ever.

Dessert came and went, and they still talked. It wasn't until the other diners began to leave that she realized how much time had passed. Flushing guiltily, she brought out several sheets of blank paper.

"I'm sorry. I was having such a good time that I forgot the real reason for this meeting."

"It wasn't your fault. I was, too." He gazed at his pocket watch in annoyance. "I have to get back to work. Do you think you could have something ready for me later this week? I plan to see Elizabeth on Friday."

Her throat tightened, but she cleared it quickly and nodded. "I have some information about Elizabeth. I'm sure I can write a poem by Friday."

"Good." He rose to his feet and paid for their lunch. "I enjoyed your company. Thank you. And thank you for your help. You don't know what this means to me."

Nodding, she jammed her papers back into her case. She did know what it meant to him.

And that was the part that bothered her the most.

Chapter Three

It wasn't like him to forget about work. As Clayton struggled into his physician's coat, he remembered the waiting room filled with patients. None of them had been too pleased to see him when he had arrived. Chagrined, he realized that he'd been too involved in talking to Victoria. Not only hadn't they worked on a love letter, but he had arrived at his office twenty minutes late for his first appointment.

Agnes, his clerk, gave him an annoyed glance, but said nothing when he hurried to the door. He would get caught up—it was just a matter of using his time efficiently. Then there was a treatise he wanted to work on later, an elderly woman he wished to see in her home, and then he had to meet Elizabeth.

Damn! But it was worth it, he decided, letting his frustration fade. It was so good to see Victoria again, to hear her laugh. He had forgotten how much they had in common, how interested she was in the people around her. He thought about the pension fund she was attempting to establish. It was a radical idea, but one that was just like her. She understood the plight of working women and wanted to help.

And it was obvious that she hadn't been out in some time. That amazed him, for he still thought she was exceptionally pretty. Yet even in school, most people hadn't seen past her dowdy clothes and hairstyle to the wonderful woman beneath.

It was incredible that she'd managed to start her own business, and an amazingly successful one at that. He was surprised that prosperity hadn't changed her, but she was as unsophisticated as ever. She even seemed interested in his work. Halfway through lunch she had begun asking him about his career, what his practice was like, how he felt about his patients. It had been obvious that she was very sincere and not just asking out of polite curiosity, and so he'd answered her questions as thoroughly as he could, gratified to be able

to share his work with her. He had found himself
opening up to her the way he did when they were
little. Only now she was a woman, and a very
attractive woman at that.

My God, what was he thinking? They were
friends, he reminded himself, good friends. He
was only reacting this way because he had missed
her, and hadn't realized how much until now. And
it was nice to be able to talk to her, to tell her about
his life.

Elizabeth could never stand to hear the slightest
thing about medicine or blood . . . feeling instantly disloyal, he dismissed the thought. Elizabeth was just squeamish, like most women. If
anything her uneasiness around delicate subjects
only demonstrated her femininity. Victoria had
been raised differently and didn't realize that such
subjects were not to be discussed.

Perhaps he would introduce her to Elizabeth,
and they could all be friends. Elizabeth would like
that, and it would help get Victoria out more.
Satisfied with his conclusion, Clayton called for his
first patient. There were times when he welcomed
the distraction of his work, and this was definitely
one of them.

"When I look into your eyes, I see
Not the loveliness of their shape, or the sweet
        fullness of your lips,
But the scarlet mists at dawn,
The joy in an old man's smile,
The soft twinkle of the stars at night.
I hear the laughter of a baby,
Smell the sweet scent of earth.

The wind seems to carry an erotic splendor in its
   rage,
Dying among the trees like a lover's lament
Until it finds succor within your arms once more."

Victoria cringed as he read the poem out loud,
repeating her own words back to her. Did he
know? Had he somehow surmised that these were
the words she longed to hear from him? Color rose
in her cheeks, but when she dared look at him he
was smiling in satisfaction at the love letter. Then
he glanced at her with an expression of gratitude.

"It's perfect. How can I ever thank you?"

The emotion tightened her throat, and she
looked away. "It's nothing. I do this for a living,
remember?"

"I know, but it is wonderful. I think it's the most
beautiful thing I've ever read. I could never have
thought this up on my own. You have the most
fantastic mind. It is something I've always admired
about you." His eyes met hers, and he gave her a
warm smile. "Elizabeth will love it. I'm sure."

"I really have to go now." Victoria picked up her
hat and coat, wanting to escape, to be anywhere
but here at his office. She felt naked and exposed,
her feelings reduced to a commodity to be sold for
money. She was aching and empty inside, and the
pain grew unbearable as she wrapped herself
awkwardly in her coat.

"Before you leave, I want to ask you something." He stopped her at the door, taking her
hand in his own. "Elizabeth is having a tea later
today—nothing big, just a few friends. I would

very much appreciate it if you could come. I'm sure she would be delighted to see you again."

Victoria stared at him in surprise. "Me? You want me to come to tea?"

"Of course." He grinned at her reaction. "That's not so farfetched, is it? My sister will be there—you remember her from school—and a few other people. Promise me you'll come."

It was so enticing—the chance to spend some time with him, to see him on a social level—but she realized that wasn't what he was asking. Elizabeth was the woman he loved. He merely wanted Victoria to come as one of his friends. Perhaps he felt sorry for her. She flushed as she thought of this.

"I—I can't," Victoria stammered, turning toward the door. "I'm sorry, but I just can't."

He stood in front of her, blocking the exit, his smile devilishly handsome and persuasive. "Why not? I know you don't have any other appointments. And if you need transportation, I can have a coach pick you up."

"It's not that." She struggled to explain. "It's just . . . I've been meaning to talk to you. I don't think it's a good idea to continue this. I've written one letter for you, and I will do the valentine, but I think we should just call the whole thing off."

There. She'd said it. She saw the hurt look on his face, but it was nothing compared to what was happening inside her. She couldn't continue this charade. She would not assist him in courting Elizabeth, no matter how much she wanted to help him. It was tearing her up inside. Worse, she was afraid he'd somehow fathom her secret, and it would end their friendship permanently. She just couldn't do it, and it was better to realize that now.

"I'm sorry, have I done something to offend you?" He looked so upset that Victoria rushed to explain.

"No, it's nothing like that. It's just . . . I don't have enough information." She grabbed onto that inspiration and continued quickly. "It's been years since I've seen Elizabeth. I really don't know what she's like now or what she's thinking. It's extremely difficult to write poems, trying to reach the essence of a person, when you have no idea of that person at all."

His smile deepened and he refused to let go of her hand. "You've just given me the perfect reason for you to come. I won't take no for an answer," he warned, seeing the protest come to her face. "This will give you the opportunity to renew your relationship with Elizabeth. I know you knew her at school. This time you can get to know her as a friend. Not only will it make the job easier, but she can help you. She knows everyone and can introduce you to society. Victoria, I want you to be happy. Say you'll do this for me."

She closed her eyes, and her resistance melted. She had never been able to deny him anything, and time had not changed that one bit. Fighting the emotions that threatened to overwhelm her, she withdrew her hand and looked at him once more.

"All right. I will come."

"Good." He stepped out of the way and opened the door. "My carriage will call for you this afternoon. Thank you, Victoria."

She rushed down the steps of his office. She had to get away from here, from him. Somehow she had to get control of her feelings.

"Victoria Wickersham?" Elizabeth looked at Clayton as if he'd lost his mind. "Why on earth would you want to invite Victoria to tea?"

Something about her tone made Clayton wince, but he realized that his request must have come as a surprise to Elizabeth. He couldn't let her know the reason he'd gone to see Victoria, and from her perspective, it did seem odd.

"She's lonely, Elizabeth. And you know so many people. I haven't seen her since school, but I ran into her at lunch the other day. I just thought it would be nice if you could help to get her out more and introduce her to some of our friends."

Elizabeth's eyes narrowed as she protested. "But none of our friends know her! She's not from the Main Line, and you know how some of them are. When they hear she supports herself by making valentines, they will think her mad and us, too, for inviting her!"

Irritation knotted Clayton's jaw, but he tried to remain patient. Elizabeth sometimes didn't realize how thoughtless she sounded. "They will not think anything of the sort unless we tell them how she earns her living. No one will automatically connect Victoria to the Wickersham valentines unless we introduce her that way. Philadelphia is a big city, and the founder of the valentine business has always been something of a mystery. The few people who have heard of Victoria were not willing to credit a female with such a successful enterprise. Her reputation, and yours, will be safe."

"I didn't mean it like that," Elizabeth said softly, aware that she'd erred. "I was thinking about Victoria's point of view. I do remember her from school, and she was always such a sweet little thing. Does she still look the same?"

Clayton nodded, frowning. "Yes. In fact, I thought you might be able to help her there as well. I always thought Victoria had a lot of natural beauty. Yet she dresses as if to hide it. Maybe you could teach her a few things, see that she meets some nice people. I'd like to see her have a chance. She's worked so hard."

Elizabeth smiled, tossing her blond curls. "You sound serious. Do I have cause to be jealous?"

Clayton grinned. She was so sure of herself, so confident. Clad in blue silk with a fetching ruffle at her throat, she was the loveliest woman he'd ever seen. Untouched by pain or poverty, she laughed often and freely, almost refusing to believe that the rest of the world didn't live the way she did. There were times when he wished she were a little more caring, but when Elizabeth laughed, he forgot his irritation and could only laugh with her.

"No, you don't have cause to be jealous, and you know it. But will you do this for me? I would appreciate it."

"Of course," Elizabeth agreed. After all, Victoria would never draw attention away from her, so she was someone Elizabeth could safely befriend. It was painless and required little effort on her part. "I will see that she meets the right people, and I'll introduce her to my dressmaker. By the time we're through, Victoria will be a new woman. Wait and see."

"And these are the Wetherills, Mr. George Harrison, Mrs. John Lewis . . ."

Victoria struggled to remember all the names. Mary, Clayton's sister, furnished her with their occupations and updated her on their lives. "Harrison—sugar. You remember his daughter from school. Lewis—chemicals. Wetherill—trading. Jayne was a physician, like Clayton, but is now making medicines." Mary smiled at Victoria's bewildered expression. "Don't worry, you'll soon know them all."

"How do you keep it all straight?" Victoria asked.

Mary giggled. "It's easy—we grew up with these people, remember? Besides, it will help with conversation if you know something about what they do. I'll help you."

Victoria gave Mary a look of sincere appreciation, then glanced down at her dress. She was wearing a dove gray gown with hoops, which Aunt Esther assured her was the latest style, but she noticed that the other women were wearing only bustles. She realized that she looked hopelessly out of date.

"Why, Victoria, I haven't seen you since school." Elizabeth smiled, and her eyes dropped to Victoria's gown. "You look . . . exactly the same."

She hadn't meant to be unkind, but Victoria realized that she was correct. She lifted her eyes and saw Elizabeth's lovely white gown with its demure lace and pink roses. The skirt swept the floor in the front and was gathered into a bustle in the back, accentuating her figure and calling attention to each lovely curve. Her hair, the color of straw in sunlight, was artfully dressed to draw attention to a face that needed little aid. For a brief second Victoria wondered why a woman as pretty as Elizabeth would work so hard to enhance her beauty, but she immediately dismissed the thought as envy. Elizabeth was simply a lovely woman who knew how to make the most of her looks.

"Clayton will be pleased when he sees that you've come. I was so happy when I heard he had seen you."

"Yes, I was surprised as well," Mary said, giving Elizabeth a curious glance. "Clayton has few friends, but he is intensely loyal to them. I remember how close you two were in school."

Victoria colored violently, then glanced at the floor, the walls, the scintillating chandeliers. Had Mary somehow guessed her feelings? Clayton's sister gave her hand a reassuring squeeze while Elizabeth smiled quickly.

"That was a long time ago," Elizabeth said. "Come and let me introduce you to the old guard. These women are very important in society. I'm sure everyone's wondering who you are."

Mary nodded, and Victoria followed Elizabeth through the gathering. Feeling more intimidated with each step, she glanced at the women in their lovely dresses and flamboyant hats, and the men in their finely tailored suits. Clayton was standing near the fireplace, his head slightly inclined as he listened to an older woman seated on a plump sofa. He gave her a dazzling smile, then nodded approvingly to Elizabeth as she took Victoria by the hand.

A group of older women stopped chatting as she approached, and Victoria felt their unspoken appraisal as they glanced in her direction. She wanted to run home to Aunt Esther and her mulberry wine, to Aunt Emma with her sharp cane rapping on the floor. She yearned to be anywhere but here, where she didn't belong. What on earth could have possessed her to agree to attend this tea? And for all Clayton's kindness, could he honestly think this would benefit her in any way?

"Martha Brooks, Winifred Biddle, and Emily Drexel, this is Victoria Wickersham." Elizabeth smiled graciously and brought Victoria closer. "You have heard of Wickersham Originals? Victoria is the valentine maker."

The women gasped collectively. Elizabeth smiled sweetly, then gazed at a man and a woman near the door. "Oh, there are the Rutledges. I must speak to them. I'll catch up with you later." She disappeared, leaving Victoria with the group of women.

"You are *the* Victoria Wickersham?" Emily asked, not hiding her astonishment.

Miserably, Victoria nodded. "Yes, I make—"

"Why, my dear, I am well aware of what you make. Everyone knows what a Wickersham valentine is." Emily's middle-aged face lit up, and she turned to the other women with a conspiratorial delight. "Do you recall that beautiful card I received from Jonathan last year? It was a Wickersham, without a doubt. It had the fleur-de-lis insignia and all."

The women crowded closer, all of them curious and obviously thrilled to meet her. "However do you do it?" Martha asked, excitement in her voice. "Those poems—do you write them yourself? And where do you find such lovely lace?"

"And the scents!" Winifred sighed, rolling her eyes. "Mine was lilac last year. Roses the year before."

"I had lily of the valley and heliotrope," Emily said happily. She looked at Victoria with a new respect. "And to think someone as young as you managed to start such a business! I told my husband that women were just as capable as men, and I am delighted to be proven right."

Everyone began talking at once, and Victoria managed to conceal her astonishment. They accepted her, were happy in her company, and obviously curious about her trade. As she explained the valentine-making process, she felt their glances of envy and interest. It was unbelievable, and her face betrayed her amazement as Mary joined them.

"Did you know this, Mary? She is *the* Wickersham—the poet who makes valentines."

"Of course." Mary smiled warmly. "Victoria is an old friend of the family."

"You must come to my brunch on Sunday, Victoria," Martha said happily. "Mary is coming, and everyone will be delighted to meet you. Wait until I tell them that I've met *the* Victoria Wickersham!"

"And you must come to my supper party on

Friday night," Emily said, miffed to have been beaten out by Martha. "Everyone is coming, and we will go to the theater afterward."

Victoria smiled, amazed at her own success. She admitted as much when Mary led her away and handed her a cup of tea and some cakes.

"Why are you surprised?" Clayton's sister asked. "Clayton has good taste in friends. I only wish you had kept in touch all the while. He's done nothing but talk about you since he ran into you recently."

Victoria choked on the tea. "Really?"

Mary nodded. "I'm glad to see him relax a little. He's so dedicated to his work and has such a kind heart that he is busy all the time, visiting a poor child or an invalid. Since he's been courting Elizabeth, his time is even more scarce. I rarely see him."

"I know, but the city needs him, and more like him." Victoria rushed to Clayton's defense. "He was telling me about some of the people he's treated in the wards. They suffer unbelievably in the sweatshops and the construction yards. I don't know what they'd do without him."

Mary smiled, a twinkle in her eye. "I'm glad you feel that way. Too often upper-class people have little empathy for the working classes. Perhaps because Clayton and I were once poor, we find their troubles easier to understand. Our parents lost a good deal of money in the panic, but fortunately, we've regained it. Still, I think it noble of Clayton not to forget." She glanced at her brother who was standing across the room with Elizabeth. Clayton was an exception in a lot of ways, she thought.

But then, so was Victoria.

* * *

"Isn't it great how easily Victoria's fitting in?" Clayton said to Elizabeth when he saw Mary glance his way and give him an encouraging smile. "She has quite a crowd around her. I think she's definitely won over the old guard."

Elizabeth gazed across the room at the women talking animatedly with Victoria. A frown crinkled her pretty face as she saw the once-shy valentine maker laughing and seeming to enjoy herself. Even Martha Brooks seemed taken with Victoria and was practically gushing.

"It's amazing," Elizabeth said. "Who would ever have thought? Especially since Victoria was so dowdy when she was in school."

"I never thought she was dowdy," Clayton said, annoyed. "You know, Elizabeth, you should think before you speak. Victoria happens to be an old friend and a good friend. I think a lot of her."

Elizabeth looked at Clayton thoughtfully. Her eyes narrowed, and an odd smile came to her face. "You're right, Clayton. I apologize. You do think a lot of Victoria. And I'll keep that in mind."

Clayton smiled down at her and slid his arm through hers.

"So there you are." A handsome young man with blond hair and a mustache gave Victoria a bold smile. "Mary, I was wondering if you were going to keep this lovely creature all to yourself or introduce her to the rest of us."

"Victoria, this is my cousin Philip. You two have something in common." Mary smiled. "Victoria's an artist, too."

"Do you paint?" Philip asked, obviously delighted.

Victoria shook her head. "No, I—"

"She's the valentine maker," Mary said.

"Are you serious?" As he glanced from his cousin to Victoria, Philip's smile broadened. "I heard some of the women talking. You really write love poems?"

Victoria nodded, a little ill at ease with his attention. "Yes, valentines—cards. You know."

"I've seen them," he continued, impressed. "They are spectacular. Nothing quite like them. How did you get started?"

Victoria answered his questions, accepting a second cup of tea and a cake. It was easy, much easier than she had anticipated. She was beginning to enjoy herself when she saw Clayton watching her with an expression that was not entirely pleased. After excusing themselves from their friends, he and Elizabeth joined her, and Clayton gave Philip a not-too-friendly smile.

"Are you having a good time?" he asked her, turning his back to his cousin.

Victoria nodded, giggling as Philip made a face and bowed off, promising to come back. "I'm having a wonderful time. Thank you so much for inviting me."

"Clayton, that was mean of you," Mary said, though her voice held suppressed laughter. "You scared Philip off."

"Good," Clayton said, then turned to Victoria apologetically. "I didn't mean to interrupt you. It's just that Philip and I haven't been able to stand each other since we were children. I didn't want him to monopolize you, that's all."

"Clayton just doesn't appreciate art," Mary replied. "He doesn't know genius when he sees it."

"Neither does he," Clayton muttered as Philip waved in her direction.

Something was odd here, something she didn't dare hope. Mary gave her an encouraging smile, one that Clayton fortunately didn't notice. It wasn't possible, and yet—

"Victoria," Elizabeth interrupted. She looked lovelier than ever, though her smile seemed forced. "It seems you are a success! Why even Philip seems smitten." Giving Clayton an intimate look, she slid her arm through his, showing in that small gesture that he belonged to her. "Can we tell them now?"

Clayton looked anything but pleased, and he shrugged. "I would prefer—"

"Oh, do let's tell," Elizabeth interrupted, brimming with excitement. "Clayton sent me the loveliest poem this morning. Once I read it there was no longer any question. I've agreed to become his wife."

Chapter Four

It was Mary who recovered first. Taking one quick glance at Victoria's ashen face, she looked as if she could cheerfully have strangled Elizabeth. Instead, she clasped her hand in a sisterly fashion and gave her a strained smile.

"How wonderful for you! Congratulations. When is the wedding?"

"Not for at least six months," Elizabeth said happily. "There's just so much to do, and you know how my parents are. They've been planning this for a long time."

"I can imagine," Mary said with an odd tone in her voice. "They must be very pleased. Clayton is quite a catch."

Elizabeth's smile vanished, and she gave Mary a cold look. "Well, so am I, they say."

Clayton grew obviously uncomfortable, glancing at his sister in bemusement. Finally Victoria broke the tension. "I'm sure everyone will be very pleased, and you will both be happy. Now if you'll excuse me, I did tell Aunt Emma that I would be home early."

"Please plan on coming to the wedding," Elizabeth said, her smile returning. "Now that we've become reacquainted, it will be splendid to have you there."

Victoria nodded, forcing a smile. She had to get away from Elizabeth's glowing happiness. Mary's sympathetic glances only made her feel that much worse. Clayton's sister must have figured it all out and was now feeling sorry for her. It was humiliating, to say the least.

"I'll escort you to your coach," Clayton said firmly, taking her arm. Victoria began to protest, but he insisted, leading her away from the others and ordering the butler to bring her cloak.

"It really isn't necessary—"

"Victoria, I'm sorry." Clayton took a deep breath and gave her a rueful smile. "It seems your work had the desired effect, but I would have preferred to tell you myself. Elizabeth just doesn't think sometimes."

"She didn't say anything improper," Victoria murmured.

"I know she was excited, but still . . ." His voice trailed off, and she saw the annoyance in his face when Elizabeth approached another group of people and covert glances were sent his way. Turning back to Victoria, he helped her on with her cloak, then waited while she buttoned the neckline and smoothed the collar. "I will call on you tomorrow," he said softly.

"But you no longer need my help." She indicated his fiancée. "Surely, there's no reason—"

"Ah, but there is." Clayton's smile grew even more rueful as he sought to explain. "Elizabeth was so enchanted with the poem that she wants me to continue wooing her that way. Our engagement won't be officially announced until Valentine's Day. Although she's pledged herself to me, she wants a courtship, wants to be gently wooed the way a woman of her class deserves. It seems the letters must continue."

The back of her throat constricted, and Victoria glanced away. Part of her was happy at the prospect of seeing him again, for the ending of their newfound friendship would have been too final. But the thought of writing more love letters to Elizabeth was almost unendurable, especially knowing how it would all end.

"I don't know—"

"Please, you must help me," Clayton pleaded. "You know I can't write them myself. My only alternative would be to tell Elizabeth the truth, that I didn't compose the poem she read today. I don't think that would be the best idea, do you?"

Victoria glanced at Elizabeth. She was surrounded by admirers and was in her glory, shining like a golden sun. No, she didn't think Elizabeth would appreciate hearing the truth, especially when she thought the love words were Clayton's. Closing her eyes, she nodded.

"I will come tomorrow in the late afternoon. Is that convenient?" When Victoria agreed, Clayton squeezed her hand. "You are the best friend I've ever had. What would I do without you?"

Somehow she managed a smile. Thankfully, the carriage arrived and she fled from the house. I will not cry; I should be happy for him. But she knew what was wrong; it was so obvious that even Clayton's sister could see it.

She was falling in love with Clayton all over again. And he was marrying Elizabeth Chester.

"Aren't you Mary Girard?" Esther ushered the woman into the shop, bobbing her head approvingly as she examined the lovely hat and dress that Clayton's sister wore. "I remember you as a little girl. My, aren't you pretty? Don't you think she's pretty, Emma?

Emma glanced up sharply, then indicated a chair. "Victoria will be straight down. Would you like tea while you wait?"

"Please," Mary answered. She glanced around the room, amazed at the obvious success that Victoria had wrought. She could see the finished cards and the assortment of valentines still in progress. Esther was happily stitching ecru lace onto a red heart, and she gestured to a pile of orders.

"She hasn't even had time to go through them all. This will be the best Valentine's Day ever. The orders are just pouring in."

Mary nodded and smiled. "I'm glad for all of you. Victoria deserves it."

"Yes, we think so, too," Esther said in agreement.

Mary accepted a cup of tea from Emma and sipped quietly. The sun poured in through the windows, making the satins shimmer and the sequins sparkle. The room was in disarray, but it was clearly the result of constant and frenzied work. She saw a lace shawl lying over the side of a love seat, the well-kept look of the house, and once again appreciated the struggle for a woman to manage such a feat. Many men starved or worked at anything in a desperate attempt to feed their families. Thank God Victoria had the talent and the ambition to run such a successful enterprise, Mary thought.

"We've got to go through these orders today. There'll be more in the mail, and I need to order pink thread. . . ." Victoria entered the room and stopped when she saw Clayton's sister. "Why, Mary," she said in surprise. "How nice to see you."

"We got her some tea, dear. Did you see her hat? Just lovely." Esther beamed. "Why, when I was a young girl and the men used to court me, I had a hat just like it."

"Now, Esther, let's leave these two alone to talk." Emma took her sister firmly by the hand and led her to the door. "Good day, Miss Girard. It was lovely to see you again."

Esther followed, looking miffed, as Emma disappeared into the kitchen. The door closed behind them, and Victoria glanced at Mary apologetically.

"I'm sorry. They are sometimes . . . different."

"I think they're charming," Mary said sincerely. "Especially Esther. Victoria, you've done a wonderful job of keeping all of you together. You are to be envied."

No one had ever said anything like that to her before. Victoria didn't know whether to be proud or embarrassed at the attention. Taking a seat, she smiled and shrugged. "I really didn't have much choice, but I'm sure you didn't come here to talk about that. I'm sorry I rushed out of the party the way I did, but I needed to get back to my work. I've really neglected it lately."

"I know you're busy. I won't keep you, but I do wish to talk to you about a few things." Mary hesitated, then went on in a rush. "Victoria, how do you feel about my brother?"

Victoria couldn't hide her shock. She folded her hands in her lap, squeezing her eyes shut in embarrassment. "Is it that obvious? I care deeply for him, but I never meant to make it seem—"

"No, don't say that. That was rude of me, but I'm so worried." Mary put her teacup aside and leaned forward earnestly. "Please don't take what I'm about to say the wrong way, but it is my concern for Clayton that makes me speak. He can't marry Elizabeth; he just can't."

Hope sprang up inside Victoria, and she stared at Mary in bemusement. "But why—"

"She's all wrong for him. You see that, too, I know it. Oh, it's not that Elizabeth isn't a nice girl. I'm sure she'd be the perfect wife—for another man. But not for Clayton. Elizabeth doesn't have the temperament to be a doctor's wife, especially Clayton's. She's like a little girl. She wants to be petted and admired, but she doesn't know what it means to truly love. Once Clayton gets over this infatuation with her, the marriage will be a disaster."

"I don't know," Victoria replied, remembering the way Clayton had spoken about Elizabeth. "He said she was the most beautiful woman he'd ever known."

Mary nodded. "I know, and she is. Unfortunately, for all his brilliance Clayton is much the

same as other men. He can't see past her looks.
They can't get married; they just can't."

Victoria glanced away, afraid of the quickening
joy inside her. She squelched it firmly, reminding
herself that Clayton wasn't hers, that he belonged
to another. "But they will," she protested. "You
heard them yesterday."

Mary nodded. "But that's where you come in. I
know you're helping Clayton court her—I saw the
poem." When Victoria shook her head, Mary interrupted with a smile. "I've known my brother all
my life, and he never penned that letter to Elizabeth. As soon as she showed it to me, I realized
that only Victoria Wickersham could have written
it. It became very clear why Clayton renewed his
friendship with you, though I think he would have
done that eventually anyway."

"What are you suggesting?"

Mary's eyes twinkled, and she fought to keep a
smile from appearing on her face. "Let me help
you court Elizabeth. I'll give you advice, and you'll
give it to Clayton. In the meantime, I'd like us to be
friends, real friends. You can see Clayton more
often and give him the opportunity to make a real
choice."

"I couldn't!" Victoria stared at her, horrified,
dimly aware of what Mary was proposing. "You
mean to trick him."

"I won't be exactly tricking him," Mary said
sweetly. "I just want to give him the opportunity
to see Elizabeth at her worst. This is a marriage
we're talking about. If we don't interfere, you'll
write him into her arms."

"I can't deceive him." Victoria shuddered. The

idea was tempting, but the thought of hurting Clayton . . . "It just wouldn't be right."

"Think about it." Mary rose with a confident smile. "After all, if he ends up marrying her, you'll be partly responsible. If you think it's hard to do this now, think of how you'll feel then." Gesturing to the orders, she grinned. "I know you have work to do, but why don't you call on me later, at home? Clayton's seeing Elizabeth tonight, so it will be safe."

Victoria found herself nodding, and Mary swept out the door and into her carriage. A small smile crept across Victoria's face as she realized that for some reason Mary wanted her and Clayton together. It was a marvelous dream, but it was just that, a dream.

"My dear, what's the name of that young lady Clayton Girard is courting?" Esther asked sweetly, pausing in her work as she sifted through the mail. She held up a letter with a frown, then glanced at her niece. Emma looked at her as if she was mad.

"Elizabeth Chester. You know that, Esther. We spent an entire day digging up information about her."

"That's right, we did. It's just so very odd. I thought that was her name, but none of this makes sense." Esther looked bewildered as she studied the papers before her.

Victoria frowned. "What doesn't?"

"Well, didn't you tell me, dear, that this Miss Chester had agreed to marry Clayton?"

Victoria rolled her eyes, fighting to keep her patience as she stitched. "Yes, Aunt Esther, you know that. Clayton plans to marry Elizabeth in six months. I told you all this earlier."

"Esther," Emma said sharply, "are you still drinking that mulberry wine at breakfast?" She sniffed the contents of Esther's teacup suspiciously while the plump woman grew indignant.

"I should say not! I drink it at night, as you well know, and strictly for medicinal purposes." Her annoyance fading, Esther continued in the same tone. "But I am wondering why Elizabeth Chester would be receiving more than one valentine if she's practically engaged to Mr. Girard."

"What?" Emma and Victoria dropped what they were doing and stared at Esther in astonishment.

"Why, yes," Esther answered, befuddled. "I have the orders right here. One from a Mr. Charles Ingersoll. He's that nice young man we saw in church, remember, dear? And the other is from Nathan Biddle. I'm not certain I know him. My, she is popular, isn't she?"

Emma and Victoria exchanged a glance. Then Victoria picked up the orders and read them herself. There was absolutely no doubt. Both of them were for Elizabeth, both from suitors wishing to express their devotion. Both of them had ordered love letters; explicit letters that indicated a relationship. That could only mean . . .

"She's seeing other men," Emma said triumphantly.

Victoria heard Esther's intake of breath as the sweet old lady realized the import of her discovery. "You can't mean . . . Oh, this is terrible. And Mr. Girard is such a nice young man." Turning to Victoria, she said in a worried whisper, "Will you tell him, dear? I believe he's calling today."

"I can't." Victoria put down the orders. Emma gave her an exasperated glance.

"Why not? Don't you think he has a right to know? Elizabeth is deceiving him! She's seeing other men behind his back—we have the proof! Are you still going to help him court her?"

Sighing, Victoria shrugged. "What else can I do? You don't understand, Aunt Emma. He is my friend, first and foremost. It would crush him to find out about Elizabeth's duplicity. I can't do that to him."

"But it gives you the perfect opportunity—"

"No!" Both women looked at her in astonishment as Victoria spoke vehemently. "I won't use that information for my own gains. I can't hurt him that way, and I won't. If Clayton wants to find out what Elizabeth is like, he can do so himself. If he chooses not to, then he's so much in love with her that the truth won't make any difference anyway. Please don't mention it again."

Emma sighed, put down her sewing, and she went to stand beside Victoria. "I admire your values, but how can you continue to help him court her under the circumstances? Do you think that's entirely honest?"

"No," Victoria admitted. "But I don't see how I can get out of it. I've already agreed. If I back out now, he'll know there's a reason."

"Then what will you do?"

Victoria thought for a moment, then smiled softly. "I believe his sister may have come up with a solution."

Chapter Five

"Now, Victoria, you have to hold your breath while I tie the laces. Don't make that face." Mary laughed as she pulled the corset impossibly tight, then slipped a pretty lavender silk dress over Victoria's head. When the yards of fabric drifted down, she settled the dress around Victoria's slender body and adjusted the bustle. "There, now. What do you think?"

Glancing into the mirror, Victoria gasped as she observed the low-cut square neckline of the dress, showing a generous portion of her bare skin. The corset made her waist look wasplike, and the bustle added delicious curves. "I can't possibly . . . It's too, too . . ."

"It's the latest style," Mary said emphatically, smoothing the material. "And a little daring. Of course, Elizabeth will be wearing something very like this, but if you really don't want to—"

"I'll wear it," Victoria said grimly, picturing Elizabeth clad in something wonderful, looking like a fairy princess. Her face changed as she thought of the valentine orders, and she turned to Clayton's sister in concern. "Why do you think she would do that? Pretend fidelity to your brother while seeing other men?"

"She's probably holding out for the best catch." Mary shrugged as she placed another pin in the bustle. "Her other suitors are very wealthy men. If neither of them proposes, she still has Clayton."

Victoria shuddered. It was so hard to imagine anyone acting in such a calculating way, especially with Clayton as a suitor. She glanced back into the mirror and frowned. "Are you sure this is appropriate for the Powells' luncheon and reception?"

"It's absolutely fine," Mary said confidently. "Now, did you tell Clayton about the flowers?"

Victoria nodded, her nose wrinkling in confusion. "Yes, but I don't understand. Daisies are a nice gift—I thought you wanted Clayton's courtship to be unsuccessful."

Mary giggled, then assumed a straight face as she did Victoria's hair. "They are—except when they make one sneeze. However, there is no way Clayton could have known that."

"Oh, that's right!" Victoria gasped and Mary laughed out loud.

"Of course! She'll take one look at that bouquet and express her true feelings, I'm sure." Mary smiled confidently. "Now, did you finish the poem?"

Victoria unfolded a sheet of paper and handed it to Clayton's sister. "I wrote what you told me. Do you really think we should do this? I heard Elizabeth is sensitive about her large feet."

Mary's mouth twitched suspiciously. "Let's just say her feet are her most noticeable feature. And yes, we should do this. Clayton needs to see what she's really like—otherwise, he'll be married to her in no time. You haven't shown this piece to Clayton yet, have you?" When Victoria shook her head, Mary nodded. "Good. I think the reception would be the best place to give it to him. Make sure you bring it. There." Placing a finishing touch to Victoria's dark curls, she presented a mirror, smiling in satisfaction at the young woman's surprise. "What do you think?"

"I look . . . nice." Victoria stared in amazement. It was true; the upswept hairstyle brought out the best of her chestnut hair, making the curls glisten in the morning light while accentuating her high cheekbones and pretty mouth. With the spectacles gone, her eyes were suddenly noticeable, as clear and as blue as Aunt Esther's. Mary pinched her cheeks, making them bloom with color, then stood back in satisfaction, admiring the result of her work.

"You look more than nice. Clayton won't be able to take his eyes off you. I have a feeling this will be the most entertaining reception I've been to in a long time."

The Powells' residence was even more impressive than the Girards' or the Chesters'. Victoria glanced around in amazement at the marble floors, the tall Grecian windows draped in Parisian lace, the gleaming rosewood furniture. Chandeliers glittered, while gorgeously gowned women and handsome men sipped champagne and nibbled on elaborate tea sandwiches.

"Come on, now, don't worry," Mary admonished as Victoria stared dubiously at the crowd. "You can do this. Walk the way I showed you, shoulders back and head up."

"It's a lot of work having money." Victoria stifled a giggle as she followed Mary's instructions. "I think it's easier to make valentines."

"Of course it is," Mary agreed. "Let me introduce you to the Widners and the Harpers. Both of the men gave a lot of money to Clayton's hospital, and their wives are dying to meet you. Just remember, smile and look pleasant."

Victoria followed Mary's lead, amazed that if she did as instructed, success followed. It was so simple, she thought as she bowed gracefully, smiled, nodded, and appeared interested in the recitals of their vacations to Cape May and the state of the economy. She held her cup the way Mary had shown her, limited herself to one tea sandwich, listened politely, and nodded when appropriate. As before, her reputation as the valentine maker created a topic of discussion, and all of the women expressed their appreciation of the cards.

It was wonderful. Victoria had never before been accepted like this. Her smile grew brighter as Philip joined them, exclaiming over her hair and gown, while several other attractive men found excuses to furnish her with more tea or a dainty sandwich from the cart. She was giggling at something Mary had said when she spotted Clayton and Elizabeth at the other side of the room.

Her heart pounding, she tried to look away but couldn't. Elizabeth was so breathtakingly beautiful that she almost looked unreal. Her pale blue gown enhanced her blond loveliness, and her smile was radiant. She clung to Clayton, obviously proud of him, her laughter like a tinkling bell in the room.

Victoria glanced at Clayton. He was looking at his fiancée in adoration. He leaned forward to whisper something in her ear, and Elizabeth laughed again, blushing beautifully.

My God, what's wrong with me? Victoria wondered. Clayton loved Elizabeth—it was as simple as that. No plan that Mary concocted would make a difference, and she had been foolish to think that it would. Glancing down at her borrowed gown, she cringed. She wasn't pretty enough to compete with Elizabeth, wasn't funny enough or sophisticated enough. She was fooling herself to even think that he might ever come to prefer her. Frantically, she saw them making their way toward her, and she wanted to run from this place and hide in her shop.

"Why, hello, Victoria," Elizabeth said brightly, eyeing the lavender gown. "You look lovely. I think I recall that dress. Mary, wasn't that one of yours?"

"Why, yes." Mary gave Elizabeth a less than friendly look. "Isn't it wonderful that Victoria and I are the same size? She's going to my dressmaker and has ordered the most beautiful clothes. She'll be all the rage this summer."

Elizabeth smiled, her eyes crinkling. "We'll have to see that she meets all the eligible men. We wouldn't want Victoria to be alone too long, would we?"

"I don't think that's a concern." Mary glanced meaningfully at the men who stood a short distance away. "It seems Philip is already insane about her, and his friends are just as bewitched."

"Damned fool," Clayton said, giving Philip a

hostile glance. He turned around, his gaze sweeping over Victoria with open amazement. His eyes lingered a moment on her neckline, and she could have sworn she saw disapproval there, along with something else that made her heart pound faster. "That is a pretty dress, but you might have lent her something a little more conservative. You know how some of these college men are."

"Oh, stop it," Mary said, delighted. "Victoria isn't about to fall in love with all of them, are you, dear?"

Victoria was about to say no when Mary sent her a look that meant everything. For the first time in her life, she used the feminine wiles she'd been born with, recalling the conversations of dozens of women—women she'd written valentines for, women who were successful at love. Hiding a smile, she cast her eyes downward, promising to confess all this at church the following morning.

"Well, not all of them. But they are very nice, especially Philip. He wants to take me out riding tomorrow. Do you think that's proper?" She gave Mary a wide-eyed look, and Clayton's sister grinned in encouragement.

"Oh, yes. He is very popular. And he is so taken with you. I think it's a great idea. Don't you, Clayton?"

Clayton muttered something unintelligible while Mary beamed. It was Elizabeth who distracted him, indicating a servant at the other side of the room.

"Why, Clayton, isn't the butler trying to get your attention?"

Clayton dragged his eyes away from Victoria

and saw the butler gesturing to him. With a grin, he turned to Elizabeth and placed a kiss on her hand. "I'll be just a minute. Will you excuse me?"

"Don't take too long, darling," Elizabeth said sweetly. "Just a moment away from you is an eternity."

Clayton smiled uncomfortably, then strode to the butler while Elizabeth turned her attention back to the young card maker. "He really is so sweet. He's written me another poem, you know. He's going to read it to me in the solarium."

"I'm certain he'll sweep you off your feet," Mary said blandly while Victoria choked on her tea. "By the way, Elizabeth, didn't I see you at the opera the night before last with Charles Ingersoll?"

Elizabeth didn't bat an eye, but returned Mary's smile. "Yes. He is an old friend, as you know. I believe he's here today."

"What a shame that Clayton couldn't join you at the opera. But his medical practice keeps him so busy. It's unfair, don't you think?"

Elizabeth lost her smile, and a sparkle of annoyance showed in her beautiful eyes. She was about to reply when Clayton rejoined them, his arms full of daisies. When he presented them to Elizabeth, his fiancée's eyes widened in horror.

"Daisies! Oh, my God, Clayton, how—how could you—" She sneezed hard, and a shower of petals sifted into the air around her. "Take them." She thrust the flowers angrily at Clayton, who gazed at her in confusion. "Get them out of here! I can't—" Another sneeze convulsed her, then another. Her eyes streamed, and her nose pinkened. "Now!"

Clayton took back the flowers, gesturing to a waiter for some water while Elizabeth sneezed again and again. Mary sighed sympathetically, then proffered a handkerchief. "Poor dear. I'm afraid my brother's bungled it. Daisies! What kind of a tussie-mussie is that?"

"Don't ever give me daisies again!" Elizabeth said between sneezes. "Dreadful weeds!"

"I apologize," Clayton said. "I wasn't aware of your sensitivity to flowers. I was only trying to court you, as you asked."

"I know, I . . . *a-chew!*" Elizabeth sneezed, aware that she sounded ungracious. From Clayton's tone, she knew she had offended him, but the sneezes came fast and furious. Excusing herself, she stormed off to fix her appearance while Mary shrugged, the picture of innocence. Clayton followed his fiancée with his eyes, a strange expression on his face. A slight twinge of guilt assaulted Victoria, but she reminded herself of those valentines. Elizabeth was merely showing him her less than pretty side. It was something that Clayton needed to see.

"The dainty splendor of a woman is not expressed
in her pretty speech or charming manner,
but in the slender lines of her legs,
the delicate structure of her ankles,
and the softness of her petite toes.
Oh, yes, let me say there is nothing so beautiful
As the well-shaped arch of a woman's tiny foot."

Elizabeth had risen and was now standing in the solarium, a not so angelic expression on her beautiful face. She had finally managed to stop sneezing and to restore her appearance and had rejoined Clayton, expecting another love poem. Gasping with fury, she wrung her hands as if undecided whether to hit him or to exact some other kind of revenge.

"How dare you?" Her eyes flashed a cold gray. "How could you do this?"

"What is the matter?" Clayton folded the poem and slipped it into his pocket, staring at his fiancée as if he thought she was mad.

"That . . . that thing you wrote!" Elizabeth stamped her foot. "I don't think it's a bit funny, and it's in extremely bad taste!"

"What on earth are you talking about?" Clayton snatched her hand to detain her when she would have fled. "It's a little different, that's true, but there is nothing wrong with the words or intent."

"Really?" Elizabeth spat, then lifted her dress. Clayton's eyes dropped helplessly to the floor. He was totally perplexed—until he saw her feet.

Elizabeth's slippers were anything but dainty and delicate. Astounded, he realized that she had quite the largest feet of any woman he'd ever seen. The humor of that struck him, and he burst into laughter.

"It's not funny!" Elizabeth pummeled his chest with her fists, growing angrier by the moment. "You are the rudest, most thoughtless man I've ever met! I'd die before marrying you!"

The smile disappeared from his face and he stared at her with an expression that made her anger quickly disappear. "I'm sorry you feel that way," he said coldly. "The poem was obviously a mistake, but I didn't think it a fatal one. Evidently, my proposal doesn't mean that much to you."

"I'm sorry," Elizabeth said quickly, realizing she'd made him angry and exposed her true nature. Forcing herself to smile sweetly, she gave him a coquettish look. "It's just that I'm sensitive about my feet."

"I see." He allowed her to enfold his hand between her own, but he still looked at her as if seeing behind a mask. Elizabeth smiled, tossing her hair, then pressed a quick kiss on his cheek.

"It was foolish of me, darling. You forgive me, don't you?"

At her childlike actions, he smiled and gave her a nod. "Yes, let's forget it. I believe they're all going in for luncheon. I think we should join them."

Mary and Victoria saw Clayton appear from the solarium, his shoulders stiff as he escorted his fiancée into the dining room. Mary had somehow arranged for Clayton to sit beside them at the table. Her smile was radiantly innocent as she asked about their walk among the wonders of the indoor garden.

"I hear the Powells' ferns are lovely," Mary said sweetly. "Did you find them so, Elizabeth?"

Clayton gave her a look revealing his lack of appreciation, while Elizabeth coldly excused herself. Watching her leave, Clayton sipped his wine and stared at his sister thoughtfully.

"I'd almost swear something was going on here," he said. "You don't have anything to do with this, do you?"

"What are you talking about?" Mary asked sweetly. When Clayton refused to answer, she continued in the same tone. "Stop frowning, Clayton, and pass the sandwiches. You look so much older when you scowl. Don't you have to leave for work?"

He nodded and withdrew his watch, verifying the time. "With the cholera epidemic, the hospital is overcrowded. We're all assuming extra hours. We really need volunteers."

"Is it that bad?" Victoria asked.

Clayton nodded. "I've never seen it like this. All of the beds are filled. We can't get enough medicine, enough food. These people are violently ill—men, women, even little children—but most of them are poor and the money is limited."

As Elizabeth returned, Victoria shuddered, picturing the sick people. "Do you need help? I don't know much about nursing, but I can give medicine and change beds."

"I would be glad to help as well," Mary added sincerely.

Clayton smiled. "That's very generous of you both, but the hospital is not a pleasant place for a woman. I don't know if you would be able to tolerate the conditions."

"Oh, rubbish, Clayton," Mary said firmly. "It won't kill us, and we want to help. Plenty of women nurse, and it doesn't bother them. It's all settled. We'll come this afternoon." Giving him a firm look, Mary turned to Elizabeth. "Would you like to join us?"

Elizabeth blanched. "I . . . couldn't. Seeing all those sick people would give me the vapors. I would be in bed all day." She smiled at Clayton, then shrugged delicately. "You don't mind, do you?"

"No, I understand." There was an odd note in his voice as he rose from the table, giving Victoria and his sister a warm smile. "I'm looking forward to seeing you both later. Good day, Elizabeth."

Chapter Six

The hospital wards were even worse than Clayton had led them to expect. Victoria choked at the sight of grown men wasting away, unable to keep any food in their stomachs while their wives and children suffered much the same fate. The beds needed to be changed constantly, the linens washed, the floors scrubbed. Poverty and suffering were everywhere. The sickly sweet odor of medicine and illness permeated the wards, and more than once she had to leave the room when a woman or child gave up the struggle for life and passed peacefully into sleep.

Yet Clayton did this on a daily basis. Victoria marveled at that as she wrapped a woman in a blanket, then tried to get her to take a few sips of water. He was compassionate with the infirm, listening to their complaints, making them as comfortable as possible while he did what he could to ease their suffering. He was wonderfully patient, even when a man confessed that he hadn't taken his advice and was still drinking from the filthy wells. He understood them, and the people sensed his empathy and trusted him.

He looked dead tired by late afternoon. Mary had taken her leave a few minutes before, and now Clayton joined Victoria, wiping the sweat from his face as he glanced around the ward.

"You've done a great job today. How can I thank you?" He indicated the spotless floors, the clean beds and fresh linens.

Victoria smiled and lightly touched his face. "It's you I should thank. I have to confess, I never had a full appreciation of your work until today. My God, it hardly seems possible that this epidemic is so devastating."

"I know." He wiped his hands on a towel and gestured to the beds. "I tell them about the water, to only use fresh and to boil that, but they don't understand. It's hard to convince them that something they can't see can kill them. But they're dying in unbelievable numbers. It really is hard to take."

"But you've made such a difference," Victoria said softly. "They trust you. Surely that has to help."

"It does." He agreed, then gave her a smile. "I'm sorry, it's just painful to watch them suffer. Connell Boyle there has a large family, and the prettiest little girl I've ever seen." The smile faded as he paused, seeming to look inside himself at some awful scene. "God, I only hope they don't all get ill."

Victoria laid a consoling hand on his arm. "You can only do so much."

"I know, and that's the frustrating part. It's one of the reasons I go to the receptions and the teas. Many of our acquaintances have money and can help, but they have to be convinced. I do the convincing." He smiled ironically, helping Victoria with her cloak. "They're getting more charitable. Our donations last year were remarkable."

"I'm glad." Her eyes met his, and for a moment it seemed as if time stood still. Emotion overwhelmed her and she was forced to look down, away, anywhere but at him. "I have to go," she whispered softly. "I have to finish the cards."

"Can you come for coffee?" He shrugged when she looked back at him and he gave her an enchanting smile. "Just one cup? I won't keep you long. I just hate to be alone after a day like this."

Smiling, Victoria nodded. She could understand that, especially after being exposed to the work herself. Glancing up at him, she saw that his hair had become disheveled from work and that a charming lock had fallen across his forehead. She wanted to touch him, to brush the hair from his eyes, to smooth away the sweat and make it all right. His eyes were so warm, and the dark jacket he wore fit him extremely well. She could almost picture slipping it off his shoulders for him and making him feel comfortable and at ease. What was the matter with her? He's engaged, she reminded herself. Yet she felt so close to him.

"Shall we go, then?" He held out his arm, and Victoria took it.

* * *

She was so pretty, and yet she had a strength he couldn't help but admire. Clayton watched Victoria, seated across from him in the coffeehouse, her smile tired but genuine. She'd worked like a servant at the hospital that day, never minding the more arduous chores, and she had managed to say something special to each patient, something that made them remark to him later that she was an angel of mercy.

A Wickersham Original. She had an ability to reach out and comfort people, to make them feel wanted and appreciated. It was that which made her cards special, and made her special. Her gift was evident in her valentines, but it was even more apparent in her work with the ill today. She was dressed in a simple gown his sister had lent her, and he found himself watching the way it pulled on her body, showing her slender figure and enticing curves. He wanted to hold her with gratitude, and with something more. . . .

Clayton frowned at his own thoughts. What was wrong with him? He was practically married to one of the most beautiful women in the city, and yet all he could think about was Victoria. He found her physically beautiful, true, but it was more than that. She touched him on many different levels, and she meant more to him than he'd ever realized.

"Why are you smiling?" Victoria asked, smoothing her hair. "Do I look a fright?"

He wanted to tell her what he was thinking. Instead, he sipped his coffee. She'd never believe him.

"Mr. Girard?" The waiter approached their table, obviously reluctant to intrude, but there was a look of urgency about the man's face that Clayton recognized. Something was wrong. He'd seen the waiter quite a few times before when he'd come here late at night, and although the man always had time for a brief smile, he'd never approached him. Until now. Putting his coffee aside, he almost knew what he'd hear.

"There's a small boy outside," the waiter told him. "Says his name is Peter Boyle and that there is a sickness. I told him you'd worked all afternoon, but he was insistent."

"It's all right, send him in." Cursing inwardly, he pictured Connell Boyle. His sickness was advanced, and there was little Clayton could do. The man's stomach was already distended from prolonged illness, and he knew it was only a matter of time.

Damn! He felt so ineffectual. He gave Victoria a look of apology, but she pressed her hand to his as if in comfort.

A little boy in a ragged coat stood in the foyer, entering reluctantly as if he feared that his presence would soil the place. He saw Clayton first and pulled his cap from his head, revealing a shock of red hair.

"It's them, sir. Me family. They've all taken ill. I'm sorry to trouble you, but me pa said to call for you if it happened." Tears slipped down the young boy's face, and he peered up at Clayton. "Megan is crying."

"I'll come. You say they're all ill?" The little boy nodded, and Clayton cursed again under his breath. The Boyle family was large. To treat all of them, administer medicine, provide them with care, would be a monumental task at best. "You live in the Irish ward, east of Spring Garden?" The boy nodded, and Clayton grimaced. That section had been particularly hurt by disease. "Let's go."

"I'll go with you." Victoria rose and picked up her cloak.

"No, you worked all afternoon. And you have your business to attend to."

"Clayton, I can help." She gave him a firm smile and continued quickly. "You saw that today. And I'm on schedule with my own work. I got quite a bit done in the last few days. I won't take no for an answer."

He looked at her, wavering. "I could use the help—"

"I'm going." She marched ahead of him, taking the little boy by the hand, whispering words of comfort and assurance.

Clayton smiled, then quickly joined them. Victoria could be a tough woman when she wanted to be, and he was definitely not about to cross her.

The Boyles' house was in a ramshackle tenement in the worst part of the ward. Appalled, Victoria kept her feelings to herself as she saw the broken windows, the leaking roof, the drains that smelled of sewage and the rats that scuttled in the corners. There was simply no money for medicine, sheets, or any of the basics.

Inside the row house, Rose Boyle lay flushed and sweating on her bed, too weak from illness to do anything for her family. Victoria glanced about

and saw the children, choking from sickness, pale
and distraught at the realization that they might
not get better. Neighbors came and went, whispering among themselves, trying to help however
they could.

Megan, the youngest, lay pathetically on an old
couch, her head propped up with her father's coat.
Black hair framed a face that was like a china doll's
in its beauty, and her eyes were a startling blue, as
serious as an adult's. Clutching an old rag doll, she
barely made a whimper as Clayton tended the
others, then came to stand beside her.

"Well, well, it's my little girlfriend." Victoria's
throat tightened as Clayton bent over the child, his
face knotted with emotion. "I hear you're feeling a
little sick. Is that true?"

Megan nodded, holding the doll tighter. "My
pa . . ."

"He's in the hospital. We're taking good care of
him. Now, how long have you been ill?"

Clayton listened as the little child recited the
history of her illness in forced whispers. Her heart
breaking, Victoria closed her eyes as she heard the
dreaded symptoms. Surely God couldn't do this,
couldn't take this little child, a child who had never
really lived. Glancing at Megan, Victoria thought
how unfair it was that this girl would never finish
school, never marry, have children of her own.

Forcing back tears, she handed Clayton his bag
and waited while he tenderly examined the child,
talking to her all the time. When he finished, he
pulled the coat around her to keep her warm, then
forced a spoonful of medicine down her throat. A

few minutes later Megan was sleeping peacefully, and he turned to Victoria, his face pale.

"Clayton, will she—"

"I don't know yet." Obviously bitter, he ran his hand through his hair. "There's a slight chance it may be a virus, but damn it! Look at this place! They can't live like this."

"I know." Victoria took him in her embrace, needing to comfort him, to feel him beside her. "There's only so much you can do."

"I gave her a sleeping draft. I hate this, to know I can only ease their suffering a small amount. I won't know until morning if she takes a turn for the worse. I can't do much more tonight."

Victoria stifled her own pain as the little girl snuggled into the coat, looking like a sleeping princess. She walked silently with Clayton out the door, her own hands raw from cleaning what she could, from boiling water and scrubbing bottles. She couldn't help contrasting the Boyles' way of life with her own, as difficult as it had been. She felt thankful that God had given her a talent that allowed her to earn a living. Most people, like the Boyles, were not so lucky.

Outside a fine mist veiled the streetlights, and Clayton turned to Victoria, his face wretched with pain. "Please," he whispered as she reached for his hand. "I know I have no right to ask you this, but would you stay with me for a little while? I just can't go home."

Victoria nodded, her own tears spilling forth. She would have done just about anything for him—she admitted that now. "Come back to the shop. Aunt Esther and Aunt Emma are staying with some friends tonight and won't be back until morning. We'll be alone, and we can talk."

His hand tightened around hers, and he helped her into his coach, handling her as if she were made of delicate china. It seemed an eternity before they reached Second Street. The neat little brick row houses seemed like another world after the tenements, and Victoria stepped inside, lighting the lamps and heating some water.

"Please." He came to stand behind her as she lifted the kettle, and he put his arms around her, holding her tightly. "I just want to hold you. I have to feel—"

She knew what he meant. Her heart constricted, and she put down the teapot and turned in his arms, wrapping her own around his waist. It was wrong—he wasn't hers—but he needed her and tonight, she needed him. The pain was too awful, too devastating to ignore, and the uncertainty of waiting to hear Megan's fate was even more horrible than the truth.

When his lips touched hers, Victoria sighed, then opened her mouth, kissing him back. Clayton groaned, caught between the sweet anguish of desire and the conflict inside him. Gasping for breath, he pulled her closer to him, wanting to feel her against him, needing her in a way he had never imagined.

"God, Victoria, if you know how much I've wanted this . . ."

She melted in his embrace, knowing she wanted this, too, wanted to know him, to hold him and love him. It no longer mattered that he was pledged to another; he was hers and always had been.

"Kiss me, Clayton, please."

Her urgent whisper made his blood flow hotter. His mouth met hers in a kiss that was gentle yet full of passion and emotion.

Then he swept her into his arms and carried her to the love seat in the sitting room. She was powerless to protest and didn't want to in the least. Barriers dissolved as they fumbled with their clothing, frantic to remove anything that stood between them. When he covered her naked body with his own, Victoria cried out with the pure, primal pleasure of it, wanting all of this new experience, wanting to reach out to him and express all of the emotion she'd kept hidden for so long.

"Victoria, I want to be gentle, but I don't know if I can. I want you so badly. . . ."

"I want you, too. Please . . ." She arched against him instinctively as he caressed her, making her cry out incoherently when he finally buried himself in her. Lifting slightly, he brushed a tear from her face, overwhelmed by her reaction.

"Did I hurt you? I'm sorry—"

"No." Victoria met his lips with her own, silencing his apology. "I need you, I need to feel you . . . God, how I've wanted this."

Raw emotion overcame him, and he wrapped himself around this remarkable woman and loved her with all the depth of his feelings. She eagerly met his passion with her own, and together they reached fulfillment, man with woman, softness yielding to hardness. Time stood still as his heartbeat raged against hers, and he pulled her closer to him, reveling in their unity.

She was his.

Chapter Seven

It was the tabby cat who woke them, clambering onto the back of the love seat while chasing a satin ribbon. When the cat tumbled onto the entwined couple, Victoria opened her eyes with a laugh while Clayton lifted the furry animal to the floor.

"Damn beast." He grimaced, then rose slowly and handed her the knitted shawl to use as a cover. He saw the flush of color come to her cheeks as she wrapped herself in the fine garment, obviously never having been in such a situation before. He slipped into his clothes, finding them scattered haphazardly, forgotten in the heat of what had passed between them just hours before.

Cursing inwardly, Clayton realized that he'd just complicated his life tenfold. She'd been a virgin; there was no mistake about that. Yet he'd needed Victoria. Clayton wasn't foolish enough not to realize that what had happened between them was special. They had connected on a primitive and emotional level with a passion he'd never hoped to feel toward anyone. Yet it all came down to honor. He couldn't just walk out on Elizabeth.

He was pledged to her, an oath that meant something to him. Their families were already planning the wedding, and Elizabeth had her heart set on it. . . .

"Clayton?" Victoria saw the anguish on his face and reached out to him, clasping his hand within her own. "We need to talk."

He nodded and sat beside her. The confusion he felt was obvious, and before he could explain, Victoria stopped him.

"About last night . . ." She gave him a smile so full of emotion that it caught at his heart. "I don't want anything from you. I know you're engaged to Elizabeth. What happened between us . . . just happened. It was a terrible night, and you needed someone. I understand that. I never meant to make you break your vow."

Emotion filled him, and as he looked at her he thought of how incredibly special she was. "Victoria, please. You didn't make me do anything I didn't want to do. There is more to it than that. You mean something to me. I just don't know what to do or say. I've never gone back on my word or deliberately hurt another person, and yet I don't regret a minute of what we had. Do you understand that?"

"Yes." Victoria nodded. Clayton was a good man; it was one of the reasons she loved him.

"I'll never forget you, Victoria." Touching her hair lightly, he brushed aside a tear that escaped when she closed her eyes, unable to stop the emotion. Tearing himself away, he stood up and paused before the door as if wanting to say something, then stepped outside and closed it tightly behind him.

The walls seemed to close in on Victoria. The tears came freely now, and she didn't try to stop them. She didn't need to. Instinctively she had known it would end like this, had known what kind of a chance she was taking, but last night, for a few brief special hours, he had been hers. And until the day she died she'd carry that memory with her, knowing that at one time, she, Victoria Wickersham, the valentine maker, really did have a man, really did reach out to him and hold him near. . . .

And loved him.

Clayton rode silently in his carriage. Pain knotted his stomach and made his head throb, but try as he would, he couldn't rid himself of the guilt.

Victoria. God, she had been so noble, letting him go without any angry words or desperate pleas. She had understood how he felt and what he had to do. She had refused to indulge her own feelings and, with a strength he was forced to admire, had sent him back to his fiancée.

A sinking feeling went through him as he thought of his upcoming wedding. Valentine's Day was just a few days away; Elizabeth's parents would announce the engagement, and it would be official. Once he would have been delighted with the prospect of marrying her. But now . . .

Now he would have to live with the knowledge of what could have been. And what he would never have again.

* * *

"Oh, that's so pretty, dear. I daresay you've outdone yourself."

Aunt Esther smiled happily at the finished valentine that Victoria placed on the counter beside the endless rows of cream-colored envelopes and satin cards. Lace was strewn everywhere, from the counter to the walls, over the chairs, and on the floor where the tabby cat made a tangled web of the sheer fabric. Rolls of pink ribbon unfurled in every direction, while silk and laquered roses adorned everything from the cards to the love seat.

The three women worked furiously, finishing up the last of the cards. Aunt Esther's words were the first ones she'd spoken in over an hour, as all of them realized that time was running out. Esther was in charge of poems, while Emma assembled the silks and laces. Victoria addressed them all by hand and did the final inspection. Not one would be sent if it wasn't just perfect. These were, after all, not just greeting cards but expressions of love.

"Yes, this one is nice," Victoria agreed, gazing at the red silk card. Her glasses slipped down her nose, and she removed them, wiping them clean as she rolled her tired shoulders. Turning up the lamp, she glanced down at her order book and sighed with satisfaction.

They would make it. Somehow, in spite of everything that had happened in the last two weeks, they would finish the cards. It was gratifying to know how many women would receive an outpouring of love on the very next day, Valentine's Day, the one day that was close to every female's heart.

For the briefest moment, her thoughts drifted to Clayton. She really hadn't expected to hear from him, and it no longer mattered at this point. Clayton would do the honorable thing. He had to.

"Come now, ladies," Aunt Emma said in her practical voice. "We have to get these valentines out. Three hundred! This has been a banner year for Wickersham Originals."

"Don't forget the stamp, dear," Aunt Esther reminded them as she held up the elegant fleur-de-lis and the gold ink. It was the final touch for a Wickersham, and she busily applied the imprint.

Valentine's Day arrived with a blast of cold wind and snow from the north. Aunt Esther shivered as she helped stack the cards, sorting them by address numbers so that the street urchins they'd hired to deliver them could work more efficiently.

"They're finally done." Aunt Emma looked at the rows of cards, neatly tied into bundles with red ribbons. Even the packing looked good. She drew her shawl more tightly around her as she examined the ledger, then grinned as she saw the final results. "We are well over last year. I believe you should have enough money now to start your pension fund."

Victoria nodded, sifting through the letters. "It's more than enough. Between that and what Clayton gave me, I'll be able to provide a nice little income for them. And as profits grow, I can increase the fund by percentage without hurting the business. It's so nice to be able to do something to help, after all this time." She smiled fondly, then continued in the same tone. "Did I tell you about the Boyle girl? Clayton said Megan's going to be fine."

The two elderly women glanced at each other at the mention of Clayton's name. But Victoria seemed happy. There was a wistfulness in her expression, but otherwise, she was radiant. Scratching her head in confusion, Aunt Esther shrugged.

"That's nice, dear. You should be proud. I still think it's a shame, however, that Mr. Girard is getting engaged to that woman today. I can hardly bear to think about it."

"Esther!" Emma said sharply, then turned to her niece. "I'm sorry, Victoria. Esther sometimes talks without thinking."

"I do not!" Esther huffed, but she glanced apologetically at her niece, who was busily stacking more cards.

"It's all right. It doesn't matter," Victoria said softly, giving them both a reassuring smile. "Clayton is an honorable man. He is promised to Elizabeth. He never lied about that or ever pretended anything else. I have his friendship again, and that is more than enough."

Emma nodded, while Esther glanced away. Friendship was not enough; both of them knew that. But Elizabeth Chester would pledge herself to Clayton today.

And there was nothing anyone could do about it.

Clayton stood on the white marble steps of the Chester mansion, glancing at the card he held in his hand. It was a Wickersham valentine, and he smiled as he envisioned the card inside.

It was lovely. Victoria had outdone herself this time. The card was white with red laquered roses, trimmed in lace, and inside there was a poem that would melt any woman's heart. He had read it carefully, grateful that it didn't have anything to do with feet, and he couldn't stop the smile from coming to his face.

That poem hadn't been accidental; he knew that now. He had confronted his sister, and she had confessed all, asking him bluntly when he was going to wake up and realize that Victoria cared about him. But to Mary's chagrin, he explained that he was promised to someone else, and he couldn't break his vow.

His heart sinking, he knocked on the door, the cold wind howling behind him. This was wrong, all wrong. He couldn't stop the feeling, nor could he find anything in the situation that was reassuring. He would formally propose today, and Elizabeth would accept. She would become his wife, his partner and mate. She would live with him for the rest of his life, bear his children, help him with his work, listen to him when he came home at night and just needed to talk. . . .

The butler ushered him into the drawing room, and he waited, the card feeling heavier in his hand. Somehow he couldn't picture it. He tried to envision Elizabeth as his wife, but all he could see was her expression the day he'd given her the daisies. He thought of the countless times he had tried to tell her about his life, his work, and he remembered her delicate shudders, which he'd always attributed to her femininity. He realized now that even when he tried to talk with her about his fears and ambitions, she would grow impatient and turn the conversation back to herself.

Elizabeth entered the drawing room and closed the door behind her. The beautiful smile was gone, the sparkle in her clear gray eyes had diminished, and there was no gay toss of her curls. Today those eyes looked hard and brittle, and the look she gave him was glacial.

"Clayton, we need to talk."

Sighing, Clayton nodded, aware from her tone that she was angry. "Elizabeth, if it's about the other night—"

"Yes, and more." She cut him off, the gaiety gone from her voice. "We were supposed to go out that night, to the Morrises' dinner. I understand that you felt it more important to work."

"Elizabeth, the Boyle family was ill. I couldn't let them suffer through the night."

"But it's perfectly all right to upset and disappoint me."

"I didn't say that." Irritation swept through him. The dinner had been important to her, but a child's life had to take precedence. Why couldn't she see that? "You know how bad this epidemic has been. It's my duty to help them, you know that. And little Megan—"

"Clayton, I'm afraid I'm just going to have to come out and say it: I don't think we have a future together. You're too wrapped up in your work, and everybody knows it. Frankly, you're becoming a bore. All you ever talk about is the hospital, those sick people, and your prissy friend Victoria."

She glanced at the valentine in his hand and gave a short laugh. "Keep that, Clayton. Or give it back to Miss Wickersham. I'm sure she'll appreciate it."

She swept out of the room without looking back. Dumbfounded, Clayton stared at the card. He could still smell her perfume, still hear her voice as she directed the butler to show him out. As he stepped into the hall and waited for his coat, he saw the silver serving tray on the Sheraton table near the door. There were two more valentines on the tray.

Wickersham Originals. He could never mistake the beautiful handwriting, the elegant creamy envelopes, the fleurs-de-lis embossed on the backs. A wry smile came to his face as the situation became abundantly clear.

Elizabeth didn't love him; she never had. She wanted him the same way she wanted a possession. He was simply what she felt she deserved for a husband—but she had several other prospects. And when he couldn't give her constant adoration, she had found it elsewhere.

He should have been crushed, but instead, relief poured through him. He was free, free to do what he wanted more than anything else, free to have love in his life, real love. As he opened the valentine he still clutched in his hand and read the poem, he realized with a painful clarity that the words had been written for him. This woman, this unique and caring woman, loved him unconditionally, and he had been blind. She had known about Elizabeth's fickle nature and had kept it to herself, not wanting to hurt him.

Tucking the card inside his jacket, Clayton practically beamed at the confused butler who was going to offer him a sympathetic glance. He felt as if he'd been given back his life.

And this time he was going to keep it.

"And did I ever tell you about the time my Jonathan sent me flowers? Bluebonnets they were. I remember them well."

"Esther!" Emma interrupted, rapping her cane on the floor. "The last thing Victoria needs to hear today is any reminiscences about your old romances. Do you mind?"

Esther looked hurt, and Victoria smiled fondly. "I don't mind. Today is the perfect day to relive old loves. Go ahead and tell me, Aunt Esther."

The old woman beamed, and after sending Emma an "I told you so" look, she proceeded to dream out loud about the one man whose memory filled her life. Victoria smiled as she counted out the receipts and balanced the books. The fire crackled, and the tabby cat purred on the hearth as the three women shared a peaceful evening.

The day had been a great success. Already, thank-you notes had begun pouring in as grateful women everywhere received their valentines. Victoria's eyes filled when she saw just how much her work meant to these women, how she'd managed to brighten their day and make them feel what every woman wanted to feel—cherished and appreciated and loved.

Even the men were grateful. Some of them had received their own valentines and had scribbled her short notes expressing their astonishment at their beauty, while others thanked her for helping them say the right thing to their beloved. It was a wonderful feeling to have touched so many people, and Victoria marveled at the realization that she, Aunt Emma, and Aunt Esther had done just that.

There was a knock on the door, and Esther rose to answer it, certain that another well-wisher had stopped by. Victoria, buried in her work, didn't notice the man until he had stepped into the room and given Esther his coat. Glancing up, she froze as she saw Clayton Girard enter the room.

"Victoria."

She stared at him, wondering for a wild moment if she had conjured him up out of one of Aunt Esther's dreams. The two aunts gave each other a knowing smile, and this time Emma didn't have to urge Esther to disappear as they headed toward the kitchen.

"It's that nice Mr. Girard. We'll go fix tea and some cakes, if you don't mind."

Clayton smiled as the two women hurried out of the room, leaving him alone with Victoria. Her heart pounding, she rose, trying to steady her hands as her mind clouded with confusion.

"Clayton? Did everything— I mean, are you engaged? Did Elizabeth like the card?"

He chuckled, and the sound was so infectious that Victoria found herself smiling even as she stared at him in bemusement. Drawing her out from behind the counter, he led her to the love seat, the same place where he'd loved her so intimately just a few short nights ago. More confused than ever, she saw him withdraw an envelope from his coat and hand it to her.

"Open it."

She stared dumbly at the card until, still chuckling, he helped her open the envelope and withdraw the valentine. Her hands felt heavy and awkward as she stared at the beautiful hand-painted heart, the lace, and the roses in the center. Joy began to flow inside her, and hot tears sprang to her eyes. This couldn't be happening; this didn't happen to her.

"Read it," he said softly, watching her face as she opened the card and gazed at it as if it was the most precious thing she'd ever held.

It was a poem. A billet-doux. A love letter. The tears came freely now as she read the words, a simple outpouring of his love. Emotion choked her, and she turned to him, burying her face in his coat while he held her so tightly she thought she would die from the pleasure of it all.

"I know it's not as good as yours, but I wanted to write it myself. I mean it, Victoria. I love you, and I have to have you in my life. Please marry me."

"Clayton." Her tears were so filled with joy that she couldn't have stopped them even if she'd wanted to. She was laughing and crying at the same time, holding him and trying to wipe at her face while he, in much the same condition, fought to find a handkerchief.

"Does this mean yes?" he asked hopefully, wiping away her tears while Victoria hugged him.

"Oh, yes, Clayton. You know I will. My God, I thought you were lost to me."

"Never," he said fiercely. "Never again. I was so blind, so incredibly stupid. Please forgive me. I love you, Victoria. I think I always have. I need you. You are so incredibly special."

"No, you are." She laughed as he pulled her impossibly close to kiss her, his mouth possessing hers, wanting her, needing her, expressing everything inside him. When Esther and Emma appeared a moment later with the tea tray, it was Esther who turned to her sister with a wise expression and nodded.

"I think, dear sister, that we should rearrange the tray."

Emma nodded, a grin coming to her face. "I believe, dear Esther, that you are absolutely right."

TEMPTATION'S BRIDE

by

Maureen Child

Dear Reader,

I love romance. I always have: Wonderful
books to keep and re-read for years; great old
movies that never fail to touch your heart;
puppy love, brides and grooms and fiftieth wedding anniversaries. They all hold the magic of
romance.

And, although there's nothing like a good cry,
I prefer my love stories served with humor.
Which is fortunate, because so many odd things
seem to happen around me.

I met my Valentine, my husband Mark,
twenty-two years ago. A friend and I were having
an argument about something that seemed very
important at the time and she decided to stop
by her friend Mark's house to have him settle
the bet. Since he had to be at work at three in
the morning, he was sound asleep when we
arrived, but that didn't discourage my friend.
She pounded on his window until he was wide
awake. (A family of five sons kept his parents
from being the least bit surprised at such a late

visit.) Anyway, Mark settled the bet, (I won), and we met.

Even on that first night, he impressed me with his sense of humor. It seemed to me then that nothing could upset him. (In fact, it took our children to accomplish that.) And on our first date, when he very seriously informed me that we would be married and have six kids, I *knew* he had a sense of humor!

Twenty years of marriage and two teenagers later, we still laugh together. I do believe that laughter is necessary for love to last. And when you have children, a sense of humor is essential!

So, in honor of my wonderful husband and my crazy family, I wanted to write a story about the funny side of love. About the fact that sometimes, no matter how hard you try, nothing works out the way you planned. In "Temptation's Bride," two people who really love each other find out just how strange love can be.

And, though the characters are fictional, The Bees *were* born from reality. My father was a police officer in my hometown. Every time he went to court, he had to pass by a park bench where two lovely old gentlemen spent their days. The men would question my dad and the other officers about their pending cases. Anything interesting would get the men up and moving for a front row seat.

I really enjoyed the time I spent in Temptation, California with Jake, Rachael, The Bees, and everyone else. I hope you will, too.

—MAUREEN CHILD

Chapter One

Rachael groaned as the stagecoach jolted to a stop in front of her father's general store. She didn't care that every muscle ached or that she was covered with trail dust. She was home again. Nothing else mattered. As she glanced out of the coach she saw little Danny Hogan sneaking away from the schoolhouse. Good to know that nothing had changed.

She turned, and the smile froze on her face. Of course. *Nothing* had changed. How could she have forgotten the Bees? That they would be in their regular spot? That she would have to pass them to get home? Sighing helplessly, she gathered up her green silk skirt and shoved the door open. As she stepped down, she eyed them carefully.

Bill, Bob, and Buck Taylor. The Bees. About sixty years ago old Mrs. Taylor had delivered a boy a year, three years running. She'd named them alphabetically in order of appearance, then announced that three boys was plenty for anybody and never had another.

Rachael's gaze swept one face after the other. As

alike as peas in a pod, the old bachelors could have been triplets. But if you looked closely enough, there were subtle differences in their features. All had round faces, bright red cheeks, and pale blue eyes that never missed a thing happening in Temptation, California. The general rule of thumb in town was, if you want news spread quickly, tell one of the Bees.

She could almost see the wheels turning behind their sharp eyes. Rachael would have been willing to bet that by suppertime everyone in town would know she was back. Well, she asked herself, why not? She had every right to come home. She had done nothing to be ashamed of.

"Afternoon Bill, Bob, Buck."

They nodded, each in turn. Buck, the baby of the group, offered, "Need some help with your bags, Rachael? Or is this just a visit and you don't have many?"

She smirked at him, well aware he was fishing for information and wasn't about to get off his bench to help her. In fact, she couldn't remember the last time she'd seen one of the Bees actually move. Everyone in town assumed they went home at night, but no one had actually *seen* them go.

"No thanks, Buck. I can manage fine."

He nodded expectantly, waiting for her to continue.

Rachael shook her head and sighed. No point in making them work for the information. Might as well tell them what they wanted to know. They'd find out anyway.

"And no. This isn't a visit, boys. I'm home to stay."

The three old men turned to one another, smiling and whispering.

"You might as well let everybody know right away."

"Why, Rachael"—Bob sounded hurt—"how can you think we'd stoop to gossipin'?"

All three of them wore such affronted expressions that Rachael chuckled. "I'm sorry, boys. Of course you wouldn't dream of carrying tales."

They smiled.

"Your papa ain't in the store right now, Rachael. Went home early. Looked kinda poorly, too. Didn't he, Bill?" Bob looked at his brother for confirmation.

"Not nearly as peaked as Tom Wright did yesterday after his wife found out about him goin' to the gamblin' house on his last trip north."

"It wasn't gamblin' she didn't like," Buck corrected Bill. "It was—" He stopped short of mentioning the house of ill repute and glanced worriedly at Rachael.

Obviously she was slowing down their exchange of information. She picked up her carpetbags and asked the stage driver to leave her trunk on the walk. Glancing at the Bees, she asked, "You boys keep an eye on it until Papa comes to collect it?"

"Oh, yes."

"Yes indeed."

"Pleasure."

She nodded and ignored the whispered but frantic conversation behind her as she started down the street at a brisk walk. Her gaze lovingly touched every weathered building she passed. It was good to be home. She hadn't realized how much she loved the place until she'd been away.

No sooner did that thought blossom than she saw the lace curtains quickly drop into place over the front window of Mrs. Kelly's boardinghouse.

Rachael stopped in the middle of the street. How many other pairs of eyes were watching? she wondered. A swell of anger rushed up, then quickly faded. She'd known there would be talk. After all, she'd been gone almost a year, and the townspeople were bound to be curious.

But, she told herself again, straightening her shoulders, *she* had nothing to be ashamed of. It wasn't *she* who'd created such a spectacle last Valentine's Day.

She walked faster, feeling hidden eyes follow her every step. Throwing her chin up, Rachael reminded herself that it wasn't *she* who'd given the town's gossip mills enough grist to last a lifetime!

When she finally reached her parents' house, Rachael's green eyes were flashing. She climbed the steps to the wide front porch without noticing that the two-story house had been freshly painted a pale yellow. All she could think of was getting inside, off the one and only street of her hometown.

This was all Jake's fault, she thought as renewed anger swept through her. It wasn't fair, for heaven's sake! Why should *she* have to put up with the stares and listen to the whispers?

Charles Hayes opened the door for his daughter, recognized her expression, and gave her a wide berth. As she stomped up the stairs, Charles muttered on a sigh, "Welcome home, Rachael."

* * *

At sunset a cowboy on a charging horse rode into the yard of the Travers ranch. He jerked back on the reins and as the horse slid to a stop, he jumped down. Without bothering to tie his mount to the rail, the young man, clutching the pound bag of coffee he'd been sent to town for, ran across the porch and into the ranch kitchen.

"What in thunder's wrong with you, Frank?"

Sam Jenks, the cook, jumped a foot as the kitchen door slammed open against the wall.

"It's . . . it's . . . " The cowhand held up one hand, dropped the coffee on the table, and clutched his chest. He was having a time trying to catch his breath.

"What is it?" Sam moved closer, concern on his weathered features. "You been shot?"

Frank shook his head.

"Snakebit?"

A vigorous shake.

Sam punched the boy in the arm. "Get aholt of yourself, then, boy! I'm a busy man. I cain't stand here all day playin' guessin' games!"

Frank nodded and finally managed to pull a deep, steadying breath into his lungs. "Sam . . . you're gonna have to tell the boss. I ain't gonna."

"Thunderation, boy! Spit it out! What do I have to tell him?"

"Rachael's home."

Sam grabbed at the back of a chair and gingerly lowered himself down. He rubbed a hand over the gray stubble that covered his jaw and mumbled, "Oh, Lord. Just when things was startin' to settle down again." He glanced up hopefully. "Are you sure? Maybe you made a mistake?"

"No mistake."

"But you don't even know what she looks like, boy! You didn't start workin' here till after—"

"Didn't have to see her," Frank countered. "The Bees told me."

"Well, that's it, then." Sam slapped the table. "Never knew those old coots to be wrong about anything."

The youngster dropped to a chair and asked in a whisper, "Why's everybody so scared of her?"

Sam's laughter barked out. "Hell, they ain't scared o' Rachael! Finer woman never lived. Folks is just a little concerned about what's gonna happen when her and Jake meet for the first time."

"Why?"

"Well,"—Sam looked over at the boy, who was almost eighteen—"last year Rachael and Jake was all set to get hitched."

"Married? Jake?"

"Yes, Jake. He's a man, ain't he?"

"Yeah." The boy shrugged.

"Anyhow, him and Rachael had been courtin' for quite a spell, and they fixed the weddin' for Valentine's Day. Rachael's idea. She had that whole dang church done up in red ribbons and lacy whatnots. Everybody in town was there. All spruced up, lots of food for the party and dance after. Oh, and it would have been a humdinger of a party, too. Even had a fiddle player."

"What happened?"

"Nothin'." Sam got up and walked to the sink. "Nothin' happened. They didn't get married.

Wasn't Jake's fault, but he ended up leavin' Rachael standin' at the altar."

"Oh, my."

"Yes sir—oh, my." The old man filled the coffee pot at the pump, then turned to the stove. "Rachael was madder than spit on a hot skillet. Jake tried to talk to her, but she wouldn't let him near. Then she took off. Went to Europe with her aunt for a long spell—been back a few months now. Stayin' in Stockton at her aunt's place. "Yeah." He sighed. "Rachael's been gone almost a year."

The boy whistled softly. "Didn't Jake go to see her?"

"Hell, no. He ain't got the money to go to Europe. And Stockton's quite a ways from here. This place is all Jake's got. He can't afford to go traipsin' off." Sam took up a spoon and gave the chili pot a few good stirs. "Wrote to her, though. Must've wrote a hundred letters. They're in there"—he jerked his head toward the main room—"on the mantel. She never opened 'em. Just sent 'em back."

"Whew! I bet Jake was mad!" Frank shuddered at the thought of his boss's anger being directed at him.

"I'll swear he was. Not right off, though." Sam squinted at the ceiling. "First couple o' months he wandered around here like a lost hound. Then he started in talkin' to himself for the next few months. By the time *you* was hired, he was actin' like a grizzly with a sore paw!"

Frank nodded his agreement.

"Dammit, he was just commencin' to cool down

lately, and now she's back." The old man took his apron off and threw it down on the table. "Reckon I better just tell him and get it over quick." He glanced at the stricken cowhand and chuckled. "C'mon, Frank. Watch the fun!"

"Fun?" Didn't sound like this was gonna be fun, Frank thought uneasily. But then again, he sure didn't want to miss anything. He grabbed his hat and ran out the door after the cook.

Jake was in the paddock trying to sneak up on the meanest horse he'd ever owned. The mouse-colored hardhead had already thrown him twice that afternoon, but Jake was determined to break him.

The big animal rolled his eyes as the man crept closer. Warily the horse sidestepped, always keeping the man in sight.

"Jake!"

He turned and shushed Sam with a wave of his hand. He didn't want to be bothered now.

"Jake, I got to talk to you!"

Jake cursed silently to himself. Couldn't Sam see he was busy?

Slowly, carefully, he walked up to the horse. When he was finally near enough, his left hand snaked out and grabbed the reins. The horse reared, but Jake was determined. Getting along-side the animal, he jabbed his foot in the stirrup and swung aboard.

Immediately the horse shot up in the air, arching his back, turning, twisting, and doing everything in his power to shake the man off.

"Jake!" Sam leaned on the top rail.

"Don't you think you oughta wait?" Frank sounded nervous.

"No, I don't. I'm tired pussyfootin' around him! Maybe this'll be the best thing for him. At least it'll settle things once and for all!"

"Jake!"

The other hands were beginning to gather. Frank moved in closer to Sam. He didn't want to lose his spot.

"Dammit, Jake! This here's important!" The old cook waved one arm in the air.

Jake didn't take his eyes off the back of the animal's head, but he did manage to swear that he'd fire Sam as soon as he got off the damned horse if the old man didn't shut up! His body jackknifed back and forth, every muscle in his body screaming. His left arm high in the air for balance, he stuck as if it meant his life. He'd never been bucked so hard before. But he would stay on!

"Jake! Rachael's back in town!"

The horse bucked again, and Jake sailed over his head. He landed with a thump against the rail fence. He lifted his face out of the paddock mud and shouted, *"What?"*

Chapter Two

Jake Travers brushed at his pants, then checked the knot in his string tie. He knew it was fine. He'd already tied it seven times. Running his index finger around the inside of his collar, he considered leaving.

Then he glanced at the stack of unopened letters in his hand. No. By heaven, she would listen to him, even if he had to hog-tie and muzzle her. He grinned suddenly. Knowing Rachael, he just might have to. Lord, he'd missed her.

Quickly, before he could back out, Jake ran up the steps and knocked on the front door. While he waited for an answer, he ran his hand over the doorjamb. Still looked good, he thought. Right after Rachael'd left town, he'd spent the better part of two weeks painting the Hayes house her favorite color.

He'd wanted to surprise her on her return. But he'd never figured she'd stay away for a year. Jake gripped the letters tighter. A damn year and not a word from her. Just his own mail coming back at him.

The doorknob turned, and he snatched his hat off. Sarah Hayes, an older, somewhat paler version of her daughter, opened the door.

"Mrs. Hayes."

"Hello, Jake." She smiled and stepped onto the porch. Her gaze quickly noted his scrubbed appearance. His wavy black hair combed flat, he wore a brand-new double-breasted red shirt tucked into faded black Levi's. Even the toes of his boots had been carefully polished. A tall man, Sarah had to look up to see him clearly. His strong jaw was freshly shaven, and his lips showed no sign of the grin she'd always associated with him. She looked into his deep brown eyes and saw the hope shining there.

"I come to see Rachael, Mrs. Hayes."

"I know, Jake, but—"

"I know. She doesn't want to see me." Jake took a step closer to the door and tried to see inside. "But she's just gonna have to, 'cause I ain't leavin' till she does."

"That's not it, Jake—"

"I even rode into town by the back road so no one would see me comin' here." He looked down at the woman who should've been his mother-in-law by now. "Please."

Sarah sighed. "She's not here."

"But the Bees said—"

"Oh, she's back home." Sarah laid her hand on his arm. "But she went to the store with her father early this morning."

"The store?" Rachael had always hated being stuck behind the counter all day. Why would she go to work her first day home? Then it hit him. Of course. She went so she wouldn't have to face him. "She really doesn't want to talk to me, does she?"

"I'm afraid not, Jake." Sarah could have swatted

her daughter's backside. Twenty years old or not, she was behaving like a stubborn child.

"Prob'ly figures I won't go to the store. Won't make a scene." He was talking to himself more than to Sarah. "Well, she's got a surprise headin' her way." Jake jammed his hat back on. "Thank you, Mrs. Hayes. I'll just go see her now."

"Do you think that's wise?"

"Prob'ly not." He looked down into her kind eyes. "Every time I get around Rachael, I don't seem to do a *thing* wise." He walked to his horse, mounted, and trotted it down the street to the general store.

Sarah stepped inside, grabbed her bonnet, and, tying the ribbons as she went, hurried after him.

"Mornin', Jake!"

"Jake!"

"Come to see Rachael?"

Jake nodded a greeting to the three old men.

"She sure does look pretty today, son," Buck said wistfully.

"Rachael Hayes always looks pretty," Bill corrected.

"True, true, not like some we could mention." Bob leaned toward Jake. "Saw Myra Talbot just yesterday mornin' without all her war paint on? Liked to stop my heart! Don't know how ol' Harvey stayed married to her all those years. 'Course, he always did have bad eyes."

"Harvey was no prize, neither," Bill added.

Jake finally managed to walk past the old men into the store. The friendly aromas mingled and welcomed him—fresh coffee, sugar candy, hot bread from Mrs. Olsen's bakery. All of these things brought memories flooding into his brain.

From the very first day he'd come into this place, a twenty-year-old stranger in town, he'd felt the warmth of Charles Hayes's mercantile. Then, as the years passed, he'd begun to notice that Rachael wasn't just a skinny redhead with freckles anymore, and he'd found a different reason for spending so much time at the store.

Now he took a deep breath and looked around the familiar store. She wasn't there. Had Mrs. Hayes lied to him? No. She wouldn't do that. Suddenly Rachael stood up from behind the counter and looked across the room at him. For a moment he could have sworn he saw joy, even love, on her face. Then it was gone, replaced by the stony set of her jaw that promised trouble.

He walked toward her to meet it head-on.

Her finely arched strawberry-blond brows rose over clear sea-green eyes. Jake's gaze ran over the perfect line of her delicate nose, then rested on the full lips he longed to kiss. "Hello, Rachael darlin'."

Her eyes narrowed. "Don't call me darlin'." Lowering her gaze to the ledger on the counter, Rachael effectively dismissed him.

"You always liked me callin' you darlin'," he said, moving toward the opening in the counter.

She reached out and slammed the gate in the counter down, just missing Jake's outstretched hand.

"Jesus, Rachael!" He jumped back and stared at her, now separated from him behind the unbroken wooden countertop. "You could've cut my hand off!"

She smiled and batted her eyelashes. The bell over the front door jangled and Rachael turned, not at all surprised to see her mother.

Sarah looked quickly from one to the other, mumbled "Oh, my," and went through to her husband's office at the rear.

Rachael looked back at the man opposite her. "I'm working," she finally said. "Go away, Jake."

"No." He leaned on the counter. "I am not gonna leave till we talk."

"Fine. I'll tell Papa to leave the fire in the stove burning tonight." She smiled. "Wouldn't want you to get cold."

"Dammit, Rachael—"

The bell rang again.

"I have a customer, Jake." She turned to face the door. "Hello, Mr. Moffat. Can I help you?"

"No. No—" The banker shook his bald head. "Not really sure yet—just want to look around a bit."

Rachael's lips quirked slightly. She'd never known Mr. Moffat to browse. He generally came in, got what he wanted, and left. "Certainly. Take your time." Under her breath she said, "Go away, Jake."

"Not yet." He kept his voice low and placed the stack of letters on the countertop beside her. "Why didn't you read these?"

The bell jangled again.

"Dammit," Jake cursed quietly, then forced a smile.

"Why, hello, Jake." Mrs. Olsen, wearing her

apron and a long streak of flour across her cheek, glanced eagerly at the couple. "Good to see you back, Rachael."

Rachael nodded.

"Oof!" Mrs. Olsen grunted as the bell rang again and the opening door crashed into her.

"Well, for heaven's sake Hannah!" Myra Talbot glared at her friend. "Move away from the door!" Myra's heavily rouged cheeks looked like two campfires in the snow against the pale parchment of her face.

"Honestly, Myra." The baker pushed her hair out of her eyes and moved off to look at the pots and pans.

Jake stared open-mouthed as, one by one, practically the whole town trickled into Hayes's general store. The bell danced and clanged until he was sure it would fall off in exhaustion.

Rachael groaned and put her hand to her forehead.

"What in the blue blazes?" Charles hurried out of his office and gasped at the milling crowd.

"Oh, Lord," Sarah moaned softly.

"Don't worry, Papa," Rachael said clearly, as she glared at her nosy friends and neighbors. "I'm going home now. The show's over," she said to everyone. "I'm leaving."

"No, you're not."

Her jaw dropped. "Jake, you can't seriously expect me—"

"Rachael. You're not goin' anywhere till I say what I came here to say!"

She flicked nervous glances at the people straining to overhear. The bell rang again and her head dropped to her chest. Who was left? The entire town was already here.

Then the awed whispers started, spread through the crowd, and grew in strength. Rachael craned her neck to see over the packed room, and then she gasped in surprise. Buck Taylor stood at the back of the store, his pale eyes alight, licking his lips in anticipation.

"Good Lord." Jake shook his head unbelievingly. One of the Bees had actually moved! If he hadn't seen it with his own eyes, he'd never have believed it. He took a deep breath and told himself it didn't matter. He didn't care who else listened, as long as Rachael did, too. Tearing his gaze from the short squat figure of Buck Taylor, Jake focused on the shocked woman before him.

"Rachael."

She looked directly at him.

"Darlin', I'm so sorry."

Tears welled up in her eyes, and she bit her bottom lip. "Don't."

He reached across the counter and cupped her cheek. "Rachael, you know I love you," he whispered.

She moved away. "You love me so much you left me standing all alone at our wedding."

"I can explain."

"Then why didn't you?"

"Yeah, Jake," Buck called out. "Why didn't you?"

"Jesus, Buck!" Jake turned back to Rachael after sending the old man an icy glare. "I tried to explain." He spoke faster, sensing she was about to run. "I sent Jimmy in from the ranch with a note and—"

"I waited *two hours* at the church," she interrupted. "He didn't come."

He grabbed at his hat and pushed his hand through his hair until it tumbled carelessly over his forehead, just the way Rachael loved it best.

"His horse broke a leg. Jimmy had to walk back to the ranch."

Murmurs of sympathy and understanding filtered through the crowd. He ignored them. "I rode in myself. That night."

"He did, dear." Sarah nodded.

"See? Anyhow, by the time I got here, you were already gone! You didn't even wait to talk to me."

"That's true, Rachael," Buck intoned as he nodded sagely.

Rachael's gaze swept the fascinated group. Every ear cocked, every mouth open, they stood entranced, waiting for the final act.

Well, she wouldn't give it to them! She straightened her shoulders and lifted her chin. A year ago they'd witnessed her humiliation. But by heaven, once was enough! It was nearly Valentine's Day again, and she didn't want to relive her embarrassment!

She turned back to Jake. He looked so confident. So sure of himself. So sure of *her*.

"Oh, no," Rachael said, looking away from his dark, warm eyes. "It's not going to be that easy."

"What?" He glanced uneasily at the crowd behind him, then turned back to Rachael. "What are you talkin' about, darlin'?"

"That." She flipped the gate in the counter open

and stepped through. One finger against his chest, she continued. "You calling me darlin'. That's what I'm talking about. You think all you have to do is sweet-talk me and show me those dimples of yours and I'm gonna fall into your arms?"

"Well . . ." Jake backed up a step and flashed her a nervous grin. She was too close to the truth. That was exactly what he'd figured.

She shook her head. "Nope. It won't work. Not this time."

"Now, Rachael honey," he whispered softly, "you know I love you."

"What?" She cocked her head and said clearly, "I didn't hear you. What'd you say?"

Jake glanced at the expectant crowd. They'd moved in closer. Leaning down toward the little redhead, he said "Rach . . . this is kinda embarrassing."

"Embarrassing?" Rachael glared at him. Hands on hips, she challenged, "It's *embarrassing* to tell your betrothed that you love her?"

"Well," he hedged cautiously, "in front of everybody . . ."

Their audience shifted almost as one. A few muttered voices were heard.

"Ain't that just like a woman?"

"Take it easy on the boy, Rachael."

She held her hand up to silence the men surrounding her. Raising her gaze to Jake, Rachael narrowed her eyes at his confident smile. With the men supporting him, Jake seemed less nervous.

"Why, Jake, I wouldn't want to *embarrass* you in front of the whole town."

He grinned.

"Like *you* humiliated *me* last Valentine's Day!"

He paled. "Rachael."

She took a step closer and tried to ignore the fresh, clean scent of him.

"You left me standing in that church all by myself! Why, I might as well have been parading down main street in my—my *drawers!*"

"Rachael!" Sarah Hayes's gasp sounded over the crowd's chuckling.

Color flooded Rachael's face. She'd gone too far, and she knew it.

Myra Talbot's nervous twitter was the only sound in the room as the others quieted, not wanting to miss a word. Rachael's eyes, filled with unshed tears of frustration, moved from one fascinated face to the next. She heard her own heartbeat pounding in her ears. From the corner of her eye, she saw Jake's hand move toward her. She stepped back and took a deep, steadying breath. Then, chin lifted, eyes straight ahead, she swept through the dumbstruck crowd.

As she marched through the doorway, she thought she heard Buck say, "Have mercy! The fur's gonna fly now!"

Chapter Three

"Rachael, this can't go on."

She kept her eyes on her supper plate. Idly she pushed at the untouched meal with her fork.

"Rachael. Are you listening to me?"

"Yes, Papa."

"Charles, I really don't think this is the time—"

"I disagree, m'dear." Charles looked from Sarah to his daughter, frowned, then turned back to his wife. "It's been a week now, Sarah. And I haven't gotten a lick of work done in all that time." He dropped his fork on the table and leaned back in his chair. "Every time I turn around, Jake's there. I tell you, it's as if the man's a ghost haunting me! And as soon as Rachael sees him, she goes to the back and stays in my office, leaving me alone in the store!"

Sarah hid a small smile. "But, Charles," she said softly, "you said yourself that business was slow this week."

"Slow!"

Rachael turned startled eyes on her normally placid father. She watched as he yanked at his cravat. "Business has stopped! I haven't sold so much as a piece of candy all week!"

"Then what can it possibly matter if Rachael leaves you alone with Jake?"

"It's not just Jake!" He jumped up and paced around the table. Late afternoon sun filtered in under the half drawn shades covering the bay window. The two women turned in their chairs to follow Charles with their eyes. "The store is packed tight with people every day! Finally had to take the blasted bell down from the door! About drove me out of my senses—clanging and clanging all day long."

"But, with so many customers . . ."

He shook his head wildly. "Not *customers*, Sarah! Busybodies!"

Rachael winced.

"Folks coming and going, mostly coming. Drinking my coffee, nibbling on crackers right out of the barrel. Laughing and carrying on like they were at a church picnic!" Suddenly weary, Charles rubbed his eyes and said in an astonished tone, "Do you know Myra Talbot and Hannah Olsen actually brought their mending with them yesterday? Plopped right down like two nesting hens and didn't stir an inch all afternoon!"

"Surely a few older women can't be that much bother."

"It's not just the women!" Charles ran both hands through his graying hair until it stood on end. "Moffat's there all the time, too. It's a wonder the bank hasn't gone out of business, it's closed so much lately!"

"Even Mr. Moffat?" Sarah asked in a shocked whisper.

"And the list doesn't end there."

"Perhaps if Rachael stayed home—"

"Lord, no!" Charles walked to his daughter's side and stared down at her until she finally raised her gaze to his. "We tried that two days ago. Remember?"

Rachael said nothing. Her mother finally spoke to end the silence.

"Oh, yes." Sarah sighed as the recollection came rushing back at her. She hadn't accomplished a thing all day. More women had dropped by to call that day than when she'd been laid up with a broken ankle the year before. And she'd never get over the shock she'd experienced when she opened the door to find Bob Taylor on the front porch.

"And the Bees, Sarah." Charles threw his hands up. "It's getting so a man can't depend on anything anymore! A week ago, I'd have bet my life that nothing short of the Second Coming would have gotten those old coots to move! But today Bill Taylor came *inside*! Big as life. Every day one or another of them strolls into the store, and they actually seem surprised when folks stare at 'em. I tell you, Sarah, it's more than a little scary how those three are up and moving all of a sudden."

Abruptly Rachael stood up and moved toward the stairs.

"One moment, young woman!"

"Charles! Please. Your tone."

"*Hang* my tone."

"Charles!"

"Papa!"

He looked from his wife's crossed arms and tapping fingers to his daughter's surprised expression. "Forgive me," he said suddenly, shaking his head. "I shouldn't have spoken so to either of you. It's just that . . . well, I'm not myself right now, and . . ."

"I know, dear." Sarah patted his arm gently. "Why don't you sit down now and finish your meal in peace?"

"Yes. Yes, perhaps I will. Thank you, m'dear."

Leaving her husband at the supper table, Sarah followed her daughter and caught her at the foot of the stairs. She stared up at the pretty young woman and wondered again at how fast time had passed. It didn't seem possible that her little girl could actually be at the center of such extraordinary occurrences.

"Rachael, something simply must be done." She took a deep breath. "You're going to have to settle this situation with Jake and settle it soon. I won't have your father upsetting himself so. Why, the poor man's nerves are almost destroyed."

"I know." Rachael reached for her mother and gave her a quick hug. "But, Mother, I can't promise that anything will be settled. Ever."

"That's nonsense, dear." Sarah patted her daughter's hand. "Why, you know as well as I do, Jake loves you to distraction."

"Distraction is right." She picked up the hem of her skirt and half turned toward the staircase. "He was so distracted he forgot about his own wedding."

"Rachael, how long are you going to make him pay for that one mistake?"

"Mother! I thought you understood. That you agreed with me."

"Well, dear, I did. Last February." Sarah looked down at the newel post as her fingers slid over the polished mahogany banister. "In fact, I understood all summer long and into the fall. But, honey, it's been almost a year!"

"But—"

"And you've been away all that time with your aunt Libby. According to her, you spent most of your time in Europe crying your eyes out, too. Then when you got back to California, Libby said if your cousin Preston hadn't come home from the university when he did, you might never have left the house."

Rachael lowered her eyes, unable to deny the truth. Her trip to Europe was nothing but a blur in her mind. She had almost no recollection of that time at all. She'd been much too miserable to enjoy herself. And once she came back to California, Preston *had* insisted on her getting out. He'd spent nearly every waking moment with her. In fact, she'd come home only because she'd had more than enough of her cousin Preston. He was a nice boy, but . . . annoying after any length of time.

"I know you were hurt, darling. But so was Jake. You weren't here. You didn't see how poor Jake just wandered around like a lost soul."

Rachael's eyes snapped up. Lost soul indeed! Whose side was her mother on, anyway?

"*Poor* Jake?"

"Yes." Sarah nodded emphatically. "Why, he even painted our house your favorite color as a surprise for you on your return. Though I suspect the poor boy did it more as a way of staying close to your father and me during your absence." She looked up and met her daughter's narrowed gaze. "I admit, he did embarrass you terribly. But you should at least have listened to his explanation."

"How could he possibly explain—"

"You'll never know that until you hear him out, will you?"

"But—"

"No." Sarah reached out and cupped Rachael's cheek tenderly. "No more arguments, dear. There is only one question you must answer. And only you can. Do you still love Jake Travers?"

After giving her daughter an encouraging smile and a soft pat on the cheek, Sarah Hayes went to rejoin her husband. Rachael simply stared after her, too stunned to come up with a reply.

The world had gone crazy. That was the only possible explanation. Never would Rachael have believed that her own mother would take Jake's side against her. Of course her parents had always been fond of him. They'd both been pleased when Jake asked for Rachael's hand.

But for heaven's sake, after what he'd done, a body would think they'd show a little more compassion. More concern. She picked up the hem of her skirt again and slowly began climbing the stairs. It wasn't just her parents, either. She suspected the entire town stood firmly on Jake's side.

And now with Valentine's Day almost here, everyone was obviously expecting her to forgive and forget.

Didn't *anyone* understand?

She smiled. Cousin Preston had understood perfectly. Annoying or not, he'd held her hand and murmured all the things Rachael's hurt pride had wanted to hear. He'd cursed Jake and flattered her. Never mind that his soft hands were always sweaty, his wire-frame spectacles had the irritating habit of sliding down his too sharp nose, and he had an unfortunate tendency to spit every time he said a word containing the letter *t*. No matter that his insistence on following her everywhere like a lapdog made her want to scream in vexation.

At least *he* hadn't left her standing all alone at the altar surrounded by red hearts, white lace, and paper cutouts of laughing Cupids! Rachael reached the landing and walked to her room. Her mother was wrong. It wasn't a question of loving Jake. She always had and always would. It was really a question of how much he loved Rachael.

And what he was willing to do to prove it.

Chapter Four

The back door flew open and crashed into the kitchen wall. Sam Jenks jumped, looked up, and swallowed his curses unuttered. It was Jake. And if he wanted to punch holes in his own walls, Sam figured that was his right. Besides, his employer looked exhausted.

Jake plopped down onto a chair and nodded his thanks when Sam brought him a cup of coffee.

Easing himself into the chair opposite his boss, Sam studied the younger man.

The poor fella looked like hell. His hair was in a tangle, his eyes were puffy, and his mouth was flattened in a frown. His head propped on his hand, he fiddled idly with the handle on his coffee mug. Sam shook his head and hid a smile. Love. Thank the good Lord he was too old for such nonsense. And boss or no, it was time for Jake to hear a few things, whether he wanted to or not.

"Did you talk to Rachael?"

"No." Jake looked at him, a smirk turning up the corners of his mouth. "She won't hold still long enough for me to open my mouth."

Sam slapped his dish towel down on the table. "Boy, it's high time you got this mess straightened out!"

Jake's eyes narrowed. "What the hell do you think I've been tryin' to do?"

"Ain't sure. But I can tell you what you're gonna do if you can't put a stop to this nonsense."

"What?"

"You're gonna lose this ranch."

"Is something wrong? The bull?"

"Right kind of you to ask, boy." Sam leaned back. "That there is the first time in a week you've even remembered you own a ranch."

"What's that supposed to mean?" Jake stood up and glared down at his cook and friend.

"You know damn well what it means—and don't give me that fish-eye look, neither." Sam grabbed a cookie from the plate in the center of the table. "You can't fire me, Jake. I wouldn't go."

Jake smiled reluctantly. "All right, Sam, have your say."

"Intend to." He munched on the cookie and reached for another. "There ain't no problems with the ranch."

Jake sighed.

"Yet." Sam paused and met the younger man's gaze. "But there will be. You're just buildin' this place up, boy. Startin' to look like you could maybe have a first-rate place in a few years. But you got to be here. Workin' it. Watchin' everything. Worryin' over it. Like a mama with a new baby. This place needs your attention—and it ain't gettin' it."

"Yeah. I know. But Rachael—"

"Is as mad as a wet hen." Sam nodded. "And she's got a right to be. You held her up to laughter, boy. A woman don't forget somethin' like that. A woman can forgive her man a little private humiliation—and most times does, else there'd be mighty few husbands wanderin' around. But, boy, you did it in front of the entire town."

Jake hung his head for a moment as Sam's flatly stated truth sank in. Finally, though, his arms crossed over his broad chest, booted feet wide apart, he took a deep breath and forced himself to ask, "What can I do? She won't talk to me. Her father's sick of the sight of me. The whole damn town pops up everywhere I go—"

Sam chuckled. "Hell, boy. It's a small town. When somethin' excitin' happens, folks want to be in on it."

"*Exciting*?"

"Sure. This here's the biggest thing that's happened around here since Myra Talbot caught poor old Harvey with that fancy woman and chased him down Main Street swingin' the business end of a broom at him!"

"I guess so." Jake pushed his hand through his hair. "Even the Bees are up and around."

Sam snorted, got up, and went to the stove. He lifted the lid on the bubbling pot of beef stew and gave it a few quick stirs. The rich aroma filled the kitchen, and the windows misted over with sudden moisture. "Don't know why folks are so surprised. They think those old coots was born on that bench or somethin'?"

"I sure did."

"No such thing." Sam dropped the lid back into place. "Why, I knew those boys when they was young and frisky. 'Course, so was I." He shook his head slowly, in fond memory. "Them three was the wildest hares around for miles, as fast to sweet-talk a woman as they were to start fights. Mighty fun bunch, them three. We had us some times, all right—" Sam noticed Jake's open-mouthed stare and changed the subject. "Anyway, that ain't what I wanted to talk about."

"Rachael."

"Wrong. You."

"Me? What'd I do?"

"It's what you ain't done, boy!"

"Spit it out, Sam."

He laid the big metal spoon down on the stove top and poked a gnarled finger into Jake's chest. "You're goin' about this all wrong, son. Don't follow the woman around like a big ol' dog, apologizin' and whinin'. Hell, she knows you're sorry. She ain't stupid!"

"If she knows I'm sorry, what's she waitin' for?"

Sam sighed. "It is a wonder to me how you ever managed to get such a fine woman in the first place!"

Jake's eyebrows arched.

"Now, don't get on your high horse. You ain't got time. You got to get busy."

"Doin' *what*!"

"Courtin' Rachael."

"Courtin' her?" Jake's arms flew up. "I already done that! Dammit, she knows I love her! And I know she loves me!"

"Sure, sure. Everybody in town knows that. But after what happened last year, you're gonna have to show her again." Sam cocked his head and stared at him. "You remember how, don't you? Gettin' all slicked up, actin' nice, talkin' pretty?"

"Yeah." Jake grinned. Courting Rachael had been the best and most nerve-racking experience of his life. "I remember."

"Then you'd best get at it. You got to show her how bad you want her. And you got to make sure all the folks in town see you do it. They laughed at her, boy. Never forget that. Rachael won't."

"I know."

"Good. The whole town's got to see you tryin' to win her back. A woman's got to be able to hold her head up. And Rachael's a proud woman. A good woman. Too damn good for you."

Jake grinned. He understood. If Sam was right, and Jake was pretty sure the old man knew what he was talkin' about, then Rachael wanted him to prove himself in front of everybody. Hell, he could do that. He'd dance naked in the middle of Main Street if it would make her come back.

"Now you git. I got to get ready to feed the hands."

"Yes, sir." Jake turned away, then stopped. Looking back at the old cook, he asked, "Sam, if you know so much about women, how is it you never got married?"

Sam snorted. "'Cause I know so much about women."

"Mornin', Rachael."

"Miss Rachael."

"My, you look fine today, Rachael."

"Thanks, boys." She stopped outside the store and smiled at the Bees. She couldn't help it. As far back as she could remember, they'd been a part of her life. And even though she'd never known anyone nosier than the Taylor brothers, she also knew they didn't have a mean bone among them.

"Goin' in to work now?"

"Yes, Buck."

"When do you reckon Jake'll be in?"

Rachael turned to Bob. "I wouldn't know."

"Well," Bill said, "we only wanted to know so's we can tell folks not to bother comin' in too early."

Hands on her hips, she faced the three gray-haired cherubs. "Why don't you just tell them not to come in at all? Unless of course they want to buy something!"

Buck chuckled. "Now, Miss Rachael, you know that wouldn't do no good. Folks is curious."

"Nosy, you mean."

"Now, I wouldn't say nosy, exactly," Bob offered, "except maybe Myra and Hannah. But you know how women are."

Rachael stared at him, stunned.

"Why, just the other day, I caught Myra peekin' around the corner tryin' to see if that nice new teacher was kissin' the Anderson boy." Buck shook his head sadly. "I shooed her right off, though, Miss Rachael, before the boy got to the schoolhouse. 'Course, if they don't want folks to see them kissin', they ought not to stand right in front of the window."

Rachael rolled her eyes heavenward. It was no use.

"It's high time that Anderson boy started after a female. Some folks was gettin' right worried about him."

"No such thing, Bob." Bill wagged a finger at his brother. "But that young teacher there, she could straighten out any fella with a problem."

"Oh, for heaven's sake!" Rachael picked up her skirts and started for the door.

"Miss Rachael!"

She sighed and turned to face the little boy running toward her. "Yes, Danny? What is it? Do you want to know when Jake's coming to town, too?"

"Heck, no!" He screwed up his face and shook his head. "I just seen Jake."

"You did?" Instinctively she raised her eyes and looked over the nearly deserted street. Nothing. She turned back to Danny.

"Yes'm. He give me these to bring to you." He pulled his arm from behind his back and held out a small, scraggly bouquet of bright golden yellow wild mustard blooms peppered with a few deep orange desert poppies.

"Jake sent these?" Rachael looked at the bedraggled flowers but made no move to take them.

"Yes'm. And they wasn't easy to find, neither. Not in January. But Jake says that rain we got an' then the hot weather made some of 'em bloom early."

"Did Jake have you pick them for him, Danny?"

"Hell—I mean, heck—no. I wouldn't pick no flowers for no girl."

"Jake picked 'em?"

Danny nodded at Buck. "You shoulda seen him. He musta looked through three meadows 'fore he finally found enough to make up a bunch." He shook his head, disgusted with the memory of his hero picking flowers for a female! "Took him forever."

"My, my. Ain't that interestin'?" Buck sighed and tilted his head back. "Since it's comin' on to Valentine's Day, you reckon ol' Jake's gettin' sorta romantic?"

Rachael shot Buck a withering glare, but knew it was useless. The flower story would be all over town in minutes, and everyone would remember *last* Valentine's Day as well as she did. It should have been so different. So beautiful. They should have been together. Married. On the most romantic day of the year.

"Miss Rachael," Danny said impatiently as he waved the bouquet, "would you take these here, before somebody sees me?"

Rachael's fingers curled around the scrawny stems, and she fought down a smile. She remembered the first flowers Jake had given her. He'd scoured three meadows then, too. But then it had been spring. And the bouquet he'd brought her had filled three vases. These poor flowers would fit in a water glass. But that didn't matter. What did matter was that he had remembered.

She lifted the flowers to her nose and inhaled their familiar scent.

In Stockton, Cousin Preston had presented her with roses quite often. In fact, he'd made a point of telling her how he'd thoroughly inspected the flower shop in order to acquire the most perfect blooms. It would probably never have occurred to him to go out to the surrounding hillsides and pick flowers himself. How did Jake know that she'd missed the sight of acres of wild mustard dancing in the wind? And the poppies—Such delicate-looking yet sturdy little plants. There was so much about this place that she'd missed.

Exhaling a sigh, she opened her eyes to find only two of the Bees watching her. Buck was gone, busy spreading the latest news. She thanked Danny and ignored the two remaining Taylor brothers. Lifting her chin, she went inside the store to prepare her father for the crowd that Buck would no doubt be bringing back with him.

Chapter Five

"Oh, Rachael," Myra Talbot twittered excitedly, "here comes another bunch!"

Rachael sighed and looked up. Danny was indeed coming through the front door with another small bouquet. Glowering ferociously at the chuckling adults who surrounded him, he resolutely made his way to the counter and held the bedraggled blossoms out. "Here," he said gruffly. "They're from—"

"Jake," she interrupted. "I know."

Danny waved the flowers a bit testily and scowled when several petals fell onto the counter.

Rachael took the flowers and swept the fallen petals to the floor. She watched as Danny brushed his small hands together as if glad to be rid of the bouquet. When the boy made no move to leave, Rachael leaned over the counter and whispered, "Any message this time?"

Danny sighed heavily and nodded. "Yes'm." He glanced over his shoulder toward the expectant crowd, then turned back to Rachael.

"Will you whisper this one? So no one else will hear?"

Hope flashed across his face momentarily, but

then he shook his head. "Nope. Can't. Jake'd have my hide."

Rachael rubbed the bridge of her nose. What a day. Since she'd received the first bunch of flowers, more and more people had filtered into the store. She'd spent most of the day making coffee and serving the cookies her mother had made. Her father had given up all pretense of running a business and was now involved in a highly contested chess match with Cyrus Moffat, who had once again declared a bank holiday.

The general mercantile resembled nothing less than the scene of a box social. And from the looks of things, no one had the slightest intention of leaving. Rachael looked down at the little blond boy and smiled. It certainly wasn't his fault.

This was Danny's fourth trip to the store. Each time he'd brought a few more tired-looking flowers, together with a message from Jake. And the embarrassed child had been given orders to deliver Jake's message in a clear, loud voice.

Rachael shook her head, remembering how well the boy had performed his chore. She smiled as she recalled the first message. Poor Danny's face had been a deep scarlet when he'd announced, "'I love you, Rachael.'" Mind you, the impact of the statement had been somewhat lost as the child's voice was flat as a pancake.

The second message, an hour later, added still another shade of red to his poor little face. "'Forgive me, sweetheart.'" Danny had pursed his lips as if he'd just bitten into a lemon. By the time the third bouquet arrived, Rachael's sympathies for the child had escalated at the same pace as the townfolk's laughter.

But that time Danny hadn't seemed worried in the least. That should have warned her, she acknowledged now. She'd never forget that horrifying moment when his piping voice shouted out, "'Remember that night in the valley!'" Her face had gone two shades darker than Danny's had ever been. Eyes wide with shock, she'd dropped behind the safety of the counter and made a great pretense of straightening shelves.

She couldn't believe Jake had sent that message! Good Lord, wasn't one humiliation enough? How would she ever explain that statement to her parents—much less to the interested bystanders? Even through the embarrassment, though, the memory of that night flooded her body. Closing her eyes, Rachael could feel Jake's lips at her throat. His breath, warm and sweet. His heart pounding in tandem with hers. The valley below Jake's ranch had been filled with hushed murmurings and unspoken promises that night. Even now it shamed Rachael to admit that it had been Jake's will alone that had kept them from enjoying an early wedding night.

"Rachael!"

She groaned at the sound of Danny's shrill voice. Opening her eyes to the present, she pushed the sweet memory back into the depths of her mind. She surrendered to the inevitable and faced the boy. Heaven only knew what the message would be this time. She eyed him warily. "All right, Danny," she said softly. "May as well get it over with."

"Yes'm." He cleared his throat, straightened his narrow shoulders, and lifted his chin. " 'Rachael,' " he began, " 'would you do me the honor of walkin' out with me tonight?' "

There was a collective sigh from the women in the room.

Rachael expelled her pent-up breath in a rush. "Is that it?"

"Yes'm. 'Cept Jake said to tell you if you said yes, that he'd come by the store for you at closin' time."

She nodded and chewed her lip thoughtfully. Danny, and indeed everyone else in the store, awaited her answer. She felt their eyes on her and sensed their expectation. But Rachael didn't care about any of that. Her mind was filled with images of Jake. She turned her back on the waiting crowd and absently tucked the latest bunch of flowers into the vase with the others.

As her fingers toyed with the delicate orange petals of the California poppies, the memory of her first meeting with Jake rushed back. She was twelve that summer, and Jake Travers had just purchased his ranch. On his first trip to her father's store for supplies, Rachael had fallen helplessly in love. Never mind that he was twenty and she twelve or that Cynthia Evans, the town flirt, had staked him out as her claim immediately after his arrival. When he'd winked playfully at Rachael and tweaked one of her braids, she'd decided then and there that Jake would be hers.

And though it had taken a few years to grow up and make him notice her, she'd done it. Rachael had gone after him with a single-minded determination that had become legendary. Now, though, it was Jake doing the chasing. Could it be that he was just a little worried? After all, she *had* been gone for a year. Humming softly to herself, she remembered that Jake was aware that Aunt Libby had a son just two years older than Rachael. She smiled, feeling thankful that he'd never actually met Cousin Preston.

It wouldn't do any harm at all, she told herself, to let Jake Travers think there was something specific to worry about.

She smiled again and turned back to face Danny and her waiting audience.

"Danny," she said softly, "tell Jake I'll be ready."

A loud sigh of relief swept the crowd.

"Yes, ma'am!" Danny grinned, then turned and sprinted for the door.

Rachael ignored the frantic whispering and low chuckles and stepped out from behind the counter. She caught her mother's eye and said, "I'm going home to change my dress."

"But Jake—"

"I'll be back in plenty of time, Mother. Don't worry." She grinned and walked through the store with a quick, light step.

"Whoo-ee! Ain't you somethin'?" The old man nudged his brother. "Did you ever see Jake lookin' so slicked up when it weren't even Sunday?"

"Nope," Buck said, shaking his head. "Can't say I did. Somebody die, Jake?"

"Nobody died, boys. Hell, if they had, you'd be the first to know." Jake grinned at the two men. They knew good and well why he was all fixed up.

Hadn't he been running Danny Hogan's legs off all day just making *sure* that everyone in town would know? Then he realized suddenly that there were only two of them on their bench. "Where's Bob?"

"Oh . . ." Bill threw his head back and stared at the sky while Buck whistled tunelessly. "Reckon he's around. Somewhere."

Jake glanced uneasily over his shoulder. Fine. Now he'd have to worry about Bob Taylor sneaking around corners, spying on him and Rachael. How was a man supposed to get any serious courting done with folks forever about? Then he shrugged. Nothing to be done about it.

He pulled at the lapels of his new black coat and ran his hand over his still-damp hair one last time. Taking a deep breath, he pushed through the mercantile's door and wondered vaguely why he was so damn nervous.

Jake kept his gaze straight ahead. He didn't glance once at the people whose whispered comments filled the friendly old store. As he neared the counter, Rachael stepped out of the doorway leading to the back office. He couldn't hear the voices anymore. The eager citizens of Temptation faded away until it was as if he and Rachael were alone.

She looked more beautiful than ever. He knew nothing about ladies' fashions, but he was sure her dress was new. A soft pale green, the fine material hugged her upper body and fell to the floor in delicate folds. Jake's breath caught in his throat. He couldn't speak. He couldn't tear his gaze from her shining emerald eyes. He couldn't imagine how he'd lived the last year without her.

Someone coughed.

"You figure he's gonna stand there all day with his tongue hangin' out?"

"Surely looks that way."

"You hush," Hannah Olsen whispered. "This is love, you ninnies! Haven't you two got any heart a-tall?"

Jake shook his head. He had to get her away. Someplace where they could be alone. To . . . talk.

She walked to him slowly, and somehow he found the strength to move to her side. She smelled like apple blossoms. "Are you ready, Rachael?"

"Should be—she's been primpin' for the last hour!"

A sharp slap followed Tom Wright's observation. Rachael threw him a quick glare.

"Yes, Jake. I'm ready. Shall we go?"

He nodded.

Rachael held herself like a queen and walked to the doorway with Jake only a step behind. Once outside, they strolled down the boardwalk past the Bees' bench. Two low whistles were the only comments from that quarter.

"You're beautiful, Rach."

"Thank you." She looked up at him as she slipped her hand through his crooked arm. "Do you like my gown, Jake?"

"Oh, yeah." He grinned appreciatively.

"I'm so glad." Rachael turned her gaze back toward the street. "Cousin Preston helped me pick it out. It's so helpful to have a man's opinion."

The arm beneath her hand stiffened, but he kept walking. "Cousin Preston?"

"Oh, my, yes. Though he's only my third cousin, twice removed, I think Mother said. But he's so attentive. So kind."

"Uh-huh."

"Why, he was such a dear, Jake. Escorting me all over town, to concerts, plays, and things. The time just flew past!"

"Yeah."

Rachael glanced at him out of the corner of her eye. His jaw was tight.

She smiled.

Chapter Six

The bright yellow contraption caused quite a stir as it rolled down Main Street. Jake nodded proudly at the open-mouthed people he passed and snapped the reins of his high-stepping horse. He was quite pleased with his invention.

He'd taken two discarded buckboard wheels, attached them to a sturdily built oak box, added a couple of soft cushions, and topped the whole thing off with a coat of sunny yellow paint. The whole idea had worked out real well, he thought. He just knew Rachael would love the little hand-made cart.

Jake had built the rig as a wedding present, knowing that it would be much easier for her to handle than the huge ranch wagon. And it was pretty comfortable, too. All she had to do was be real careful getting in and out. The cart was fine once it was moving, but it did tend to teeter some when a body stood up in it.

But even at that, he'd like to see Cousin Preston try to build one! Jake scowled, his jaw clenched. The way Rachael went on about the fella, you'd think he was a mix of Abraham Lincoln, Jefferson Davis, and God Almighty! Even the man's name irritated Jake. Preston! What the hell kind of name was that? And what kind of man would go around spouting *poetry*, for God's sake!

Rachael'd talked about the blasted man so much that Jake had finally been forced to kiss her into silence. Of course, he hadn't minded that. But if she started in on wonderful Cousin Preston again today—he shook his head and took a deep breath to calm himself. No use getting all worked up over some damn fool who lived all the way up in Stockton.

And if Cousin Preston knew what was good for him, Jake told himself grimly, he'd stay there. Lord help him if he ever set foot in Temptation.

It was a fine day, though, and he refused to let thoughts of "wonderful" cousins spoil it for him.

Jake grinned and looked up at the clear sky. Perfect picnic weather. He still wasn't sure how he'd persuaded her to go with him. Maybe their little walk together hadn't been satisfying for her, either.

He patted the basket on the cushion beside him.

Sam had outdone himself making up the hamper. Fried chicken, biscuits so light he had to weight them down with napkins, a cold jug of sweet tea, and even heart-shaped chocolate cookies dusted with powdered sugar.

Jake knew how much Rachael loved chocolate. Hadn't he already sent to Los Angeles for a box of candies for her? It should be arriving by stage any day now.

He heard a splash and felt a solid jolt. "Well, dammit," he cursed softly. "That's what happens when you don't pay some mind to what you're doin'!"

Disgusted, he looked down at the right wheel. It was splattered with mud. He'd driven right through the big pothole by the livery stable's water trough.

"Ought to keep your mind on business, boy!"

Jake frowned at the barrel-chested man. "Thompson, when're you gonna fix that mess?"

"Ain't." He spit a stream of tobacco juice into the dirt and wiped his mustache on the arm of his faded blue shirt. "Town business. Town street. Town hole."

"But it's in front of *your* place."

"In the road."

This particular battle had been waging for over a year now. Otis Thompson was waiting for the town to get busy—and the folks in town were determined to wait him out. Thompson was such a notoriously lazy man, Jake figured it would be a long wait.

"What the Sam Hill you ridin' on, boy?" Otis took a step closer, his brow furrowed.

"Like it?" Jake grinned. "I made it for Rachael."

"That door"—the man pointed at the back of the cart—"s'posed to do like that?"

Jake looked and saw the hinged door swinging back and forth. He frowned, pulled the door closed, then twisted the latch down firmly. "No, it ain't *supposed* to. Got a bad latch I keep meaning to fix. Your durn hole knocked it open!"

"Town's hole."

"Hell." Jake shook his head resignedly. It was useless to argue. He snapped the reins again, and the horse trotted on toward the Hayes's house.

"It's so beautiful, Jake."

His gaze moved over her profile. In the winter sunshine, a few golden freckles were blossoming across the bridge of her nose. When she took a sip of tea, he had to fight down the impulse to kiss away the remaining drops glistening on her lips.

"Jake?"

"Hmm? Oh." He shook himself mentally. "Yeah. Yeah, you're right, Rach. Beautiful."

Her lips twisted wryly. "I was talking about the view." She spread her arms wide, encompassing the entire valley.

Jake ignored how her sudden movement pulled the white shirtwaist tightly across her breasts. Grinning, he answered, "You pick your view, I'll pick mine."

"I, uh, think we should be heading back now," Rachael said, packing the last of the leftover food into the basket.

"In a bit." His fingers moved lightly over the back of her hand.

"Be sure to tell Sam how good everything was."

"Uh-huh." He leaned closer, pushing the food hamper out of his way.

"I really enjoyed the picnic, Jake."

"I'm glad." His breath moved across the sensitive skin at the back of her neck.

"And I just love the cart. It's so pretty and easy to hand . . . mmmm." She sighed as his lips moved over her throat.

"Good." His fingers moved to the tiny row of buttons.

"Jake, I don't think—" She turned her head, offering his mouth the soft flesh of her neck.

"That's right, darlin', don't think." Finally the last button was freed. His hand slipped inside her shirt and under the fine material of her camisole. Tenderly he cupped her breast and rubbed his fingertips over the sensitive nipple.

"Jake . . ." She shuddered and arched against him.

Slowly he eased her down onto the blanket. "Ah, darlin', I've missed you so." He pushed the thin white fabric down, baring her body to him. As his fingers gently kneaded one tender breast, his lips claimed the small pink bud on the other.

She gasped and wound her fingers through his hair. Pulling his head tighter against her, she moaned softly as his teeth nipped lightly at her erect nipple.

Jake shifted position slightly. As he moved to taste her other breast, his free hand swept her skirt up. When she began to protest halfheartedly, he suckled her and sighed at her eager response. Her body moved against his, and it was all he could do to retain control of himself.

Rachael felt the sun's warmth on her inner thighs as Jake's hand eased up her leg, urging her to part her thighs for him. His suckling seemed to pull through the very center of her. It was as if he were drawing out and drinking her soul. She couldn't even remember how this had started. She only knew she never wanted it to end.

Then his searching fingers found the core of her, and she jumped, startled at the intimacy.

"Jake, no. I . . . You . . . We can't do this."

He pulled his hand away immediately, raised his head, and stared into her passion-softened eyes. "It's all right, Rachael. There's nothing wrong in this. We love each other." He grinned and kissed the tip of her nose. "Hell, by rights we should be gettin' ready for our first anniversary. We could've been doin' this every day and night."

It was as though she'd been doused with ice water. Jake watched the change sweep over her and still couldn't believe it. In seconds she'd pushed him away, straightened her skirt, and buttoned her shirtwaist.

"Rachael, what is it? What'd I say?"

"You're right, Jake. We should have been married by now. But the plain fact is, we're not! And whose fault is that?"

Damn his big mouth anyway. Jake sighed and stood up. "Hell, Rachael, I've tried to explain what happened—"

"Don't bother. I already told you I'm not interested."

He snorted. "That ain't the idea I got a minute ago."

She flushed. "That has nothing to do with anything."

"Like hell it don't!" He grabbed her shoulders. "It proves to me that you love me!"

She pulled away. "I never said I didn't." Turning toward the cart, she added, "Please take me home now."

"Goddammit, Rachael! If you love me, why're you so dang mad at me all the time?"

She tossed him a disbelieving glare and kept walking.

He snatched the blanket off the grass, grabbed the hamper, and started after her.

The strained silence after their short but passionate encounter was almost too much to bear. Jake shifted uncomfortably. He'd pushed her too far. He hadn't meant to. He'd only wanted to kiss her some and sweet-talk her a little. She could hardly blame him if just being around her was enough to set him on fire!

He slowed the horse to a walk on Main Street, trying to lengthen their time together.

"Rachael honey," he said softly, "I'm sorry about—"

"Let's not talk about it, Jake." She gave him half a smile. "I'd rather forget it."

Oh, fine! She'd rather forget his lovemaking! Hearing something like that'd do wonders for a man, he thought grimly.

"What's going on at Otis's place?"

He followed her gaze as they came up to the

livery. The reins hung lax in his hands. "I don't believe it!" He glanced at Rachael excitedly. "Remember those Hereford cows and the bull I bought last year?"

She did indeed. He'd spent nearly every cent he had in the world on the prime cattle in the hope of building them a solid future. "Yes."

The horse moved on slowly.

"Well, it looks like Thompson's got himself a Hereford bull, too! If I can arrange something with the ornery cuss, my breeding stock will get even better!"

"You mean borrow his bull for your cows?"

"Yeah. And let him have the loan of my—I mean *our* bull." Jake's face was alight, his eyes sparkling. His grin was contagious, and Rachael found her own enthusiasm building.

Suddenly Jake stood up to call out to Otis. At the same time, the cart dipped into Thompson's pothole, the latch sprang loose, and Rachael let out a sharp squeal of outrage as she fell through the open door into the mudhole. She landed with a loud, undignified thump. Jake grabbed the reins and pulled. Reluctantly, he turned to look.

Rachael was sitting up now, her legs stretched out and wide apart, her hands braced on either side of her. She was covered with thick black mud. It seeped into her once pristine shirtwaist, dripped from the back of her head, and sloshed over her skirt.

Vaguely, Jake heard folks talking and laughing. From the corner of his eye, he could see a crowd beginning to gather. But he couldn't pull his gaze from Rachael's. He'd never seen her eyes go so darkly green before. Looked like a forest at night. He saw how hard she was trying to keep from screaming. Her jaw was locked so tight it was a wonder he couldn't hear her teeth grinding together.

"Ought to keep your mind on business, boy."

Jake glared at Otis.

"Rachael, you want some help?" Bob Taylor stretched out his hand hesitantly, not really wanting to touch all that grime.

She waved him off. Her eyes never leaving Jake's, she pushed herself to her feet. Her sodden clothing weighted her down so that moving was difficult. One step at a time, she started for her home.

"Rachael—" Jake tried.

"Best leave it go, boy," Bob warned him.

"He's right, Jake," Hannah offered, "now's not the time."

He knew they were right, but he hated seeing her go off like that. Then he noticed Myra Talbot hurrying up to Rachael, and he took a step or two closer.

"Rachael!" Myra stopped alongside her and wrinkled her nose. "Heavens, child! What in the world?"

Rachael wiped a blob of mud from her cheek, leaving a dark streak down the side of her face. "What is it, Myra?"

The older woman held out a squashed red heart-shaped box trimmed with mangled white lace. "This came in on the stage for you. From Los Angeles."

Jake groaned.

"The driver said to tell you he sure was sorry, honey. Seems this little box fell off the stage, and a couple of the horses stomped it 'fore he could pick it up." She shrugged. "But the chocolate's prob'ly still good."

Rachael looked over her shoulder at Jake. "Chocolates?"

He nodded. Wasn't much else to say.

Rachael patted Myra's hand absently, oblivious of the dark wet patch of mud she'd smeared on the woman. "You keep 'em, Myra. Happy Valentine."

All eyes were on the rigid spine of Rachael Hayes as she walked away from the crowd.

Chapter Seven

"I really appreciate this, Rachael."

"It's all right, Sam," she answered, "but are you sure Jake's not there?"

"Sure as can be." The old man rolled his eyes and hoped that the Lord wouldn't hold this lie against him. But hellfire, it seemed there was nothing else to do. Jake was driving the hands loco, wandering around the place yelling at anything that moved.

He stole a quick glance at Rachael. She didn't look any too happy, either. So maybe Jake was right. Maybe they did just need a little time alone to talk this all out. Sure as hell couldn't hurt anything. But it did go against the grain, lying to her.

Telling her he wanted to take her out to see all the work Jake had done to the ranch. How nice the place was fixed up. And all the things done with her in mind. Well, that was true, at least. She should see all them things. It was the other part of the boss's plan that rankled. Telling this sweet little thing that Jake and the hands was all gone for the day.

Well, the hands were gone. Jake had made sure of that. But not the boss himself. No, he was sittin' inside the house like a spider waitin' to pounce. Sam shook his head. He sure hoped the boy knew what he was doing.

"Why'd you bring the big wagon, Sam?"

He fought down his noisy conscience and returned her smile. "Jake don't want the cart used again till the latch is fixed proper."

Her eyebrows shot up. Swallowing a chuckle she asked, "Did he tell you what happened?"

"Tell me? Hell—I mean, heck, he's done nothin' but shout about that dang mudhole for two whole days!"

Her laughter bubbled up, and Sam couldn't help thinking what a pretty sound it was.

"It was awful, Sam! I was covered with mud. Could hardly move, and everyone in town there to see it!" She gulped in air and laid her hand on his arm. "You should've seen Jake's face!"

He looked at her in surprise. "You mean you ain't mad?"

She shook her head. "Not now. Oh, I was then.

But it wasn't Jake's fault." Her expression sobered, and she stared off into the distance. "Poor Jake. He tried so hard." A smile touched her lips again. "And those chocolates! My Valentine, getting stomped by horses! Imagine him sending away for those candies especially for me. It was so sweet of him."

Sam grinned at her easy laughter. Maybe the boss was right after all. Once Rachael and Jake were alone at the ranch, they'd straighten this mess out.

In the ranch yard, Rachael stepped down from the wagon and looked up at the house. Sam hadn't exaggerated. There *had* been a lot of changes.

The place had been painted a bright, clean white, with yellow shutters and trim. Jake had added a wide front porch, and a table and chairs were clustered there in the shade. Hollowed-out gourds filled with water hung from the porch rafters, where the wind would keep the water nice and cool. Everything was as neat as a pin.

And so quiet. The ranch seemed almost eerie, with none of the men around, making noise.

"You go on in, Rachael." Sam picked up the reins. "I'll just put the team away, and then I'll be along."

"All right." She lifted her skirt slightly and climbed the steps to the porch. After opening the door, she stepped into what should have been her home.

Rachael sighed in appreciation. The floors were varnished to a high shine, and the handmade tables glistened. Two settees faced each other

before a wide stone fireplace. A big rocking chair
with a flowered cushion sat nearby, and there was
even a small upright piano standing in a shaft of
sunlight from the front window. She moved to it
slowly, as if expecting it to disappear.

A long time ago she'd mentioned casually that
someday she'd like to own a piano. As her fingers
moved gently over the keys, she blinked to clear
her suddenly blurry vision.

She glanced out the window, then looked again.
She didn't believe it. Sam was driving the rig down
the road. She hurried to the front door and threw
it open. Racing into the yard, Rachael called out,
"Sam! Sam!" It was no use, though. The big wagon
was almost out of sight already.

"Well, what in the world got into him?" she
mumbled. "And how am I supposed to get back
home?" Shaking her head, she walked back to the
house. She'd just have to wait for the men to come
back. One of them would take her to town.

But as long as she was there, she thought she
might just as well look around. She went down the
hall into the kitchen. A new pump had been
installed over the old stone sink, and as she
peeked into the well-stocked pantry, she noticed
the small cubbyholes and drawers that had been
added. Wandering on, accompanied only by the
sound of her own heels on the floorboards, she
looked into an empty bedroom, then another room
that was obviously the ranch office. Farther down
the hall there was one more door left to open.

When she did, the first thing she saw was Jake
sitting in an overstuffed chair by the window.

"Jake!"

He jumped up and crossed the room. Pulling her inside, he pushed the door closed behind her.

"What is going on here? You're supposed to be gone for the day!"

"Well, I'm not, but everybody else is."

"What do you mean?"

"Just what I said." His hands moved up to cup her face. "I sent Sam and the boys out to ride fence today. They won't be back till late."

She swallowed and pushed his hands away. "Why?"

"I think you know why, Rach."

"I have to leave."

"Not yet." He pulled her close against him and laid his arm over her shoulders. "Don't you want to see our room?"

She shook her head.

He laughed gently. "Sure you do, Rachael. I heard you lookin' through the rest of the house. Don't want to stop now, do you?"

Rachael looked up into his eyes and knew she'd lost. "All right, show me around. Then take me home."

"Sure, darlin'. If that's what you want."

He led her to a series of doors on the far wall. Opening them one at a time, he displayed two big closets—one for each of them, he explained. Then, behind the last door, he proudly showed her the huge claw-footed tub in the center of a small room. Racks held towels within easy reach of the tub, and he'd even rigged a tiny trapdoor under the tub drain to let the water run out right to a flower bed at the back of the house.

"What do you think?" His mouth was too near her ear.

"It's wonderful, Jake. But isn't the tub awful big?"

His tongue traced the outline of her earlobe. "Got the biggest one I could find. Figured we could cool off together when it got too hot for us."

She gasped for air, suddenly very warm indeed. Backing away from the tub and all its implications, she bumped into the bed. Rachael jumped.

A brightly colored wedding-ring patterned quilt covered the immense mattress. The four bedposts bore intricately carved flowers and birds. Against the headboard lay an inviting mountain of pillows.

Following her gaze, Jake deliberately pushed the pillows aside and showed her the headboard itself. The unknown wood-carver had been at work here, too. Their names, Rachael and Jake, were carved deep into the dark wood, the letters intertwining.

"Oh, Jake."

"I love you, Rachael."

"I love you so," she whispered as she moved into his arms. She didn't want to fight him anymore. She only wanted his arms around her.

Their mouths came together hungrily, frantically. There was no delicate toying with each other now. There was only a desperate need to touch and be touched. To love and be loved.

In moments their clothing was lying on the floor and they were stretched out on the fresh-smelling sheets together.

His hands were everywhere. Rachael ran her fingertips over his strong shoulders and shuddered slightly when his lips fastened on her breast.

The tip of his tongue teased her already sensitive nipple, and she heard herself moan aloud.

Nothing else mattered. Nothing outside that room existed. It was just the two of them, together, as Rachael had always known it would be. She gave herself to him freely, eager for him to teach her all there was to know of love and passion.

His lips found hers, and she opened her mouth to him. Their tongues met in a wildly exciting duel of warmth, and when his fingers found the core of her desire, he swallowed her gasp of pleasure. Rachael's head tossed against the pillows, her body writhing, her breath coming fast and shallow. She opened her eyes to find Jake's passion-filled gaze locked on her features.

His thumb moved in slow circles over the bud of her sex as his fingers dipped into her warmth. Rachael arched against him, desperate for an end to the glorious torment her body suffered.

"Please, Jake . . . please." She ran her tongue over her dry lips and pressed him to her. The coarse, dark hair on his chest rubbed against her soft flesh, and she tried to get closer. To feel more of him. To be one with him, somehow.

And then she was. He'd slipped inside her body in one breathless motion. There was a brief, momentary twinge of discomfort, and then nothing but the glory of being joined at last. They moved together in unison, each struggling to capture the fulfillment just out of reach.

Her body's delight built to an unbelievable pitch. When Rachael thought she could stand no more, an overpowering, shuddering pleasure shot through her. She cried Jake's name and held him tightly as they both tumbled over the edge of desire into contentment.

Late-afternoon sun slanted in through the curtains, and Rachael stirred slightly. Jake kissed her tenderly, then smiled as she stretched luxuriously.

He hadn't gotten a wink of sleep. He'd lain awake beside her, unable to keep from touching her. Everything was perfect now. She was with him. Where she belonged. In their home. He grinned. And if they were lucky, they'd already made their first baby.

He was so relieved that the whole mess was over. Now they could get married and forget about the nonsense that had been going on lately. Maybe even the town could get back to normal! But right now, as much as he hated to do it, he had to get her up. Sam and the boys would be back soon, and he didn't want any of them guessin' what had gone on here today.

"Rach? Rachael darlin'. Come on, now. You got to get up."

She smiled and reached for him.

Jake chuckled and slipped out of her grasp. "There's nothin' I'd like better, darlin'. But the boys'll be back soon, and—"

Rachael sat straight up. "Good heavens!" A quick glance down reminded her that she was stark naked. And so was Jake! She turned her head slightly. "Jake, put some clothes on. And hand me mine!"

"Not till you turn around again."

"Jake—"

"We've got no secrets, darlin'." He reached across the bed and turned her face to kiss her.

She smiled. "Guess it's a little late to be acting embarrassed, isn't it?"

"I'd say so." However, he turned his back as she began to dress. Pulling on his shirt, Jake said, "Rachael, now that we've got ourselves all sorted out, I'd like to explain to you why I missed the wedding."

Silence.

He turned and found her watching him.

"All right, Jake, I'll listen."

Breathing deeply, he said, "Our Herefords? Remember the cows were pregnant?"

"Yes, but what—"

"I'm comin' to that." He ran a hand over his face. "One of the cows went into labor the night before the wedding. Well, hell, we all expected her to deliver long before church time. But she didn't. The day of the weddin', she was still strainin'. She was havin' trouble." He looked up and wasn't pleased with Rachael's expression, but continued anyway. It had to be said. "Rachael, you know I put near every cent I had into those animals. They're our future. Well, I couldn't go off and leave her. I had to stay with her till she calved. I couldn't afford for her to die givin' birth."

"A pregnant cow?"

"An expensive cow."

"You left me waiting at the church for a pregnant *cow*?"

"Now, Rachael." He backed up a little and grabbed his pants off the floor. "I sent one of the boys to town. But his horse broke a leg. Wasn't nobody's fault. Just happened."

She advanced on him. "Two hours I waited in church for you. With the whole town whispering and laughing. And you were here playing midwife to a *cow!*"

"Come on, Rachael! You're gonna be a rancher's wife. You got to understand these things."

"Who said I'm gonna be a rancher's wife?"

"What?" His eyes wide, he shouted, "*I* said it! Hell, we just had the damn honeymoon!"

She flushed and hurriedly buttoned her blouse. Pushing her hair out of her eyes, she said, "That was no honeymoon. That was good-bye!" Rachael turned away and moved toward the door.

Hurriedly Jake tried to pull on his pants. He hopped on one foot as he tugged at his clothes. She was going to leave. "Dammit, Rachael, wait a min—" He felt himself falling and couldn't do a thing to stop it. He slammed his forehead against the doorjamb on the way down and lay stunned and quiet on the floor.

Rachael was already out the door and flying down the road. She was going home if she had to walk.

Chapter Eight

"No, Sam. You talked me out of going last night, but it ain't gonna work again."

"I still say you ought to cool down some before you go talk to Rachael."

"Cool down?" Jake shouted then groaned softly. His head was still pounding. He took a deep breath and continued more quietly. "If I wait till I cool down, we'll both be old and gray!"

The old cook shook his head. It was no use. Jake was bound and determined to go into town. And Sam couldn't really blame him. This whole mess had gone on long enough. It was time to settle up. Past time. He glanced at his boss. The knot on his forehead looked even bigger today. Sam was sure curious about how he'd gotten that lump, but Jake wasn't talking.

"Sam! Sam!"

"Oh, Lord, what now?" the old man mumbled as he opened the kitchen door. Frank jumped off his still-moving horse and headed for the house.

"Sam!"

"I hear you, boy, keep it down. Some folks has got headaches this morning."

Jake scowled at him.

"Sorry, boss. Didn't see you," the young cowboy said.

"What is it, Frank?"

The kid stepped inside the kitchen and stared down at his employer. He sure wished he didn't have to be the one to bring the boss this news, but he had to know.

"There's some city fella hangin' around Miss Rachael."

Jake's head snapped up. "What do you mean, 'hangin' around'?"

"Well, I saw 'em sittin' real close on the porch swing. Townfolks *say* he's her cousin, but he don't act like no cousin I ever saw. Moonin' and talkin' poetry—"

"Preston." Jake jumped up, knocking his chair over in the process. "That's it, Sam. I've had it. I'm goin' to town, and me and Rachael are gonna get this settled. Then I'm gonna settle with Cousin Preston."

" 'What light through yonder window breaks? It is the east—' "

Rachael flinched at the final *t* and moved back a bit. Honestly, whatever had possessed Preston to come down here? And why now, of all times? She watched him push his spectacles back up his bony nose and tried not to yawn. He'd been at it for hours—reading Shakespeare's plays, then a sonnet or two, then back to the plays. Well, at least while he was reading, he didn't expect anything from her but silence.

She'd walked most of the way home the night before. Then, luckily, Cyrus Moffat had passed her on his way back from a visit to the widow Croft. He'd driven her the rest of the way in. But between the walk and her encounter with Jake, Rachael was exhausted. And it hadn't helped her disposition any to find Preston waiting for her when she returned. For some unearthly reason, he'd decided that she was madly in love with him!

Well, she'd had about all she wanted of men lately.

She glanced up at the sound of pounding hooves. Recognizing the rider, she jumped up and started for the door. But Jake was too fast for her. He leapt off his horse and caught her in a few easy strides.

"See here, my good man," Preston piped up.

Jake looked away from Rachael for a moment and let his gaze sweep over the skinny little dandy puffing out his narrow chest. He asked, "Cousin Preston?"

"Oh, Lord," Rachael groaned, vividly remembering how she'd talked about her cousin in such glowing terms.

Preston cleared his throat nervously. "I am Rachael's cousin—third cousin twice removed, that is."

Jake chuckled. "Hell, Rachael, he's so skinny, if they'd removed him more than twice he'd have disappeared!"

"Who are you?" Preston demanded in a voice that cracked.

Shoving Rachael behind him, Jake walked up to the little man. "I'm Jake Travers. Maybe you know the name?"

"Well . . . uh, yes—that is, I'm sure Rachael . . ."

"Jake—"

"It's all right, Rachael. I won't hurt him."

Preston's eyes bulged, and he ran a finger under his suddenly too-tight collar.

"As long as he leaves on the afternoon stage," Jake continued.

"Jake!" Rachael pulled at his arm. Not that she wanted Preston to remain any longer, but really, she couldn't very well let Jake order a member of her family to get out of town!

"Today?" Preston squeaked nervously.

Jake blinked. "Yes. Today. Good-bye, Preston."

"Well . . . uh, if I'm not wanted . . ." Preston walked a wide circle around Jake and stopped in front of Rachael. "Rachael, I'm afraid this doesn't bode well for our future together. Mother will be most disappointed in you."

"Why you little—"

Jake cut Rachael's speech short by plucking the scrawny man up by the back of his collar. "All right, Preston." He half carried, half pushed his captive toward the front door. "You go on in and pack now. Your mama prob'ly misses you something fierce."

That chore accomplished, Jake turned back to Rachael.

"Can you believe that worm? I'm going to be a disappointment to his mother? For heaven's sake! I've got a good mind to—"

He pulled her up against him, lowered his head, and kissed her long and hard. When he finally let go, Rachael was weak in the knees. Easing her down onto the porch swing, Jake said what he'd come to say. "Enough about Preston, Rachael.

And enough of everything else that's been going on."

"You tell her, Jake!"

Irritably, he glanced up to find the Bees and three or four others standing in the street, watching him with smiles of anticipation. The hell with it! He was gonna end this, no matter who watched!

"This is Saturday. Monday is Valentine's Day. There's a dance that night. You'll be goin' to it with your husband."

"What?"

"Monday morning, nine o'clock sharp, Rachael. You be at that church. You're gettin' married. Now, maybe it's a year late, but by thunder, this weddin' is gonna happen on Valentine's Day!" He kissed her one last time, then left the porch and swung astride his horse. "You be there, Rachael. 'Cause if you ain't, I'll hunt you down and *carry* you there myself!"

Shouts of laughter and excitement filled the air as Jake rode away from town. Rachael hardly heard them.

"Look all right?" Jake asked.

"You look right handsome, son," Sam assured him. "I do, too, if I do say so myself."

Jake grinned at his old friend. The two of them made quite a sight as they rode toward the church all decked out in their Sunday best. He glanced behind him. All twenty of his hands were grinning back at him. They were as anxious as he was for things to get back to normal. He faced forward again.

In just another hour or so he'd be a married man.

They came around the bend in the road to find the entire town all dressed up and lining the streets as if they were waiting for a circus parade. Jake smiled and called out greetings to his friends, but he kept right on riding.

Once he reached the church, he climbed down, tied his horse to the rail, and paused for a moment to listen to Hannah Olsen's organ music. He grinned. Everything was going along just as it should. After slapping Sam on the back, Jake strode across the grass and climbed the steps to the church door.

There wasn't a soul inside. That shook him a bit until he remembered that the townsfolk were still outside. The little church looked real pretty, though—even better than last year. The stained-glass windows along both sides of the building threw a rainbow of sunshine on the pews and walls.

Hannah turned from her sheet music to give him a smile, but she kept on playing her heart out.

The ladies in town had done up the inside of the church with pink ribbons and lots of red paper hearts. He was sure Rachael would like it. Just as he was sure she would show up.

She loved him.

After a while, people started filing in. Quite a few people were mumbling in the background, and even Hannah's playing lost some of its vigor. Jake pulled his watch out and checked the time. Nine-twenty.

She was late.

Well, hell. Womenfolk always took a long time getting dressed, even when it wasn't a special occasion, he told himself. On her wedding day, it was bound to take Rachael some extra time. He smiled at the folks and went to the pulpit to speak to the Reverend Mr. Danfield.

It was getting awful hot in the church, with all the people packed in tight. A few uneasy grumbles were heard, and Jake glanced at Sam. The old man shrugged his shoulders. The organ music stopped quite suddenly. Jake turned to Hannah and saw her rubbing her fingers.

"I sure am sorry, Jake," she whispered loudly, "but my hands are beginning to cramp."

He checked his watch again. Ten o'clock.

"It's all right, Hannah. You take a rest. In fact," he spoke up, letting his voice carry over the crowd, "why don't you all just settle back for a few more minutes? I'm gonna go see what's takin' my bride so damn"—he looked at the preacher—"so dang long."

Jake marched up the center aisle and didn't bother to look behind him. He knew that everyone in that church was hot on his trail. He also knew that it hadn't taken Rachael a whole extra hour to get ready!

His new black coat flapping in the wind, he walked at a furious pace. Vaguely he heard a few of the women in his wake complaining about his speed.

He reached the Hayes house and took the steps two at a time. Pounding his fist on the door, he tried to see through the filmy curtains.

Charles opened the door abruptly. "Morning, Jake."

"Morning, Charles." Jake slipped past his future father-in-law and moved to the foot of the stairs. "Morning, Sarah," he said when Rachael's mother stepped up to join her husband. "You look real pretty today."

Sarah blushed. "Why, thank you, Jake. We were all set to go, you know. But Rachael . . ."

He smiled. "I know." Turning back to face the staircase, Jake bellowed, "Rachael!"

No answer. He tried again. "Rachael!"

Myra Talbot snickered. "Reckon she's hiding, Jake. You gonna go get her?"

He glanced at the woman and then at the others who had filed into the house behind him. "I just might have to, Myra."

"Rachael!"

Finally she appeared at the head of the stairs. She was wearing a simple blue day gown, and her hair fell in loose curls over her shoulders.

"What do you want, Jake?"

He took a step up. "You know damn well what I want, Rachael."

"How did you like it, Jake?"

Another step. "Like what?"

She grinned and tossed her hair over her shoulder. "Standing in the church all alone on Valentine's Day. Waiting for someone who didn't show up."

"Truth to tell, I didn't much care for it." Another step.

"I'm not surprised," she said softly. "I didn't

care for it myself. Of course, I tried to send a message—"

"Oh, did you, now?"

"Uh-huh. Didn't the messenger show up, either?"

Another step. "Nope."

"Now, that's a shame. Why, I sure hope nobody laughed."

A chorus of laughter from her delighted audience followed that statement.

Another step.

"Isn't that a nice sound, Jake darlin'?"

Another step.

Suddenly very aware of his nearness, Rachael tried to back up. "Now, Jake, you stay there. I'll go get ready, and in an hour or so we'll—"

He took the last few steps at a run. Sweeping her up in his arms, he said, "Nope. You're as ready as you're gonna be."

More laughter.

She pushed futilely at his chest. "Jake! Let me down! At least let me fix my hair and put on my wedding dress!"

He kissed her. "Your hair is the way I like it best, and you're wearin' your weddin' dress!" Leaning toward her, he claimed her lips. Rachael wrapped her arms around his neck and kissed him back with all the passion she possessed.

"Whoooee!" Sam hollered. "Best get these two to a preacher right quick!"

Scattered bits of applause broke out, and soon the whole crowd was cheering.

Sarah Hayes fanned herself frantically as she watched her daughter's display.

Finally Jake ended the kiss and whispered, "You can wear your weddin' dress to the Valentine's dance tonight, all right?"

"Uh-huh," she answered softly.

He started down the stairs, holding Rachael tightly against his chest.

"You're not really going to carry me all the way to the church, are you?"

"Yep."

The crowd kept pace with the young couple, and as they entered the church, the townspeople took their places excitedly.

Standing at the front of the church, Rachael still clasped in his arms, Jake said, "All set, Mr. Danfield. Let's get this done."

"Won't you set her down now, son?"

Jake grinned down at Rachael, then shook his head. "No, sir. I ain't taking any more chances with this one. Not till we're together permanent!"

Hannah Olsen's organ blew into life, Sarah Hayes cried, her husband sighed with relief, Sam grinned like an idiot, and the Bees whispered delightedly from the front pew. The little church shook with laughter, and it took the Reverend Mr. Danfield quite a while to simmer everyone down.

But that was only because nothing ever happened in Temptation.

Please turn the page for an excerpt from Jodi
Thomas' romantic new novel

PRAIRIE SONG

Available now from Diamond Books

Texas 1866

Train tracks ribboned the west, tying together mankind as they cut the land into bite size slices for civilization to digest. With the Civil War over, this was a time for new beginnings, both for Texas and for Cherish Wyatt. She'd seen enough suffering to last a lifetime, and now at twenty, she planned to drink her fill of happiness. Cradled inside her Pullman sleeper, she closed her eyes and drifted into a sound slumber. The roll of the train and the smell of a coal oil lamp outside her compartment lulled her into a sense of safety as the train raced through the night.

Before the moon had completed its path across the inky blackness, Cherish was jolted fully awake by the sudden weight of a body falling across her. Without warning, the odor of blood and dirt overwhelmed her as someone pushed her deeper into the bed. Instinctively, she shoved against her intruder and clawed across the covers for her gun. Though slight, she could hold her own in a fair fight. She was determined that this thief would draw a full measure of resistance for his attack.

A gloved hand clamped over her mouth.

"Scream," a low voice whispered, "or make an-other move, lady, and it'll be your last."

Cold steel slid along her ribs, hesitating over each bone as if calculating the easiest point of entry. Cherish felt the point of the knife, sharp enough to run her through, and knew this would be no fair fight. With each rock of the train, the blade punctuated danger.

Cherish froze. The sleeper space that had only moments before cocooned her, now closed in like a coffin of blackness.

"That's better." She could feel the stranger's breath on her ear. "I need some answers and fast. When I lift my hand, if your voice is above a whisper, you'll be screaming in pain. Do you understand?"

Nodding, she gulped for air as the leather glove moved an inch away from her mouth. Though her eyes strained in the darkness of the sleeper, she could only define the outline of the man above her. But she could feel his lean powerful body and smell the rage that oozed from him like salty sweat from a whipped horse.

"Who are you, lady, and what are you doing here?"

Anger brushed over her fear. "I was sleeping. That's what people usually do in these new things." She ignored his first question.

"I thought this sleeper was empty."

A moment of relief washed over Cherish as she realized the man hadn't come to rob or rape her. Her voice came in nervous gulps. "I booked a ticket at the last minute."

Suddenly the train slammed to a stop and Cherish felt the intruder's weight fall over her again. She grasped how large he was, and as his long tight muscles rested on her, fear climbed into her heart. She was strong for her size, but this man could snap her in half.

He swore in pain as he lowered his head against the pillow by her ear. The knife at her side pulled back an inch but his leather wrapped fingers slid around her throat to assure her he was still in control.

He seemed to need a moment to think, as he relaxed against Cherish, imprisoning her completely with his body. His chest pressed into hers and Cherish felt a warm wet pool between her breasts. Blood! She could smell it, feel it dripping on her gown until the material clung to her skin. With each pounding of his heart against her, his blood pulsed out atop her.

Cherish twisted slightly and heard him swear again as she whispered, "You're bleeding on me." The disgust in her voice was apparent. The thought of another man dying brought bile to her throat as it had so many times during the war when there had been little medicine and men seemed to die by the hundreds around her. If she'd been ten nurses she couldn't have eased all their suffering.

With a grunt of effort, he pulled an inch away, molding his body between hers and the back of the berth. "Sorry, for the inconvenience." Laughter mixed with the pain of his whisper. His gloved hand moved slowly down to the pool of blood between her breasts. "But if I must spill my life's blood I can think of no softer valley for it to fall."

As his knuckles brushed the damp material in the space between her soft globes, Cherish was shocked by his words and movements. Never had anyone dared touch her so.

A thin light shown through from the passageway and the stranger's shadow materialized. The outline of a strong jaw and dark straight hair falling across his forehead were her only clues to his identity.

Footsteps shuffled at the far end of the car. Cherish heard the unmistakable sounds of gun hammers being pulled back to full cock.

"Search everywhere, men! That son of Satan couldn't have gone far with the bullet I planted in him." A man's voice shouted orders that rang through the car as hollow and frightening as a coyote's howl through a box canyon. "To hell with an arrest, we'll see him hang before dawn!"

The knife moved once more against Cherish's ribs. "I have no desire to hang . . . nor to harm you." His voice was only for her ears, but the emotion touched her. It seemed a plea not for his life, but permission to spare hers.

Nodding, Cherish felt the stranger's breath let out slowly against her cheek. "Roll behind me," she ordered as she reached beneath her pillow, bypassing her Colt to retrieve her handkerchief. With shaky hands, she pressed the cotton against the center of his chest, only guessing where the wound might be. Warm blood seemed to be everywhere.

Gloved fingers stopped her progress. "What are you doing?"

"I'm trying to stop the bleeding!" She pulled her

fingers from his and pressed the cloth once more against his chest.

For a moment he seemed unable to speak. "It's not deep," he finally whispered.

"Well, press this over the wound or you'll bleed all over my bed."

A low laugh rumbled in her ear as the sounds of footsteps warned of men nearing.

Vainly twisting her petite frame to try and cover his, she pushed him against the wall. The knife stayed at her ribs, less threateningly now, but his free hand circled her waist, pulling her into the outline of his body.

With trembling hands, Cherish slid the velvety curtain a few inches aside and blinked into the lantern light of the corridor. "What is it?" The terror in her voice was valid, similar to all the other shouts from passengers.

A large man removed his hat to reveal a head as hairless as an onion. He leaned forward and the badge on his vest caught a glint from the lantern. "We're lookin' for a murderer. We thought he dropped in here, but he must have just passed through the car. He has to be here somewhere. But don't you worry, Miss. Before we pull into Bryan, he'll be meetin' his maker."

As Cherish hesitated, strong fingers pulled her back, making her drop the curtain. The intruder's heartbeat pounded against her back as his hand drew the material of her gown into his fist. Cherish lay stone-still, afraid to breathe. The anger, the power of *this* man frightened her as no other could, not even a wild Comanche or a hellbent Yankee.

"Well, good night, folks." The lawman's voice

faded away as he and his men shuffled out of the car. "Sorry for the inconvenience."

Moments crawled by in silence as the stranger held Cherish to him. She could feel his breathing near her ear. His fingers pressed her solidly against him each time she would have moved away. Slowly, as the other passengers settled back into sleep and the train jerked to a start, the knife against her side eased.

Finally, she could stand the tension no longer. She pressed her cheek against his and whispered, "I didn't give you away. Now go."

The stranger shifted until he was above her once more, but without resting his full weight against her. "Thanks," he whispered. The single word seemed hard for him to say.

Anger heated her cheeks for Cherish suddenly only wanted him gone. "I want no thanks for keeping quiet to prevent getting a knife slashed through my insides. Who is it you've killed, another reluctant berth partner?"

The stranger laughed. "I'll bet you're quite a woman in the light. If you look half as good as you feel and smell, I wouldn't mind sharing a bed with you again some time."

"Try, and I'll be the one who spills your blood," she said, outraged. He was acting as though she were a loose woman of the streets who was in the habit of having men drop into her bed. "Don't mistake my silence for weakness. Knife or no knife, if I hadn't detested the thought of watching a bleeding man hang, I would have turned you in. So go! Bleed to death somewhere else and save the use of a good rope."

Low laughter was his only reply as he shifted and pulled off his glove with his teeth. With a violent movement, he gripped her face in the darkness, his fingers moving in strong bold strokes across her cheek. "If I am going to die before sunup, let me do so with the taste of you as well as the feel."

Without hesitation, he lowered his mouth over hers, silencing any cries of protest. His lips were hard and demanding; his hand held her face allowing no escape as his kiss deepened into an outlaw passion she'd never known. No stolen kiss she'd ever allowed in the shadows had demanded and given so much at the same time. His need was like a liquid fire that raced through every inch of his body and spread over her, warming her.

With a sudden moan he broke the kiss, as though it would have been too painful for him to continue. His breathing was ragged, and with a shock Cherish realized his stolen kiss had affected him more than he'd planned.

The darkness might hide his face, but she didn't miss the slight tremble of his fingers as he touched her bottom lip for an instant, then pulled away. "Until we meet again in the light," he whispered.

Jerking her head sideways, Cherish felt rage both for his advance and for her own reaction to his kiss. "When we do, I'll take great pleasure in slapping your face. I swear if you ever dare touch me again I'll see you dead."

The stranger lifted his body from her. "It would almost be worth the price."

A moment later he was gone. Just for a flicker,

the oil light in the corridor reflected on his right hand and the wide bowie knife held tight in his powerful grip. In the time of a blink, Cherish saw a scar above his wrist and committed the mark to memory.